OF RAGE

BY

STEPHANIE HUDSON

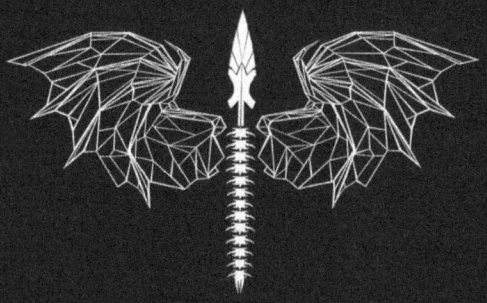

Roots of Rage
The Transfusion Saga #9
Copyright © 2020 Stephanie Hudson
Published by Hudson Indie Ink
www.hudsonindieink.com

This book is licensed for your personal enjoyment only.
This book may not be re-sold or given away to other people. If you would like to share this book with another person, please purchase an additional copy for each recipient. If you're reading this book and did not purchase it, or it wasn't purchased for your use only, then please return to your favourite book retailer and purchase your own copy. Thank you for respecting the hard work of this author.
All rights reserved.

This is a work of fiction. Names, characters, places, brands, media, and incidents are either the product of the authors imagination or are used fictitiously. The author acknowledges the trademark status and trademark owners of various products referred to in this work of fiction, which have been used without permission. The publication/use of these trademarks is not authorised, associated with, or sponsored by the trademark owners.

Roots of Rage/Stephanie Hudson – 1st ed.
ISBN-13 - 978-1-913904-83-8

*I would like to dedicate this book to all my wonderful fans,
those who are both new to the Afterlife and Transfusion world
and those who have support me for years.
I cannot thank you enough for keeping my dreams alive for so
long and I will be forever and always eternally grateful.
All my love,
Steph and family.*

WARNING

This book contains explicit sexual content, some graphic language and a highly additive dominate Vampire King.

This book has been written by an UK Author with a mad sense of humour. Which means the following story contains a mixture of Northern English slang, dialect, regional colloquialisms and other quirky spellings that have been intentionally included to make the story and dialogue more realistic for modern day characters.

Thanks for reading x

PROLOGUE

Hatred.

This was what I faced.

It was what I was told; that I needed to overcome the heart and tears of a God. But through this God's rage for injustice, a creation like no other had been born. A force formed from the anger of men and one which had sparked such power, that it had forged the Crimson Eye. A seeing glass into the souls of those it chose worthy enough to use. A key to unlock the door into the future, made by the deep and rooted feelings of the God of time and someone who believed he'd had the power to change it.

That was his lesson to learn…

Some doors were just never meant to be opened.

Because time was a dangerous thing and the one who held the power to wield it was the one who had the power to destroy the very Fates that were supposed to guide us into continued existence. And all because a God's heart bled for humankind, whilst another was playing puppeteer with rotting souls.

One power born from the Afterlife living for today's future.

And another, from the heart of Hell,
One made from the…

Roots of Rage.

CHAPTER ONE

LUCIUS

THERE IS ALWAYS TIME FOR ANOTHER 'OH SHIT' MOMENT

DAYS EARLIER

H*ere we go again.*
Another fucking enemy at my door was something I needed like a fucking hole in the head! Yet here I was, facing another threat to the most important thing in my life, making me question had word somehow got out as to who Amelia was to me?

This made me think back to moments before when walking from the throne room after nearly killing the fucking shifter with a death wish. But I had to confess to the satisfaction when a certain redheaded, Scottish asshole walked through my throne room doors and had no choice but to be forced to see the object of his desires sat on my lap, encased in my arms. But of course, I was far from a fucking saint and even though I would not admit as much to Amelia, I had orchestrated this very moment, knowing of the shifters' request to speak with their King.

The bastard needed to be put in his place...*Amelia was mine.* I also didn't give a fuck how primitive or possessive the statement sounded, for I answered to no man. Not even that of my maker...*not anymore.* No, now I was a free soul and I had worked hard to claim as much.

Speaking of which,

"They appeared from within the Echoing Forest without warning," Carn'reau said standing next to me with his winged beast waiting impatiently behind him. Its blood-thirsty nature was testing its ability to stay at its master's command seeing as the enemy was within its sights and in its mind, ripe for the taking. His beast was one of great legend and the first of its kind, hence its unbeatable strength in battle. However, for Carn'reau, I knew the beast meant far more to him than I believed anything else in his life. For it was the only being he showed any heart towards at all.

The creature was known as a Zilant, and one that owed its very existence to the Dark Fae Prince. It was also the only one that currently resided in Hell as it was another elemental being. And, other than his army, the only thing he brought with him after being cast out of his own realm. From what I could gather, it was the closest thing to family he had left and seeing the way he whispered in his own tongue back at it, was testament to this.

It was also a language he didn't believe I knew, so the caring and soothing words didn't come as a surprise to me. Not when they had been ones I had heard spoken before to the beast.

But then I also knew the benefits as a ruler when allowing those around you to believe what you wanted them to. It was also how I knew that Carn'reau was completely loyal to me, for I had heard him speaking to his men of this in his own tongue. After all, he was nearly as powerful as my brother and I, and with his own army would have had no problem trying to overthrow my rule. Especially with how little time I spent here.

However, this was not the case. No, instead he took my orders and acted on them with the loyalty of a man who owed his life to me, *which he did.* For without my acceptance of him then he wouldn't have survived long without his realm, one that was situated so close to my own. He was at his strongest back in the elemental realm and needed that smallest connection to keep him alive. But he could still leave here for periods of time, it just meant that the longer he was away, the weaker he would eventually become. Which always made me wonder, if he was as strong as he was now, then Gods, what would the heartless bastard be capable of back in his own kingdom?

A dark thought indeed.

But, like I said it was that closeness to his own realm that he could still feed from and hence why he had needed my approval. In return I had the use of his men and of his power. In all honesty, it had been the first move I had made when the power I held in Hell began to turn dramatically, and a more equal ground was starting to even out between me and my maker. Much to Lucifer's annoyance.

But Carn'reau wasn't the only ruthless bastard that couldn't give a fuck about being over ambitious in trying to take what he had the power to take. Because I couldn't give a fuck about ruling all of Hell, as it was not a Gods be damned headache I needed! Not when I had my own kingdom here and one topside. *Like I wasn't busy enough*, I thought holding back a frustrated sigh when facing yet another new thorn in my side. Gods, I'd only just got my girl back and the last fucking thing I needed now was some new threat to face!

But with regards to the shift in power, as far as I knew, Lucifer had accepted my word on the matter and believed me when I said I wasn't interested in ruling his world. How long he would continue to believe this I had no clue, but I knew the bastard was a twitchy fucker when it came to his throne. And I suppose I couldn't blame him, not after seeing how many times others had tried to overthrow him in the past and take possession of his world.

Thankfully, many had tried and just as many had failed.

In fact, the closest attempt made that had nearly been successful had been the last time. It was when Lucifer had made his one and only weakness known, despite all warnings from those closest to him, including my brother and myself. Through his love for Pythia, now his queen, he had almost failed to keep that throne and now I knew more than most what a weakness could do to a man in power.

For clearly…

It could bring a God to his knees.

It was why I went to such lengths now to keep my own secret, for no one here could know what she meant to me, for I would not make the same mistake my father did. Lucky for Carn'reau his only weakness was the beast whining at his back and nudging its demonic horned head at its master. It looked like some scaled sea snake, with the body of a horse. A beast, that if legends were correct, had once been his royal steed and he had sacrificed much to give life to the creature before me now.

Carn'reau was its maker, just as Lucifer was my own.

Now, the details surrounding it I didn't know exactly. Only that at one time the Fae who stood next to me now was once worshipped as a God. As for the beast behind him, it was the result of a prayer he heard and couldn't ignore, not from the beautiful damsel it came from.

But like I said, the details surrounding it were merely a whisper I had picked up during the times spent among his army, for none of them ever believed I knew their native tongue. But what I did know is that the mortal girl who had once been from old Kazan, had been transformed into the winged beast that was currently snapping and whipping out all eight of its black snaked tails.

"Calm yourself, Aysilu!" he hushed back at it, using its given name that meant 'Beauty as Moon' in Tatar. Historically, the term Tatars referred to anyone originating from the vast Northern and Central Asian landmass, which was then known as Tartary. This had been dominated by mostly Turco-Mongol semi-nomadic empires and kingdoms. Nations built on the blood spilt by none other than the empire of one Genghis Khan. But as for the Gods they worshipped, the Mongols were highly tolerant of most religions, meaning that man was free to believe what they wanted.

As for their ruler, Genghis Khan believed in Shamanism, a religion connected to the realm of Fae. For this was a religious practice that involves a shaman, one who was believed to interact with a spirit world through altered states of consciousness. The goal of this was usually to direct these spirits or spiritual energies into the physical world for healing, or some other purpose I couldn't give a fuck about.

All I knew was that the connections and the power obtained through these rituals were connected to Fae life. And as far as I could tell without asking outright, was that there was a reason the Mongol Empire became the largest contiguous empire in history, even after Genghis Khan's death. And why, because Carn'reau, being worshipped as a God, had made it happen.

After all, he was known as a God of War for a reason.
And speaking of war,

"What is their race?" I asked my now commander and general.

"As of yet, it is still unknown, my Lord." Again, I forced down the urge to sigh and scrub a frustrated hand down my face whilst muttering, 'for fuck sake', something I would have felt free to do in the human realm.

"And their leader?"

"Still unknown, and as for the look of things, he is either a coward or non-existent." Now this did make me raise a brow for both were uncommon in Hell. An army without a leader was unheard of and one found at the back of his army calling the shots almost more so. For no army in Hell would have respected such a ruler enough to go to war for. No, something definitely wasn't right here, and it was time to find out.

"Take your Zilant, and get a closer look, I want to know exactly what we are dealing with before our army goes into battle," I ordered, making his silver eyes flash and the black ring that usually framed the iris started to glow crimson. This was a usual reaction before going to war, and one I had seen many times before. It was a show of excitement for what would soon be delivering death on the horizon.

My general literally lived for moments like this and it was the first time that I felt anything akin to feeling sorry for him. For if death was all that heated his blood then he was fucking missing out that was for damn sure! My thoughts of last night and being seated in the warmth of my Chosen One's core was a memory that only strengthened that sentiment.

He bowed his head before turning his back on the shadow of an army barely seen from the cover of the Echoing Forest. Then he ran a gauntleted hand over the scaled head of his restless steed, before grabbing its horn and using it as leverage to heave his large body upon its back. Carn'reau and I shared a similar build, yet he was a few inches taller. Fae were known for their height of course, but were normally of a slimmer build, like most of his army. However, Fae royalty was the exception, for it had to be said the lineage of rulers were obviously known for breeding big, powerful bastards. Making me wonder what his brothers looked like?

My musing didn't last long as I watched my general take flight, with his Zilant's battle cry echoing along my lands, warning of all the rivers of blood that would be sure to follow. However, the moment the beast's body swooped low at his command I knew there was something wrong when the shadows didn't move. There were very few that wouldn't have been running by now with such a sight coming at them.

"What the fuck?" I muttered the second I saw it suddenly get as low as it could before gliding straight through the army. But the mass of bodies didn't go crashing into the forest as they should. Horns didn't spear flesh and the whip of eight barbed tipped tails were met by nothing but smoke.

Smoke and mirrors.

Fuck!

The army wasn't fucking real! I growled before letting loose a demonic roar of rage when suddenly I knew what this had been. A fucking diversion! The army around me took in my deadly demeanour quickly and in response gave me space as my demon snarled back over at my castle.

"Amelia!" After her name had left my lips, I opened up my wings and launched myself into the air. My demon roared as I felt every muscle in my body tense and crack with untapped power coursing through my veins. My rage had to be contained before I lost all control, but this was easier said

than done when I knew that the fucking army in the forest had all been a ruse.

It had all been a plan to take what belonged to me! Meaning that army of smoke may not have been able to bleed but the ones that made it most certainly would, and they would do so the second I got my fucking hands on them!

And well, let's just say that I had a pretty good idea whose blood I would soon find coating my hands...

"Fucking Witch!"

CHAPTER TWO

ICE COLD FATE

I landed outside the castle gates with a thundering crack. It was one which travelled the length of the path that led all the way to the colossal doors, splitting the wood. I knew before I even entered my domain that she had been taken, for her presence was gone. But little did whoever took her know of my means of finding her. Especially when it was so soon after feeding from her. In fact, I could still taste her blood on my tongue, something that turned bitter the second I saw my brother barking out orders in the throne room.

"Šeš! The girl, she is—" I cut him off the second I had his throat in my hands, demanding with a roar of rage,

"WHERE IS SHE!?" He closed his eyes for a moment and allowed my anger to wash over him before absorbing it and using it to stoke the embers of his own power. When his eyes opened again they flashed a deeper green before black, and with great calm and restraint, as was needed for those still around us, he replied,

"I don't know." I snarled before letting him go, wishing I could cast blame his way, when deep down I knew it was my

own doing. After all that had happened my first priority should have been to get Amelia to my tower and seal her there knowing she would be safe, for no one would be granted access. But in my haste and my anger I had foolishly thought that being within the walls of my castle would be enough. Feeling confident in this to meet the army head on and eliminate all threat before it could reach my castle doors.

Fuck!

At this rate I would end up chaining the girl to me, just so the madness wouldn't consume me, for each time this happened I was losing my fucking cool. I was losing the ability to keep my shit together and make decisions. Gods, but how any King functioned enough to rule when they had found the Queen they loved, was beyond me because right now, well I was making a piss poor fucking job of it!

"Explain!" I snapped on a growl.

"I took her to the office like you ordered and had my personal guard take post outside the fucking door, little good it did, seeing as not one survived and my office was fucking ripped apart!" Dariush growled angrily with fisted hands that no doubt wanted to punch me bloody from my rough treatment of him. I would have welcomed the fight had I not had more important shit to do, like finding my woman!

"Show me!" I barked the demand, one that became an oxymoron considering I was taking long, angry strides towards my brother's office, leaving him to catch up. I rounded a corner and the smell of death wafted up my nostrils and for once, it wasn't the welcome scent of my realm. No, all it meant this time, was that my greatest loss came with a smell, *one named failure.*

"Do you believe this was the work of the witch?" my brother asked, making my lip curl at the mention of the bitch, one that should have died by my hands long ago. But then, looking around the broken hallway, and I wasn't so sure. The pale stone walls were marred by a lightning bolt of cracks that were still crumbling due to our heavy footsteps coming closer. The bodies of the guards were long gone due to their vessels turning to ash upon their deaths, but seeing their remains now floating on pools of water was surprising.

I bent down on one knee and took a closer look, leaving the sight of the broken office beyond and instead focusing on these strange puddles. Each patch of water was surrounding an island of melting shards of ice, ice that seemed to have come from nowhere. Now I was quickly asking myself where I had seen this same evidence before and not long ago at that. It was déjà vu all over again, for once more I was looking for anything that may lead to signs of who took my girl. Which was suddenly when it came to me and a low and dangerous growl rumbled from my chest.

"What is it?" Dariush asked given my vicious response.

"I have seen this before," I told him as I stormed inside the office to find even more evidence to suggest my theory was correct. The section of the wall behind the splintered desk had been split open enough to create an opening to the outside. Again, my boots kicked up water and crunched what was left of chunks of ice as I walked further inside the room.

"Where the fuck did all this water and ice come from?" my brother asked, not yet knowing what I did. I turned to him and growled only one word,

"Cockatrice..." This was quickly followed by,

"...I will fucking kill him this time!"

The memory of seeing the way he looked at Amelia flashed in my mind like a shower of salt in a wound he had slashed open by taking her. This of course came after remembering the same evidence I had found by the Arachne, the Spider Queen's forest. Meaning it didn't take me long to discover the culprits of this kidnapping.

Now, what their end game was still remained to be discovered, for I was hoping ransom for their souls was the only thing on their minds. But as soon as this thought entered my mind I knew that these noble idiots wouldn't have hurt and scared Amelia for their own gain. For I wasn't foolish enough to ignore the strongest of the three had developed feelings for my girl. No, this time it wasn't only about Trice's soul but instead, it was more about *his heart.*

But then again, I suppose seeing my treatment of her, collared like a pet and in my cruel grasp, it wasn't a stretch for him to believe he was saving her from me. Fuck! But either path I took with the girl had only ended up working against me. For in my stubborn belief that by treating her this way was for her own good, I had underestimated the consequences from the other side. At the very least the only comfort I could hold onto was that she would remain unharmed and protected until I could get her back, something I was on my way to doing right now!

But right now, it was time I did something I never had before…it was time to use the Eye of Crimson for the first time. Being its keeper since its beginning I thought I knew what to expect, for I had been granted the power to ask of it what I wanted to see. However, I was soon to learn that despite having no interest in being shown the future, the Eye was to have other ideas.

Now, moments later, I found myself standing at the edge of the pool of water. But with it being a sight that only a little time ago I had my girl naked and in my arms, meant that it was proving difficult to think straight.

"Where are you, my little Šemšā?" I said aloud, looking up at the ceiling and closing my eyes as if I could still feel her presence. I swear that I was starting to believe we were cursed or something, for I already knew our love had in the beginning been a forbidden one. But to keep losing her this way was a torture that was becoming a regular occurrence. Like some bullshit test the Fates were putting us through, believing that we hadn't yet endured enough!

I opened my eyes with a frown and with a mere thought shed my demonic armour, stepping forward from the mist of black particles; A dark essence of power that would sink into the shadows and follow me like an invisible cloud until I called for it back. Then once naked and free of the weight, I dove into the pool, taking the barest of moments to relish the feel of the water caressing my bare skin and cooling my rage. Seconds later my eyes opened, and I sent a wave of power surging forward. It called out silently to the Crimson Eye and in doing so revealed the underwater entrance where it was kept hidden. A glow started to illuminate the darkness just as the archway appeared, rising from the floor like a flickering ghost.

I kicked back forcing my body deeper until I was swimming under the arch and into the secret cavern beyond. Holding my breath for this length of time wasn't really a problem. But for a human, then by the time they breached the surface they would be gasping for air with their lungs burning from the strain. The light above me that seemed to shimmer was one that was only fuelled by the presence of the Keeper of the Eye, as for anyone else only darkness would have met them.

I broke through the surface and took a breath before treading water long enough to take in my surroundings. Gods, but how long had it been since I had come down here? It wasn't something I tended to do, for there was no reason to.

The Crimson Eye was safe in its tomb, living out its days unused and beyond the reach of harm's way.

Hell, but if it had been possible, I would have destroyed the damn thing and had done with it years ago! But then the endless storm that surrounded my tower most certainly came in handy, especially now when finding it as a safe place for my queen. A place I might add, being one she would soon find herself remaining in for the duration of Hell's visit. At the very least until I could sort out the fucked-up shit going on with my race.

Again, chaining her back to my bed was a welcome reminder as I heaved myself out of the water and with a thought called for my trousers, so I wasn't walking around the place naked. Once covered from the waist down, I then walked along the only space in this part of the cave that led to the Eye's tomb. Passing the archway sent a shudder of power through me from the lingering residue I knew came from the Eye. It clung onto the only being that had stepped foot inside this place, drawn to my presence the closer I got.

The only other who knew of the Eye was my brother and in my moment of weakness I had granted him permission to use it, something he had turned down. This wasn't surprising, as he knew the importance of keeping the future where it should always remain...*unknown.*

Hell, but I wasn't even sure he *could* use it. But seeing as it had been granted to me, proclaiming me as its keeper, we had just always assumed that being brothers with the same blood running through our veins, then its use between us was a given. But as neither of us had ever used it before, then this fact was still unknown.

Fuck, but even I wasn't sure if this would work or not, for I was relying on her blood still in my system to become a beacon to follow. The most we knew for certain was that it could be used to reach powerful beings, calling them through a link that connected anyone with a link to the Gods.

Like Dom for example, he would be easy to connect to, making me wonder if now was the time to do so? I knew that he must have been going out of his mind with worry, because as far as Amelia's parents were concerned, it would have been as if we had dropped off the face of Earth's realm. Which was precisely what had happened.

I mentally shook my head as I knew now was not the time, as it would only end up complicating matters. Fuck, but it had been bad enough that I had involved Asmodeus. Something I knew for certain would only manage to piss Dom off even more. It was a well-known fact that Dom and his father weren't exactly on the best of terms and were known to clash heads more often than not, something that usually ended in the exchange of blows.

Let's just say that in this case, butting horned heads was not just a metaphor.

The moment I stepped inside the tomb my breath was stolen from me. Again, this was from the strength of the power I could feel pulsating from the altar at the centre of the large open space. This also made my steps falter in the black sand that looked like charred remains of the very scorched, volcanic sands it first emerged from. Once, it had been a golden hue, the last time I had been here in fact, making me wonder what had happened for it to have turned its prison into the past of its rebirth?

Could it have something to do with the infected Tree of Souls?

I walked closer, purposely doing so slowly so as not to give into the temptation of its pull. It had been like this the last time, feeding from the life it felt in its presence and the future it presented, one desperate to tell. Like secrets spilled from the loose lips of a street rat in need of coin. London had been full of them at one time, and I remember most of my missions wouldn't have been completed half as fast without them.

But then, as tempting as it was to give into its call, I resisted. This was achieved by being strong enough to hold out against the alluring possibilities it presented, despite my reasons for being here now. It was why I had been chosen to be its keeper, as its guardian. I had the strength to ignore its power.

Now, on the other hand as for Amelia, well, no force in Hell had the power to keep me away from her, for she was my beacon and my willing addiction. Hence why I was here now, doing what I vowed I never would. But then if I hadn't only recently consumed her blood, then none of what I was about to do would have been possible.

I wouldn't even be trying and would currently be out there now the same as I had done when first arriving in Hell. Searching for her in a near blind panic and tearing apart my realm to find her. Only this time I had three shifter brothers to contend with and if they were in their most powerful and combined form, then I had no fucking hope without this Eye.

They could have been anywhere by now!

So, with this in mind, I finally allowed it to draw my steps closer, coming to the end of holding back. I had no choice but to give in to its pull, feeding my need to reach out and touch it. I hated the weakness it caused me to face, and just to prove to myself that I could beat it, I snatched my hand back. At least now feeling somewhat satisfied enough that I could deny its controlling essence.

"Fuck, you're a powerful fucking thing aren't you?" I said aloud just to hear my own voice in this dark situation. It glowed brighter and more intense as if responding to me in its own way.

"Right, well let's see if you can find what I am looking for…" I paused so I could concentrate on finding her blood inside me. I started feeling for the slightly foreign essence, one that in all my years as a Vampire, was a blood that had never affected me in the same way as others.

Hell, but it fucking sang in my body and lit up my insides! Because of this it wasn't a surprise where it remained centred inside me. For naturally it was one I could find beating at my core and around the heart of my vessel. But because I wasn't sure if being in my body was enough, I pulled it back, drawing it to my hand so when I bit into it, both my own and hers would make a connection with the Eye.

Once I knew it was where it needed to be, I released my fangs and bit down into my palm, letting it quickly fill with blood after cupping my fingers. It was only then that I reached out and took possession of the Eye, once and for all feeling its power.

"Show me the girl!" I commanded, and in a blinding flash of light it did as I demanded of it.

Only in doing so, it then showed me a lot more.

More than I ever wanted to see.

It showed me Amelia's future and in doing so, it also showed me…

Her Death.

CHAPTER THREE

FATES' CLAIM

The second I saw the last image the Eye forced upon me I tore my hand free and staggered backwards, not stopping until my back hit the wall of the tomb. For the first time in my supernatural life I felt as though I couldn't breathe! I even found my hand fisted at my bare chest, as I felt the pain of what I'd just seen as though the spear of destiny was no longer embedded in my spine but instead in my heart. It was as if my whole body was fighting against what the Eye had shown me.

My large frame shook, and my free hand had to steady myself against the wall for it felt as if my legs were soon to give out. The only feeling akin to this was when I felt Amelia's death closer to calling for the reaper, and I had fucking prayed for her life to be saved. But in this, I didn't find myself praying to any God, only cursing the name of one...

Janus, the God of time.

I don't know how long it took me to compose myself, but the moment it happened was when anger started to replace the blind panic. I found my fingers curling and breaking through the rock as it cracked before crumbling in my hand. I turned quickly and punched the hand that had been at my chest into the wall, because it still wasn't enough.

I needed to feel that destruction by my hands. I needed to crush the implanted thoughts out of my mind. I needed to eradicate the mental image of Amelia's sacrifice from my very soul. Which was why, before I could stop myself, my furious steps took me towards the Eye and the next time I picked it up, it was only to throw the fucking thing against the wall. A hopeless prayer that the heart of fate shattered taking with it that of its unwanted foretold future. One that…

I. Was. Not. Going. To. Let. Happen!

"FUCK YOU!" I roared as it hurtled across the open space hitting into the wall and like my fist had done, creating a hole in the stone. The Eye however, remained untouched as it landed on the sand turning it golden the moment it touched it. I growled and dragged a hand through my hair in anger, nearly tearing a fist full of strands from my head.

"NO! No! No fucking way am I willing to accept that! Fuck the Fates…FUCK THE GODS!" I roared snarling back at the new source of my anguish. Then, when I had panted through the worst of my rage, without touching it again I used my powers to lift it and put it back on the altar with a snarl of disgust. This was fucking why I never had anything to do with the fucking Fates and had never once before been tempted to look at the fucking thing! Because they twisted truths and forged the path for others to take, like fucking puppet masters tugging on the strings of souls!

Well, I wasn't like Dom! I wasn't going to be drawn into that bullshit and give power to their divine intervention by believing in it! I was going to find my girl and do as I intended by keeping her safe. I would act as if I had not seen a thing, so as not giving her the chance to fulfil some fucking prophecy they had designed for her.

I would save my own fucking people and if that sacrifice had to be my own life, then so be it! But there was one thing I was absolutely certain of…

Amelia would live.

Which meant that she wasn't going anywhere near Tartarus. And if anyone was going to sacrifice a piece of themselves it would be me. After all, I had already lost a hand once, and granted if the image was anything to go by then what they would demand for saving my people was something I couldn't give and ever walk away from.

Not when what they wanted sacrificed was none other than…

The beating heart of a true born Vampire.

Once I was free of the water, my impatience to be rid of the Eye's pull was stifling and had me summoning my armour instantly, doing so with some hope the extra layer of power surrounding me would help. I cast a hand out behind me after leaving the pool to seal off the entrance to the tomb and at the same time angry strides took me across the bathroom. I reached the top of the staircase with only one destination in mind.

To find my heart's keeper.

Which meant that after taking the last step, I launched myself up in the air and twisted my horns around so they pointed upwards. This was done to protect my body, covering it with my wings in a cocoon of demonic skin the second I burst through the obsidian crystal. Then the second I was through, my horns shifted back at the same time I uncurled my wingspan and cut through the air as quickly as possible, needing to get away.

I didn't know how long it was until I found myself stopping enough to take a breath and holding myself suspended in the air. The sight of her sacrificing herself again clung to me like a fucking web of lies! I had thought the more distance I put between myself and the Eye then the better it would be. But the truth was the vision fucking haunted me! Like the ghost of a soul before death. I even found myself dropping a metre or two as my wings lowered in defeat.

"No...no, it won't happen...it can't...I won't let it happen," I muttered to myself before my head snapped up and my wings lifted with my surge of determination.

"Speaking of which, time to get my girl back!" I snapped at no one before gritting my teeth and getting my ass in gear. Because despite the fucked up shit the Eye had shown me, it had first done what I had asked of it. It had shown me where the shifters were taking her and thankfully for me, as a combined entity, they were slower than I was. So, it was time to put the sight of a fate I would never allow to happen behind me and concentrate on my current mission. One that meant getting my Chosen One back and the price being…

Three dead shifters.

Thankfully, it took me no time at all to get to the wastelands and beyond that, were the soul fields. A place which was where the Eye had shown me I would find them. This meant that I wasn't surprised when I found all four forms below, as the vision had shown me such.

It had granted me the sight of them as they are, back as men and no longer as their combined beast. This was lucky on my side for that would have been a much harder battle to face, and not one I was confident I would have walked away from unscathed.

Of course, the situation wasn't made any better when I saw the actions below, although seeing my girl slapping the redheaded bastard Trice across the face eased my fury a little. But then a few moments later and just as I was getting closer their angry exchange morphed into one that made my blood boil.

"Oh, fuck no!" I snarled the second I saw him with his arms around her from behind, but then on my descent I heard her tell him,

"I was already free, you just didn't get to see it." So that was what this was about. It was as I suspected, the brothers thought they were saving her from a tyrant King. But of course they fucking did!

Fuck!

She turned in his arms and the second her hand cupped his cheek I roared in undiluted anger. It cut through the air like thunder, meaning that when I landed on the ground, I did so as if lightning had just struck it. But then the Cockatrice must have had a fucking death wish after all, for he made yet another colossal mistake. This was when he tried to position Amelia behind him as if protecting her from me!

I was going to tear him to fucking pieces!

I snarled low and dangerous, a warning of what was to come, feeling the weight of my fangs as they pushed through my gums. Gods, but I could almost taste the shifter's blood as the thirst for it was that great. But then, as Amelia tried to get around him to get to me, this was when he got a true taste of my girl. Or more importantly, what happened when you tried to force Amelia to do anything...*you often found your ass handed to you or on the floor!*

Fuck me, but in that moment, I couldn't have been prouder of her and at the very least watching it managed to cool the rage in my blood a little. For once she was free to do so, she ran towards me and began calling my name. Thankfully, I had enough sense even through my dark, demonic nature to release my armour so when she threw herself carelessly into my arms, the impact didn't hurt her. This way I could hold her as close as possible and at the same time wrap my arms around her and lift her to my height. I cupped the back of her head, pressing her to my neck and feeling her take a deep breath. In all honesty, it was the first fucking time since the throne room, that I myself could breathe easy.

"Amelia." I let her name out as a whisper through her hair and cared little that it sounded like a fucking prayer that had been answered. One laced with the secret vow that fate could fucking burn for all I cared. Nothing would happen to my Chosen One...

She was eternally mine!

After giving me a squeeze, I lowered her back to the ground so I could see for myself that she was unharmed. I framed her face and lifted it up so I could take in every inch of her beautiful features, lingering on the relief in her startling blue eyes.

"Are you alright, Sweetheart?" I asked making her nod in return and not missing the cocky McBain brother's comment,

"Och, I think we hae missed something big 'ere, brothers." I ignored Vern's assessment of the situation as well as his brother's simple reply,

"Aye."

I ignored all this in face of Trice regaining his feet and challenging me with his furious demeanour. Fucking bring it on shifter shit stain!

"Wait here," I said sternly after releasing a growl, one she couldn't miss the meaning of... There was about to be blood...*lots and lots of fucking blood!*

"No! Lucius, no…" she started to beg at me to stop but I ignored this until I felt her running after me.

"Amelia, do as you're told!" I snapped back before she managed to catch up and was now facing me, but it was Trice's actions that cemented an already sealed fate, drawing his weapon as he spoke,

"Aye, Amelia, dae as yer Master commands!" I had to fucking give it to him, he was one ballsy fucker!

"Not helping here!" Amelia snapped back at him making me growl down at her before warning furiously,

"Get. Back!"

"NO!" she bellowed in return, pushing against my chest as hard as she could, needless to say it was pointless. So, I physically moved her out of the way by grabbing her waist and dumping her small frame to the side. After which I took advantage of her dazed state, left over from my quick actions and continued my advance on the bastard.

However, my little hellfire wasn't done with me yet.

I knew this when I suddenly felt her body impact my back before she swiftly locked her legs around me. Then she used all her weight to propel me to the ground, meaning I had no choice but to follow or I would have risked hurting her. Fuck, but she was quick when she wanted to be! And sprightly too, which was surprising seeing as she was also usually clumsy as hell.

She tried to pin me to the ground whilst shouting down at me,

"It wasn't their fault! They didn't know!" I ignored this and gave her a piece of her own actions and before she had chance to counteract the move, I flipped her to her back and thundered back down at her,

"They knew that they were acting against their King!" And this was the truth. Because no matter how noble an act they believed it to be, there was no escaping the fact that they had turned against me. But I knew Amelia wouldn't understand this, for she didn't have the grit for it. She didn't fully understand what it took to rule, especially down here... not in my realm of Hell.

Furious that I was being forced to act in front of her, I growled in frustration as I pushed up from the ground where I had held her caged with my body. Then the moment I was upright I let my own weapon emerge from my body, with the darkness of Hell's fury seeping from me. I had my opponent in my sights, seeing that he too was getting ready for the fight ahead, with his sword now being raised, prepared for the first strike. But then came a formidable voice behind me, the barest hint of it wavering told me of the emotions being held back as she issued her threat.

"If you do this...if you fight him or hurt any of them... then I swear to you, Lucius, I will never fucking forgive you! NEVER! Do you hear me?!" I couldn't help but cease my threatening steps from going any further, questioning now what would such actions really cost me?

I looked back over my shoulder at her to see her own shoulders slump in a pained way as her voice softened in her next plea,

"Please...don't do this, don't make me hate you for hurting them." I frowned, knowing that in her eyes she was speaking the truth, that she really could hate me for such a thing. That she had it in her not to forgive me if in that moment I made this bloody choice in delivering my revenge.

In fact, I was so lost in her pained beauty that in that moment I lost all thoughts of the enemy at my back, one who was silently advancing. And the only reason I knew this was Amelia's reaction started to change and her eyes became focused on Trice. They did this before widening in shock and then in...*horror.*

But the horror was not at the sight of what could befall on me. No, the horror belonged solely to Amelia. Because this was all before they then morphed into crimson pools of blood lust and hatred!

"Impossible." I barely had time to utter this before that same impossible turned into something more disbelieving. This was because Amelia, my geeky little mortal, transformed into a Hellish version of herself seconds before releasing a wave of power of the likes I had never known or felt before!

For that split second, she looked like some kind of blood-soaked goddess. An image I would surely never forget, with her hair flaming out behind her and with the barest hint of a pair of large crimson wings haloed at her back...*she was incredible!*

But my astonished stare only lasted a single heartbeat for the second she screamed the wave hit into us all like a fucking mountain! In fact, all I saw before I had to fight to stay on my feet was a blood misted silhouette of her gaining in size and speed until it reached us like a fucking tornado!

I had braced for the impact, but admittedly, it was a force I fought against with everything in me. And even then, I suspect I only managed it because unlike the others, I somehow absorbed the power. I knew this because the moment it passed through me, I felt as though I could have picked up a fucking city with just the powers of my mind! I felt as if I could have beaten, well...*even Adam in his other form.*

Gods, but I had never felt anything like it before... actually, no, that's not true. The last time I felt anything remotely like this was when...

When Lucifer first changed me.
Fuck, but what did it all mean?
Who...*Who was this girl?*

I knew without looking that it had knocked the other three off their feet and on their asses. Honestly, had I not felt the tug of their souls connected to my own then I would have in fact, believed them dead. A testament really to how strong they were to survive such an attack, one from the looks of things had shocked Amelia just as much as it had me.

But then I strangely felt the power evaporating behind me, like the once ignited sparks against my skin were now dying down to a tingling. It was as if wherever her power had come from, it had somehow been connected to my own blood. That's how I knew without looking that it was all over.

However, the power hadn't left my vessel completely, as I still felt the strength in the hit, and I had to wonder how long it would last for? Fuck, but it was like my own abilities had been zapped with a fucking power cable and charged beyond capacity. I felt like unleashing some kind of Hellish untapped power upon the world just to see what I was now capable of. Fuck, but I felt as if I could take out a fucking army with one thought!

In fact, I had to shake these thoughts from my mind because my main focus right now needed to be on my girl. They needed to be on Amelia, who was now stood there in utter shock and panting through her strange ordeal.

"Luc...ius, I..." she started to stammer before looking down at her shaking hands as if unable to control herself. I made it to her in a heartbeat, ignoring how much quicker I appeared to be. I took her hands in my own at the same time telling her,

"I am here!" Then, seeing as she still couldn't seem to

catch her breath, I took her in my arms and spoke to her in a soothing way that I made sure masked my concern.

"Breathe, Amelia…just breathe now…calm, calm for me." I then encouraged her to follow my rhythm and breathe with me as I held her to my chest, making sure to keep relaxed myself. Something that wasn't easy considering my fear and concern, now wanting nothing more than to give in to impulse by crushing her to me and taking flight.

"That's it…deep breaths, just in and out again," I told her before snarling a warning at Vern when he asked in clear astonishment,

"Whit th fck wis that?!"

"Silence!" I snapped before I asked her if she was alright, recognising that her breathing was now steadier. Yet despite this she only nodded as if too afraid to speak.

"Ah thought she wis mortal?" This came from the next brother who wisely hadn't yet approached, and it was from one whose head I still wanted to see severed from the rest of his big, bastard of a body!

"She is mortal," I snapped back whilst holding her tighter to me. But it was when the last and biggest member of the McBain clan stepped forward did the truth really come out,

"Aye and she's also yer Chosen One." I closed my eyes in frustration, ignoring the clear shock from the other two and gritting out another threat,

"Yes, she is and if a word of this is—" He quickly cut me off,

"We wull nae speak a word o' this, we care fur th' lassie." I would have added more, like 'make sure that you don't, or it will be on your life,' when a hand cupping my cheek stopped me. I looked down at her beseeching wide eyes as she pleaded their case,

"Lucius, please don't be angry at..." She stopped mid-sentence and frowned in confusion before adding,

"I...I...feel..."

"Amelia?" I said her name to prompt more from her, just as that same slice of fear cut through me. Because something was clearly wrong as all the colour started to drain from her face and her eyes lost all focus.

"Whit's wrong wi' her?" I ignored the Wyvern or the appearance of his brother when Amelia's legs suddenly gave way and she collapsed in my arms.

"Amelia?!"

"Turn her aroond." Trice barked an order down at me, his accent heavy with his own concern. This was also said after I had lowered her to the ground and if she hadn't been in my arms, I would have embedded my fist inside his chest cavity and ripped out his heart. However, unable to do that I was left with no other option than to demand he explain himself,

"Why?!"

"Just dae it!" he snapped back, and before telling him to fuck off, I bit back the threat when I took note of his features...

He knew what this was.

So instead of taking control of the situation, I gritted my teeth and did as he asked. But the moment I moved her, the sound of her screaming in agony tore through my heart the second it pierced the air. This was because Trice had ripped open the material concealing her back before I could demand what the fuck he was doing. However, the second I saw the problem for myself those words were ones I nearly fucking choked on!

Gods, but it looked excruciating!

I started cooing down at her as her screams turned to small whimpers of pain. Trice dragged air through his teeth as his face said it all whilst grimacing down at the Hex that looked to be burning deeper into her flesh.

"What is it?!" I snapped using a free hand to drag him closer by the leather strap across his chest, one that held small daggers to his frame. But that was when I started to realise the full extent of what had been cast upon her soul. As the witch was far from through with her and I was soon to learn the full price of underestimating my enemy.

Trice included.

Because as it turned out, I couldn't kill the bastard yet and from the looks of things, well...he was my only hope of saving her. This was made clear after first glancing back at me with his expression tight and his jaw locked. This before his grave tone only added to his anxious reply,

"The Hex...tis..."

"What? The Hex is what, fucking tell me!?" I snapped just as Amelia started to lose consciousness. This was also when he unfortunately finished his sentence.

One that ended with him being her only hope...

"My lord, the Hex...tis...

"...Tis trying tae claim her."

CHAPTER FOUR

DO OR DIE

"Fuck...FUCK!" I roared the moment I couldn't get her back to a conscious state.

"Give me some space," Trice demanded in a hard voice that made me want to rip his tongue out. Especially when he started to reach out and try and take her from me, something that wasn't fucking happening.

"Get your fucking hands off her!" I snarled making him growl back at me like a fucking dragon that was about to torch me for the threat in my tone.

"You need tae let him, m' laird, mah brother can..." I cut Gryph off with a curl of my lip as my demon snarled up at him this time before snapping,

"He can do what?!"

"What the fck dae ye think, I kin help her, that's what!" Trice barked back breathing heavily and obviously fighting with his own urges to fight me, something I had to say that right now, we both had in common.

"You have done this before?" I asked, this time knowing

that helping Amelia was all that mattered in this moment and having no choice but to put our hatred for one another behind us for the sake of my girl.

"How dae ye think it stopped th' first time, ye think I asked it politely tae!?" I growled again thinking that having shit like that thrown in my face wasn't making my decision not to rip his head off any easier.

"Trice lad, cuid ye focus less on pissing aff th' king 'n' more on helping th' lass…yeah?" Gryph wisely said, making Trice respond by granting me a pointed look before nodding down to Amelia. My Chosen One, who I currently had in my arms in a tight grip that was clearly saying not to touch her.

"Well, whit's it tae be…*mah King?*" Trice said, drawling out the title in a mocking way telling me he didn't give a shit for it. But then again, I knew how he cared for Amelia and this cold-hearted bastard act was fooling fucking no one!

I looked down at my girl and that haunting image assaulted me once more, knowing that this sight wasn't one I could ever allow to happen again. Which meant that if I had to let this asshole help in preventing that, then so be it.

"Well?" he snapped again bringing me back with a frustrated growl before I had no choice but to release my white knuckled grip on her clothes.

"Give her tae me," Trice demanded the second he saw me shift her closer, making me snarl,

"Not fucking happening, Shifter!"

"And I wull be needin' space, Vampire," he shot back, making me bare my fangs at him until once again his brother was intervening and playing diplomat,

"M' laird, ye kin trust him, isn't that so…Trice?" I shot the brother in question a look that said it all, making him reply with a short and clipped,

"Aye."

This forced me to ignore the hard set of his jaw and the menacing scar running through his face that seemed to deepen in colour. More often than not, I had a pretty good read on people and this shifter was no different. Which meant that he was getting more concerned by the minute and if I didn't hand her over soon, then it might all be too late. So, with a grit of my teeth and mentally putting a fortress around my demon so this was possible, I did the very last thing I ever wanted to do…

I let her go.

I passed her to the arms of another man, even though the pain of it I would have admittedly rather of lost another hand than do so! However, not at the cost of her life, which is why I got to my feet, dragged a hand through my hair and roared,

"FUCK!"

Thankfully, the brothers ignored me and instead focused on Trice as he rolled Amelia to her front. He was holding her in a tender way I wanted to kill him for, as much as I was thankful he was taking care with her. But then he wrapped a forearm around the front of her, across her breasts and I couldn't help but take a possessive step forward. This was when I was stopped by Gryph's meaty hand on my chest. I growled back at him in a menacing way.

"Please m' laird, let him dae whit needs tae be done."

"Then can you tell him to get the fuck on with it!" I snapped back, before shouldering off his hold and looking around his large frame to add more, only this time in Trice's direction,

"…before I kill him!" At this Trice actually chuckled as if he didn't believe I could and I had to say, with the sight of my girl in his arms and knowing this wasn't the first time, it was more than a little tempting to prove it.

But then he pulled back the sides of her torn clothes and

bared her naked back, showing the Hex as it burnt deeper into her flesh. He took a breath as if building up to something and then lowered his head further over the mark.

"A'richt lassie, time tae shudder once more," he remarked, and I lost my shit enough to snarl a warning,

"Your brother has a fucking death wish!"

"Fur bugger sake laddie git th' fck on wi' it, will ye!" Gryph snapped taking the threat seriously along with Vern who told him,

"Aye, before he tears ye head aff!"

But Trice wasn't listening. No, instead he started to blow a stream of frozen air down over her back, directing his power at the Hex and doing so enough that it stopped trying to bury itself deeper into her body. No, now instead of hurting her more it had no choice but to rise back to the level of the rest of her skin.

Fuck me, but the bastard had done it!

I don't know how because magic that strong had no weakness and a Hex was cast that way for a reason. But then I was starting to discover that this shifter wasn't exactly like the others of his kind either. That was when it started to hit me exactly who he was, for I had heard of the legends of course, *we all had*.

I had heard of the stories told among his shifter kind. One with a power like no other. For it was one that came from the frozen depths of Hell that burned with greater force than that of the heart of the eternal fires and the once great mountain of even Tartarus itself.

Which was why, without a word, I knelt enough to take back possession of my girl before standing with her in my arms. It was only then did I stare down at him and say,

"You have been holding out on me…*Dragon King.*" At this he gritted his teeth and rose back to his feet without taking his eyes from mine. Then he nodded to Amelia in my arms and said,

"We all hae our secrets…and clearly I am not th' only one keeping them from mae people." I locked my jaw as I ground my teeth before telling him,

"I do what I do to protect her." It was a statement made that didn't need to be said but was heard all the same before turning my back on him.

"Aye 'n' a bang up jab ye hae done o' that so far!" he shouted behind, making me take pause and threaten,

"Take heed shifter King, for your souls still belong to me and whilst you still have fucking breath beneath your feathers and scales, you will yield to my will and right now, there is only one command I have of you!"

"Aye 'n' what's that?!"

"To help me get this fucking Hex off my Chosen One and slay a fucking witch!"

After this I released my wings as my demonic form burst free a split second before I took flight. That part of me could be contained no longer. So, I flew back in the direction all three had fled from, knowing they would follow in their own forms. Because as much as I hated to admit it, now I knew who Trice really was, and what he was capable of, then I had no fucking choice but to put my trust in him.

I needed the bastard.

And why…because he was the only one who was immune to the magic of one of the strongest witches in existence. Meaning that right now, he was our best hope at winning this war against my people. And because one thing was for sure, this was only the start. For if anything that the fucking Eye had shown me was real, then this blood soaked future that the Fates had pathed for us, was only going to get worse.

Worse and a hell of a lot…

Bloodier.

CHAPTER FIVE

WEAKNESS IS A WITCH

The moment I landed with Amelia in my arms, I knew that to prevent anything like this from happening again I had to start trusting those closest to my rule in this world. I needed to create some inner fucking circle because doing this solely on my own and keeping my girl safe at the same time, was what I now knew an impossible task. So, I had to take a different approach to this realm just as I did topside.

Which was why, the moment my army backed away from my abrupt and furious arrival, I snapped out my orders,

"Where is Carn'reau?!" My general's second in command stepped forward, another dark Fae who was named Alvaro. And well, if the rumours were true, then he was also like a brother to Carn'reau. This was no doubt strengthened by the fact his loyalty had also been gained due to joining him when both were cast from their realm. Although his loyalty to me as King was also shown when he lowered to a knee and bowed a head.

"Rise and speak," I told him making him do as I asked, and when he did, he removed his helmet at the same time. This meant that when I was now faced with the mountain of a muscle bound Fae, I did so by staring into a pair of startling light blue eyes. Eyes that were a stark contrast to his midnight black skin with hues of blue over prominent features.

A harsh and serious story was told in his ancestry from his high cheekbones and keen gaze. The same hues of blue dusted the top of his forehead near the hairline and down the bridge of his nose. This same colour was also seen in the thick snakes of dreads that were tied back off his face and could be seen reaching his waist down his back.

"Carn'reau is dealing with the witch, my lord," Alvaro answered in that deep gravelly voice of his, though it had to be said, he wasn't your typical Empyrean being. For this was what all Fae were known as. That being if their ancestry was more than just myth.

Empyrean was known as the highest part of Heaven, thought by the ancients to be the realm of pure fire and where all light Fae had been created. But as for the dark Fae, well they had been born in the Empyrean of Hell and ironically one not made of fire, like Hell is known for, but one purely of the darkness.

The two most powerful forces of all Elemental beings. It was said that eons ago, the two Empyrean sides collided, and it created the Elemental realm. A world not of Heaven or Hell but of both. It was thought that if all the worlds combined were made up of layers, then Heaven would be at the top. Of course this also meant that the Earth realm would be in the middle and Hell situated at the bottom, meaning then that the Elemental realm would have been what was sandwiched in between. However, these realms were not made up like this, they were made from gateways and portals. Which meant that looking up to the sky and praying was utterly fucking pointless unless you thought God might be on a plane!

It was why I always shook my head and rolled my eyes when I saw humanity making these mistakes, even if we ourselves had adopted the habit. The reason these habits existed of course was that the gateways or portals to get to these other realms were usually the ones found underground, not the actual realms themselves. For no sky existed under the Earth's crust, just as lands existed in the realm of Heaven and not every Angel or God there lived in the fucking clouds!

The truth was that geographically, it was more accurate to say that most of these worlds existed side by side to one another. Admittedly Hell was the lowest of them all, which was why it was always referred to as being 'down in Hell'. And contrary to human belief, Hell wasn't all fire and brimstone either. Nor was it just hordes of soulless demons gorging themselves on the souls of others or torturing the vessels of what once belonged to the evils of mankind.

No, it was a world like any other…admittedly a more brutal one than most, but it had an economy just the same. It had a food chain among its races and creatures like the animal kingdom and humanity of Earth.

Demonic beings worked, they ate, they paid for goods, and lived in dwellings. They were part of armies that too had to be fed from those that farmed the land or kept livestock. Many were master builders and beings of craftsmanship just like the rest. Hell even had a workforce known as Ukobachs. These dwarf sized demons were usually stationed in heated environments due to their preference for the hotter temperatures, which was usually why they were found working in the boiler rooms in places big enough to need them. If not put to work, then they became scavenger type creatures that could always be found close to the flaming rivers in Hell. But a subspecies of these creatures were also known as grafters, and under strict guidance could build almost anything, for working in large groups were what they were best known for.

After all, not all castles like mine were built off the back of a mage or a witch. Which meant that not every soul that ended up in Hell was cast into a forgotten oblivion, forever doomed to a torturous life. Some were chosen for more, depending of course what level of evils brought you a one-way ticket to an eternity in Hell. In short there was a place for every type of soul that ended up here and speaking of Hellish souls, mention of the witch most certainly caught my attention.

"The witch?!" I snapped out my question,

"We believe she was the cause of the diversion and the one to create the army. Carn'reau found her fleeing into the Echoing Forest soon after it was discovered."

"Nero, whaur is she?!" The angry Scottish voice came from behind us and at the same time my men all drew their weapons and pointed them at the furious shifter. One who had now lost all that easy-going manner and replaced it with a shifter's rage...*interesting.*

I turned to the side to watch as his brothers followed seconds later in their landing, doing so as men after changing back into their human looking vessels whilst still in the air. From below it had ended up looking like two tornados not connected with the ground had consumed their bodies, as the power of their shift created a vortex of air to be sucked in around them.

This was because of the power they each held in any

realm they were in, being one of the elements. The land would crack at a mere touch from a Gryphon shifter's hand and that same land would be scorched with just the click of fingers from a Wyvern. And as for Trice, who was still uncertain just how much power he had, what I did know of him he could freeze that land at just a thought or whisper of breath. Naturally then the air around them was attracted to such a living force of nature and shifting took a lot of power and strength for such a creature as big as each of them. It was also why when combined into one it took even more and wasn't a power that could last as long.

I watched as the army started to close in around them and knew I didn't have time for this shit, which was why I snapped at who I knew Carn'reau had appointed leader in his place,

"They are not the enemy, have your men lower their weapons!" His slight frown in confusion was the only answer I received before he barked orders in his own tongue, commanding them to do my bidding. Just then a woman's terrified scream was heard above and was one that was quickly drowned out by the sound of a Zilant's roar. This was no doubt in response to Carn'reau's beast as it swooped down and landed in the spot his men had cleared for him.

It quickly became clear that the witch Alvaro had spoken of, combined with that of Vern's worry was none other than the witch I had encountered back in that shit stain of a town that was closest to the wastelands. So, she was the one who had been tasked with creating the diversion. I shook my head a little and looked down at the sleeping beauty in my arms and knew the depths a person would go to for love. And well, from the looks of things, the Wyvern and the witch were travelling that depth together.

The moment Carn'reau's beast calmed he swung his legs from the saddle and dragged the bent form of a struggling Nero with him. His manhandling of the girl had the shifter lose his mind and along with it the sight of the army at the control of the dark Fae. Because before anyone could stop him, he half changed into his other form, so when he pulled back on his bow, a flaming arrow was what was aimed at the Fae's head. This in turn caused the soldiers around him to aim their spears and swords at the new threat against their general, quickly having his back.

Not that the Wyvern even flinched at this, telling me exactly when it was that usual brutal and unyielding strength came out, along with his true power...*His only weakness.*

"Let. The. Girl. Go." This threat came from the belly of the beast as it was barely a sound you would have heard produced from a human's vocal cords. However, Carn'reau didn't look at all phased and the reason became obvious as to why. He barked an order over his shoulder at his men who all fell back a step at his command. Then, once they lowered their weapons, his grip tightened on Nero who whimpered, making Vern pull his bow tighter in reaction to his actions. But Vern had underestimated his opponent when all Carn'reau needed to do was raise a single fingertip to the tip of the flaming arrow before it extinguished into black smoke. This enraged the shifter enough that those same flames started to engulf his form, telling me this was about to get too fucking ugly and having either one of them out of commission was not an option right now.

It was time to intervene.

"Enough! You two, put a fucking leash on your brother and Carn'reau, let the witch go." My general looked to me and with a slight sadistic smirk he released his prisoner by uncurling his fist he'd had shackled around the top of her arm. She fell into Vern with a stumble, making a halo of long navy-blue waves cover half her face with the flick of Carn'reau's hand.

Vern snarled over her head after first cradling her to his chest, telling me that the bad blood between these two now ran deep due to both the events of his capture and now that of the woman he clearly loved.

Fucking peachy, I thought with an inward groan. Just what I fucking needed. But then what fucking choice did I have in the matter, for as usual time wasn't on my side here and I needed every fucker I could trust working on this!

Gods, but I missed my council and the level of trust I knew came with having them sat at my table for both decades and centuries. I missed having Adam as my second in command, knowing he would do all that was possible to get the fucking job done. Even Pip, who was as loyal as the Gods made them, despite her wacky and eccentric personality. Caspian and Liessa, Ruto and Hakan and even Percy were of those that I had come to trust with that of my life. And Clay, my head of security, who would no doubt be the first one to warn me of trusting the shifters as I was about to.

Fuck yes, I missed them all and if the fantastical notion of wishes were true then it would have been those on my council I would have wished for right now. However, that was one luxury I didn't have and being choosy right now wasn't an option.

"Carn'reau, you trust your second?" I asked not giving a shit that he was stood within hearing distance. A slight frown in question was the only indication he was surprised by the question. Then he looked to the Fae in question and said,

"With my life's blood, My Lord." His answer was good enough for me, making me reply,

"Good then bring him with you...all of you are with

me...including the witch!" I ordered before turning around and leading the way into my castle and into a place that up until now, no one had ever been before other than myself and the unconscious troublemaker in my arms...

My Tower.

CHAPTER SIX

FATED INNER CIRCLE

"Wow, this is cosy," Nero muttered after having a good look around with wide dark blue eyes. It was also obvious that she was making jokes on account of her nervousness. After all, she had gone against her King and therefore the anxiety I could scent coming off her was doing so in waves.

"Nae noo, Nero," Vern warned taking a step closer in a possessive and protective way the moment I shot her an unimpressed look that said it all. I walked straight over to the bed and with a mere thought, I forced the shards that surrounded it to seep back to the floor. This was so it made it easier for me to lay Amelia down without causing her any unnecessary discomfort.

Not that she had so much as stirred since first losing consciousness. In fact, if it hadn't been for my connection with her and being able to hear her constant and steady heartbeat then I would be far more worried. But even Trice had explained to his brothers on the way up here, that the longer she was out of it the better it was. This was because the Hex couldn't claim her whilst she was asleep and that was fine by me, just so long as she wasn't in any danger and no longer feeling any pain.

"Just give me a little longer, Sweetheart," I told her after laying her down and brushing her dark hair from her face, some of the thicker strands had become knotted due to all that she had endured in yet another fucking day in Hell. A place she most certainly didn't belong and the sooner I could get her home, the better. Something I was soon to discover wasn't going to be quite as easy as I originally believed.

This I found out shortly after re-joining the rest of them and doing so by ignoring the way they all now stared at me as though I had grown a fucking head that had been singing Sinatra. But then again, I tried to look at things from their side of the Hell they stood on. And well, seeing their tyrant King taking such care and concern over who they had first thought to be nothing more than a mortal sex slave, then yeah, it was understandable. Well, all except the McBain brothers who had guessed the truth after witnessing our encounter back at the soul fields.

But then, there was one being who had joined us just before the doors had closed and he hadn't missed the encounter...

My brother.

I would have rolled my eyes at the look he granted me but instead it was time to get this shit over with. Which meant getting everyone's ass in gear and to do that, I first needed to let them know the full extent of what we were dealing with. Starting with why freeing Amelia of the fucking Hex was the first priority!

So, I folded my arms after first shedding my skin of the

constricting armour, leaving behind a layer of black material that clung to my frame. It looked like a plain black, long-sleeved T-shirt with my cursed hand being the only piece of armour to remain. I also had summoned black trousers in a beast hide similar to the Basilisk my brother had slayed. Only due to the rarity, it was in fact from a creature known as a Vipera.

This was a demonic grass snake that had bad eyesight and usually burrowed underground. They lived by the sense of vibrations they could feel with the rattle of their barbed tails, and only came out among the soul fields when they felt no one was near. This was because they were heavily hunted despite being covered in a spiked, hard shell of bright blue scales. They were hunted for their delicious meat and their soft reddish black underbellies that felt like a combination of Earth's satin and suede. It was also currently what Amelia was lay on right now, for my sheets were made of the same material.

Shit kicker plated boots completed the look and despite feeling slightly more comfortable, I would have much preferred being naked lying alongside my girl with her soft skin cradled against mine.

"Why ur we 'ere?" Gryph had been the first to ask, making me release a sigh and say,

"This tower is impenetrable to all outside magic and therefore is the only place I trust to discuss matters."

"Ah, that explains the heebie jeebies then," Nero commented, hugging herself and rubbing her arms.

"You say we need tae discuss matters, bit whit ye pure mean is—" I quickly cut the jealous bastard off,

"Amelia is my Chosen One," I stated, and I swear it was like finally dragging the barbed wire up from down my throat for how long I had wanted to declare such a thing. The only three who naturally didn't look surprised by this were the McBains, although the narrow gaze of Trice told me it wasn't totally ineffective...

Yeah, take that sting, you bastard!

"*Holy Gorgon balls!*" Nero gasped before a shudder wracked her body and I had to say, my ego took the hit. Fuck, but what did they think I did with the one soul destined to be mine, keep her in a cage? Oh right, no they just thought I fucking collared her like a dog and kept her on a leash close by ready for when I was hungry.

Fucking Idiot, Luc!

Gods, I had really fucked this up, I thought at the same time resisting the urge to scrub a hand down my face. Instead, I told her in a hard tone,

"I can assure you, I care for what is mine." Her wide eyes shot to mine and she started to shake her head a little. But before she could speak, Trice scoffed making the bulk of his body rise and fall with the verbal disbelief that made me want to rip his fucking head off once more. Shame I needed the bastard. But despite that, I still warned,

"Remember Shifter, it's a long way down from this tower after first having your fucking wings ripped off." He snarled back but wisely took my threat as one best not responded to. Besides, my brother took that moment to stride towards me and snarl in a low tone,

"*A word, Šeš.*" I held the shifter's gaze a few seconds longer, ignoring the way Nero nudged Vern and whispered not so subtly,

"*Okay, I feel like I am missing an episode here.*" Vern didn't answer but his lips twitched as he fought a smile and it was enough for me to give up the death glare. Especially knowing that unfortunately now was not the time to force him to my will. Like making him shave his head, draw a line down the centre as his new ass crack and make him believe he needed to do a handstand every time he needed a shit!

My brother placed a hand on my arm and ground out my name,

"Lucius." I didn't respond to this how I usually would have had it been in front of my kingdom. But as it stood, in front of these six, who I had chosen to be in the know, it no longer mattered. However, the knowledge that he was my brother didn't need to come to light right now. Not for plans to be put into place regarding helping Amelia.

"Witch, see to my woman," I ordered sternly before yanking my arm free and then turning my glare back to my brother, ignoring Nero's dry, mumbled reply,

"Yeah, 'cause that is usually what I go by these days, 'cause four letters of Nero are so hard to remember for a Vamp's memory." I glared back at her to see Vern place a hand at her belly and pull her back to his taller frame before nodding to me and telling her teasingly,

"They also hae bonnie hearing, Lass," After this her sheepish gaze shot back to me and she quickly held up her hands and said,

"On second thoughts, Witch is just all kinds of Hell's dandy." I scoffed as Vern chuckled heartedly behind her and with the besotted look he was sporting, I almost felt sorry for the poor bastard.

Falling in love was fucking brutal!

"Dariush, come with me," I snapped back after turning to face the opposite direction. I walked towards the wall behind the only seating area in this sparse space and my brother followed as I knew he would. Then I continued around the seats and through the illusion wall opening that most likely made it look as though I had just disappeared. The truth was that the whole tower was surrounded by hidden doorways like this. In fact, all levels beneath my private bedchamber consisted of two layers, the first was a massive spiral staircase that framed all the rooms at its core.

There was a bathroom, living space, training room, grand banqueting hall and where we were headed now, *my office*. Now why most of these rooms even existed I didn't fucking know, as no one ever came here to fill them. But then again, during the time it was being built I don't suppose Lucifer knew what it would be primarily used for. As neither of us had ever expected it to become a living vault and used to hide one of the most powerful supernatural weapons in all the realms. Meaning it wasn't as if I was going to have a fucking party whilst hiding the damn thing under my pool!

This of course meant that most of these rooms had never even been stepped foot in since the time they were made. In the beginning there had been other ways to access my tower, like on the lower levels. But these I'd had closed up years ago shortly after the Eye had come into my possession.

This also meant that I had far better places to be having this meeting other than in my private bedchamber. But the reason I didn't was because I wanted to stay as close to Amelia as possible. And her comfort and care was naturally my first priority right now.

Dariush followed me behind the wall and down the steps into my private office and like I said, it was one I hadn't entered in quite some time. Unlike my office in Castle Blutfelsen, it also hadn't been graced with a single shred of personality. Granted it was a room I spent most of my time in when there, as running a kingdom alongside a mortal business empire took a lot of fucking time. In truth, before

Amelia had stumbled into my life as a more permanent fixture, I had been little more than a workaholic. Even my nights spent at the club weren't as relaxing as I portrayed them to Amelia during those times she had infiltrated Transfusion.

Which meant that if I was to spend most of my time in a fucking office, it would be one I felt comfortable in and less like some fucking machine behind a desk. This meant that in the Earth realm I had surrounded my personal space with things from my past. Things that essentially kept me attached to my mortality in some way. Although, I had to confess that since being with Amelia I hadn't realised just how much of that I had lost. Because Amelia to me was like a mortal overload and in many ways similar to Pip. Amelia had rooted herself in the culture and history of her world along with that of her father's. Although I knew for a fact how she struggled when growing up believing herself not belonging to it.

I also knew the fault lay at my feet for taking that piece of her and I had to wonder now if that had been the reason that burst of power back in the soul fields had been absorbed instead of knocking me on my ass like it should have?

I didn't have any answers...*Yet.* But one thing I did know for certain and that was Amelia was clearly much more than just a mortal. And being down in Hell had obviously tapped into the little remaining power I had stolen from her. Which made me question, how fucking powerful would she be now had I not done so? Gods, but it even seemed too dangerous a thought to consider. Then again, no matter how much I tried it was a difficult thought to get out of my head. Not when she had looked like some Angel of Blood sent by the Gods to deliver punishment.

Gone was the girl that I had found in a big red dress sat upon my floor playing with Lego and recreating my home in block form. Gods, how I had changed, for once upon a time her obsession in all things geek would have irritated me. Now I just found it endearing and a pleasure to watch her excitement at such things.

In fact, once this was all over, I was looking forward to indulging her in these quirks and hobbies, with the gift of her playful smiles in return. But again, I was focusing on how much I had changed since knowing her this way, being with her in what modern convention would class as a relationship. These were all things I never would have thought I would accept, much less tolerate. I had foolishly believed that when I finally allowed myself to claim my Chosen One then I would do so solely on my terms. That I would have them situated by my side with little thought to much else. Selfishly and arrogantly assuming that they would cater to my needs and yield to my rule.

Gods, but how fucking wrong could I have been!

It was fucking laughable now after being with her and discovering what type of woman she was. Oh, she may yield in the bedroom but fuck, I would find myself daily being put on my ass when least expecting it if I tried to conquer her elsewhere. And if I were honest, I wouldn't want to. Because a force of nature like hers was something to marvel in and enjoy the fucking ride, not try to mould into a box and keep it contained. Of course, if I had the choice, then her hairpin decision making I would crush in a heartbeat if it meant keeping her safe.

But that was another story.

Because I knew that I would have no choice but to take matters into my own hands after what had happened. So, whether she liked it or not, this tower had just become her new prison, at least until I could fix what the fucked-up Fates had in store for me, my people, and more importantly Amelia.

Which meant that setting up our lives together in a more permanent way would have to wait...*for now.*

"What the fuck is going on?!" Dariush snapped, bringing me back to why we were now in my office and I found myself with no other option than to shake away thoughts of better days and deal with the shit one I had been dealt...*fucking Fates.*

"I couldn't tell you," I told him after first walking over to my desk that looked like crystal melted over an invisible frame. It was black like the walls were, with only the floor being different in swirls of ash-coloured, petrified wood laid in circular slabs. A throne style chair situated behind the desk that was the size of a small car was one I stayed away from as it was made from black glass. So not exactly something I thought would survive my anger right now.

It was sculpted to look like two giant demonic skeletal remains bent over so the place I sat was at the joined pelvis. At the highest point of the chair were the two horned skulls that faced us with their shoulders fused and their ribcages making up the back section.

Overly long arms of twisted black glass bone made the armrests, and the bird clawed feet made up the bottom part of the legs. It was a hauntingly, beautiful piece of craftmanship and it was one of the most uncomfortable chairs I'd ever sat on in my whole existence. Hence another reason why I took to leaning back on the desk instead.

"Bullshit!" he snapped back folding his arms and making his muscles bulge due to the sleeveless tunic style jacket he now wore which was a typical attire for my brother. He was, as one would say, stuck in a certain time period and his vessel's Persian ancestry had ingrained early on. I released a sigh when he added,

"You didn't think you could trust me with something as

important as your Chosen One, but yet those three vagabonds out there you go ahead and..."

"They guessed who she was to me when they saw the level of my care and loyalty to her," I interrupted defending myself when I really I didn't need to. But we were alone, and he was my brother, so I believed he at least deserved some form of explanation.

"I fucking knew she meant more to you than you were letting on!" he added with a bitter growl to his words.

"It wouldn't have changed things had you known from the start," I told him, but his face said otherwise.

"The fuck it wouldn't, for starters I wouldn't have thrown her in a fucking jail cell to nearly get raped by her jailor!" he snapped back making me wince at the fucking good point he made.

"Which is why the outcome was on me, as well as the death I served," I replied, with a grit of my teeth. Dariush released a heavy sigh and rubbed the lower part of his face, which ended with him bringing his fingers and thumb together with the hair on his chin stroked down between them.

"You thought I would tell him, that's it, isn't it?" he guessed speaking of course about our father.

"I was protecting you," I stated.

"Fuck that!"

"Choose to believe it or not, my reasons were sound, for I knew you would have been bound to the truth should the question be asked and let's fucking face it here, it wouldn't be long before this shit got back to him." Dariush at least agreed on this if not with words but with his expression.

"My loyalty has and always will be first to the blood I share, not the blood that made me." I released another sigh and pushed straight from the table so I could clasp a hand on my brother's shoulder,

"I know, brother, but this way, what you didn't know, you wouldn't have been forced to lie about and no offence, my Šeš, but you're a fucking shit liar." He scoffed at this even as I laughed, a sound I hadn't heard since my girl had been awake and in my arms. I let him go, giving him back his space so I could resume leaning my weight back on the desk.

"So, she was feisty for a reason then?" I raised a brow in question, making him add,

"Well, she would have to be to put up with your shit." Now I was the one to scoff.

"She is as she should be and perfect at that," I admitted unashamedly. He grinned at the same time his eyes grew wide with surprise.

"I think that's the nicest thing I have ever heard come out of your mouth...*fuck me, it must be love,*" he muttered this last part to himself and I chose to ignore it. After this I told him everything that had happened regarding the threat against our people and the spreading infection of the Tree of Souls. Of course, it started with the box and the map leading all the way up until recent events, including Amelia's Hex.

"Have you discovered yet where this summoning Hex is linked to?" he asked, making me grip the edge of the table in anger at the thought of the fucking thing still marring her skin.

"No, but I think it is easy to assume it is to wherever the fucking witch is, as she obviously needs her blood to access the Tree of Souls," I told him only adding more strength to what I had already shared with him.

"And what of the Eye, does your Chosen One know where it is or how to get to it?" I found this an odd question so asked,

"Why would she?"

"Well, you used it to find her, so it is safe to assume it may start calling to her." I frowned in response and found the next question coming from my lips a troubling one...

"How do you know I used the Eye?"

CHAPTER SEVEN

POWER IN PLANNING

My brother's explanation to knowing that I had finally used the Eye was in his words, through the 'power of deduction'. And as my brother also pointed out, there weren't exactly lots of ways to know where the shifters had been going. Especially adding to this that speed was heavily of the essence. He also knew that if there was anything in the world to make me finally use the Eye, it would obviously be for my Chosen One's safety. And of course, he had been right, I had. But now I worried for a different reason, asking him,

"You think I should have it moved in case she is affected?"

"I think you are safe, at least until she regains consciousness, but I have to ask, did the Eye show you anything more than just where she was being taken?" It was at this point that I decided not to say more, for what the Eye had shown me was my burden to bear, and no one else's. Hell, but it was one of the reasons only a few people even knew the Eye existed beyond anything more than just a myth, let alone whose possession it was in.

I had not even trusted Dom with that bit of information. A decision that turned out for the best seeing as I knew, had he known at one time, he would have fought my armies of Hell just to get to it. Doing so in a desperate need to seek a glimpse of his Chosen One's future and of course, how to prevent it. Something that in turn would have destroyed the world and all realms beyond it.

Making what the Eye had shown me an even more bitter wound which I was still figuratively bleeding from.

"No, it showed me nothing more," I told him after a brief pause. Naturally, his gaze lingered a little longer telling me he wasn't so sure he believed me. And well, considering all I had kept from him since turning up here, then it wasn't as if I could blame him. Not when I had been cagey from the start.

But then he wasn't the only one I had been keeping things from, as Amelia was still yet to discover who 'my Šeš' really was. And putting it mildly, I didn't exactly look forward to that conversation, or explaining why I purposely missed out mentioning that I had a brother. Truth was, I hadn't exactly ever planned for Amelia to see this side of my world, despite our joking about such and in that, well...*It included my brother.*

After this we walked from my office to find everyone had occupied their own space, with the three brothers making use of the small living area. As for Carn'reau and his second, Alvaro, they were doing as they should after I had made such an announcement about my Chosen One. Meaning they were standing guard close to the bed and looking ready for trouble from the McBain clan. Nero was sat on the edge of my bed dabbing a damp cloth over Amelia's forehead and doing as I had asked of her by looking after my girl.

I said nothing before walking straight over to her, mounting the steps and taking a seat on the opposite side to Nero with Amelia lay peacefully between us. I then held out my hand silently indicating what I wanted, making Nero do a strange double take before handing me the cloth.

"She has a slight fever?" I noted after first placing the back of my fingers to her forehead and then replacing it with the cold cloth.

"It...uh...getting a little better," Nero told me in a strained voice that told me she was naturally still wary of me. This was understandable seeing as the last time she was this close to me I'd had her life in my hands, threatening to take it.

I nodded slightly without taking my eyes from Amelia, watching the drips from the cloth disappear into her hairline. She was so beautiful, even in this unconscious state. Which was why I unashamedly leant down and lay a gentle kiss on her forehead after moving the cloth, feeling the heated droplets left on her skin.

I handed the cloth back to Nero, one that admittedly had been fisted in my gloved hand as I held back my frustration at her still being in this state. Then, as I ran a single fingertip down the side of Amelia's face, I told Nero,

"Keep her comfortable."

"Erm...yes...of course, My Lord," Nero said after first shaking herself from her shock at obviously seeing this gentle side to a King she expected was as heartless as she had heard. But then, one glance at Vern watching us with a wary eye and I knew that such was the power of loving our Chosen Ones...

It had the power to bring Kings to their knees.

I walked back down the steps noting the bowed heads of my general and his second. My brother had also resumed his earlier place and was once more leaning his weight back against one of the lit shards, doing so with his arms crossed over his chest. He still looked pissed that I had kept knowledge of finding my Chosen One from him, but right now I couldn't give a fuck. I would deal with that guilt should it arise once this shit was over with. Besides, if Lucifer didn't soon come around knocking then I would know his loyalty was as he said it was.

Speaking of loyalty.

"What I am about to tell you all doesn't leave this room, is that understood?" I stated in a commanding tone that rarely was ignored…well, *unless Pip was in the room that was.* I looked to each of them and only continued when I was assured I had received an acknowledgement to my warning, one that had to be nudged from Trice by his brother Gryph. An asshole who since arriving, permanently looked pissed off. Like I gave a shit, as long as the fucker did as he was told!

"The witch that hexed Amelia is trying to gain power of the Tree of Souls, meaning that every soul connected to me is in danger," I said and the only one who didn't look surprised was my brother, who I had just informed of such things.

"Fck…that's…wull that's a wee bit shite," Vern said making Gryph scoff,

"Aye, that's putting it mildly, Lad."

"What dae ye intend tae dae aboot it is whit a'm waantin tae know," Trice said, making me grit my teeth and Carn'reau put his hand at the hilt of his sword at the same time taking a step forward. I held up my own up to stop him, making Trice look around me and wink at him in a goading way. I forced myself to ignore the idiot with a death wish and tell him,

"I had intended to deal with the situation without my fucking Chosen One being put in danger but for those that don't yet know, Amelia is as headstrong as she is brave."

"Meaning?" my brother asked,

"Meaning that she believed she was the only one with the power to stop this force from taking the lives of my people and therefore jumped into the fray before I could stop her," I replied when turning back to face him.

"And is she?" Dariush's question quickly had me narrowing my eyes as it ignited unwelcome images of what the Fates had deemed our future.

"No!" I snapped through gritted teeth, granting him a scathing look that told him not to question me further on it. His look in return said everything his lips didn't have to…he knew I was hiding more.

"And whit o' yer shitty treatment o' her, that was…?" Naturally this question came from Trice.

"It was for her protection," I informed him again with a grit of my teeth now wondering if they would survive much longer, or if the shifter would for that matter!

"Aye 'n' a bang up jab o' that." I opened my mouth ready to tear him a new one when Gryph got in there first by smacking him on the back of the head with his meaty fist and snapping,

"Yer keep pushing him tae throw your ass oot this tower wi' this shite 'n' ah might just let him, brother, fur yer nae helping th' lass." Trice pushed Gryph back with a palm to the side of his head but didn't say anything more. I just hoped his brother's words sunk in before his death, one I was about two more snide remarks away from delivering.

"If my enemies were to get wind of my Chosen One being in this realm then I would find a bigger problem to deal with than just that of my people being eradicated and I think on my list of fucked up shit to do, going to war with the other realms isn't one of them," I told them all, aiming most of it at the shit stain on the sofa.

"Hence why you had big bad here pull out of the Shadow Lands," Nero surmised making Carn'reau grant her a deadly and knowing grin at the reference made.

"I need every resource available right now," I added, making her nod in agreement before suggesting,

"I might be able to help in that department, if you could get me the supplies." I raised a brow in question making her go on to say,

"Basically, it's called a cloud spell, shit name I know but it may be a better way to contain any information of Amelia from travelling too far...basically it contains gossip," she added with a bob of her head and both hands gesturing outwards.

"This spell, how does it work exactly?" Carn'reau asked, folding his armoured arms across his plated chest as he regarded the witch. Vern, however, looked to be ready to punch the Fae, just for speaking with her. Great, what a fucking band of merry men this turned out to be, I thought with a mental roll of my eyes.

"It acts as a deterrent as soon as any keywords are spoken, like the word 'mortal' and any reference to the King being made in the same sentence. Things like that the spell would pick up on."

"And when it does?" Carn'reau pushed for more,

"It acts like a memory cloud, almost like waking up with a bad hangover and not remembering parts of the night. It clings to those who speak about it and creates a fog over the parts of information they just spoke about. It has the same effect on those that hear it...hence the shit name," she said, gesturing again with her hands which I could quickly tell was one of her habits.

"What would need to be done?" I asked this time.

"Well, it would need to be administered in every

populated area, towns and stuff, with maybe a heavier dose placed along the roads and crossover points between realms, like the known portals so for those the spell misses at least it won't leave your lands," Nero said making my eyes widen in surprise as I had to say, I was impressed. It was clear this blue haired beauty of Vern's had skills I had underestimated. I looked to Carn'reau and said,

"General?" He looked thoughtful a moment before saying,

"It can be done and swiftly, depending on how quickly the witch can cast." She coughed a muttered,

"Charming..." before she continued to say,

"That is depending on how soon this...*witch*...can get enough supplies, as with a large enough batch made, it would just be 'smash a bottle and say a few words' type of gig, which a Gorgon monkey could do...no offence, Captain," she added with a cheeky wink to Carn'reau, and a salute using her middle finger from her forehead to flick at him. This made the Fae smirk back at her, clearly up for the challenge.

"Alright, so we git th' fckin' picture!" Vern snapped, clearly getting annoyed at the sight of Nero's attention being on another male, despite how innocent it seemed.

"Carn'reau, I am putting you in charge of working with Nero and getting what she needs to make it happen," I said ignoring Vern's outburst, both before and after he stood up and declared,

"I kin git the lass whatever she needs."

"No, you three have only one job," I stated making him growl in frustration but yield to my order all the same. This was helped when Gryph grabbed his shirt from behind and yanked him back to sitting down telling him,

"Sit yer ass doon lad 'n' ney git yer kilt in a twist, fur th' Fae is only gaun shopping fur th' lass."

"And this jab would be?" Trice asked ignoring his brothers,

"The Hex, you mentioned you might know someone who could remove it?"

"Aye, bit it wull nay be easy," Trice responded, after first looking towards Amelia's sleeping form making me force myself to suppress the urge to break something on his face. Instead, I stood in his line of sight and replied in a dry tone,

"That doesn't exactly surprise me, Shifter!" I snapped at his pointless comment as it was fucking obvious that it wouldn't be. I looked behind me at my girl and said,

"Nothing important ever is."

After this we established a plan of sorts, with the McBain brothers on their own mission to find someone they believed powerful enough to remove the Hex. Although, annoyingly, they remained cagey on the details, making me question why or more like...*Who?* However, before I could express as much my brother swayed the conversation in a different direction.

"And as for the witch, do we have any idea who she could be, other than someone you obviously pissed off?" Nero and Vern both scoffed at the same time,

"Shocking."

"Aye, shocking." I shot them both a scathing look and the moment my fangs grew Nero quickly started dabbing Amelia's forehead, muttering,

"Wow, Vampires are touchy...who knew." Vern laughed at her reaction and therefore received the same treatment only prompting a wink from him in return, making me growl.

"No, her identity is still unknown," I replied, ignoring the urge to re-enact the time I had his throat in my hands and was beating the living shit out of his posh ass down in my dungeon. My brother looked thoughtful a moment longer making me turn to face Carn'reau and say,

"I want you to use whatever underground contacts you have to seek who she could be, even if it takes you beyond our realm, dig as deep as you can...understand?" It was at this moment that I felt my brother move towards me and his hand gripped my shoulder before telling me,

"Leave that to me." I raised a brow back at him before he assured me,

"Trust me, if anyone can find someone with a grudge against you..."

"It's me."

CHAPTER EIGHT

WHERE THE BLOOD LEADS

A few days later and Amelia still hadn't woken, and I was getting more worried by the minute. I had asked my brother to send word to the McBain brothers to return if they didn't find whoever it was they were looking for. I was growing restless in the knowledge that the days were ticking by and I couldn't risk Amelia waking with the Hex trying to claim her again. For as much of an asshole Trice was, right now he was the only one who could save her from being taken from me. Which if it meant letting the bastard touch her again to achieve such, then I would grit my teeth and bear it. But for that suffering to happen, I would first need him here.

I also needed to speak with my brother on other matters, like what was taking so long in discovering the witch's true identity like he boldly claimed he would. I didn't know if it was just my imagination or anxiety for Amelia's life, but it felt like he was both hiding something and stalling. For the last few days since our plan was agreed he had been avoiding me, and on the few occasions, like now, that I had left

Amelia's side, he had been nowhere to be found. I had asked him to keep me informed of his progress but still I had heard nothing.

Needless to say, that because of the fucking obvious, I walked around in a constant state of being pissed off. Doing so with outbursts of demonic fury at the simplest of things. In fact, the only time I wasn't acting this way was when I was alone with my sleeping beauty, after first dismissing Nero for the night. I would lie next to her and just, well...*talk.*

I told her about all the times I had watched her from afar. The moments observing her playing the piano, admitting that at the time, I had never heard anything so sweet. Of course, that was until the first time she ever told me she loved me and in the most unlikely of places. Or should I say, it was the first time I'd heard such coming from her lips, and not something said directly to me. No, instead this was something said when defending my honour in some fucking gas station.

But that was my girl. She could be the cutest, sweetest, and funniest girl alive, along with the clumsiest but then when it came to fighting for what she believed in or for those she cared for, well, then her courage knew no bounds! She was utterly fearless and ready to risk her fucking soul to save everyone else's. But then when I thought of the two beings that made her and brought her into the world, was it really surprising?

It was little wonder why the Fates had deemed me to be so connected to Keira for if I had never played my part then my own fate would never have happened. Gods, but I fucking hated the Fates just as much as all I had to thank them for! The bitter pill being forced down my throat was getting fucking bigger, knowing what the Eye had shown me!

On one hand I wanted to ignore it as though it had never happened, but then I also knew as Dom had once known, trying to prevent the future only ended up aiding it. After all, there must have been a reason the Eye had shown me that slither of the dark future ahead.

I dragged a frustrated hand through my hair as I left my tower in search of Dariush hoping to find him in his office. A room that a few days ago looked as though it hadn't been ripped apart by three shifters without a fucking clue!

My throne room was empty other than the usual line of personal guards that I had no fucking need for but kept around to keep up appearances. Gods, but the sooner I could get back topside the fucking better, I was done with all this royal shit!

I passed my throne and down the corridor towards his office feeling his presence in there. But then, the moment I opened the door I was rewarded with the sight of his vessel slipping through a recently made portal.

"What the fuck?!" I snapped the second the tear in our realm disappeared leaving behind no trace of his abrupt exit. I hammered a fist down on the desk, doing so just as Carn'reau entered behind me.

"I see you had the same response as I did the last time I wished to speak with your second, my Lord." I growled and ordered,

"No one is here Carn'reau, so you can cut the 'my lord' bullshit." This surprised him as I deflated into my brother's chair and scrubbed a hand down my face in frustration. I heard the Fae close the door knowing we were going to be frank with one another. Fuck, but I missed Adam, in both his efficiency and in his honesty.

"My…" he paused when he saw my scathing look of warning, when finally, I gave him a break and said,

"Luc is fine." Then I thought back to Amelia and always wondered why she never called me Luc?

He bowed his head telling me he understood, making me wonder if now I would see that fucking cold hard rod being pulled from his backside and the true Fae come out.

Not fucking likely.

"I am afraid your second in command has been disappearing quite a lot of late," he told me, making me look towards the tear in our realm that had been there moments before. I gripped the armrests of the antique chair with enough force I felt it strain in my hands.

"When?" I snapped.

"From what I can gather, it has been times he was needed to be useful in his exchange of information," he replied, making me grit my teeth and wish I had an explanation for it, or the patience, but right now, I didn't.

"Tell me of the spell's casting."

"It is being finished as we speak, for Alvaro is with our armies, administering the last of what Nero made." I raised a brow at the admiration I heard in his tone for the handy little witch.

"Nero?" I questioned seeing as he had quickly forgone the title of 'witch', now becoming more personal.

"I find her to be *intriguing,*" he admitted with a shrug of his shoulders, making me scoff,

"That she is but heed my warning Carn'reau, be sure that is all you find in her or you will find one pissed off Wyvern trying to torch the tail of your Zilant." Carn'reau actually cracked a grin and I honestly couldn't say when I had ever seen it before. But then again, it was not as if we had conversed in this manner before. It also wasn't exactly what one would call a warm sight. No, more primeval and the face of a man that would enjoy ripping your throat out with his teeth. Which meant that I also didn't think the charming, light-hearted, redheaded rogue had much of a competition on his hands.

"As fun as that sounds, I believe my efforts are best served in aiding my King on keeping his Chosen One safe." His response came with a slight bow of his head and a thankful change of subject when discussing newly recruited souls in need of training.

This conversation lasted some time, including a tour of the new training grounds and barracks Carn'reau had commissioned for my growing army. Meaning that it was a few hours later when I was making my way back up into my tower and making the next fucked up discovery. One that had me close to tearing my fucking bed apart when I found an important piece of it missing…

Amelia was gone.

"Amelia!"

I yelled her name after fisting the sheets and tearing the material in my hands, making it come apart like paper. Then I roared her name again,

"AMELIA!" I scanned the room, looking for any evidence of her and saw some clothes lay over the back of one of the chairs, telling me that she had at least woken and got dressed. Could it not be as bad as I first thought, could she have just woken and found herself needing to freshen up in my pool?

I closed my eyes and tried to locate her presence. But without partaking in the blood exchange between us since the day the Hex tried to claim her, then it took me longer and even then, the results weren't what I wanted. Yet, something was there and lingered, almost as if it were too far away to be sure. I felt a snarl rip from me before my eyes snapped open and I stalked down to the last place I felt her. Another furious question penetrated the anger and had me cracking the crystal beneath my feet,

Where the fuck was Nero?

"You'd better have a good fucking excuse, witch!" I snapped as I reached the bottom step, and only came to a dead stop the second I looked up. I frowned the moment I scented blood in the air and my relief was only from the fact that it didn't belong to Amelia.

"What the fuck?" I muttered as my mind tried to make sense of what I was smelling. Because if I had walked in here blindfolded and relied on my other senses, then I would have sworn upon opening my eyes to find myself surrounded by a pile of mortal body parts after a massacre occurred.

It was a mix of different blood types all watered down which brought my footsteps to the cause. The pool of water in front of me, even though it was now clear, I suspected it hadn't been this way the entire time. A crimson residue remained around the edge of the pool that had spilled over onto the tile. I looked behind me sniffing the air, knowing that with the lack of blood behind me it had obviously originated here.

It didn't take me too long to realise where I had seen evidence like this before. For once more it became a moment in time that all centred around Amelia. It had been after stepping back inside Dom's vault when looking for clues as to what had happened. That was when we had both seen it, for like now there had been blood and water on the floor.

What did it all mean, and more importantly...

Who in Hell was Amelia?

I took a deep breath and in doing so released it quickly, for I could now sense what else was missing from this space. Meaning that yet another panic quickly merged with another.

Amelia wasn't the only one missing.

The Eye of Crimson was gone.

This was when I didn't take another moment before I was diving into the water, only half surprised to find the hidden archway was there without needing to call for it. This could only mean one thing…

The Eye had called out to Amelia.

I pushed myself through the water, only taking breath again once I was through to the temple on the other side. I pushed my body up from the surface, ignoring the way my clothes clung to me and only shaking away the gathered water in my gauntleted hand. I stormed through the archway the second I felt that her presence was stronger through there, knowing that she had found something she shouldn't have.

Had my brother been right, had she woken and been drawn to the Eye because of my actions? I may have used it only once, but I had done so with her blood on my hands. Had this now acted like some calling card to her, tapping into her conscious state the moment she woke?

"Fuck!" I hissed through gritted teeth before emerging out of the tunnel to the other side and once I did, I was again struck rooted to the spot as ice filled my veins. Then, as if in some kind of trance, I walked over to a spot next to the altar and put one knee to the ground before digging my hand into the black sand.

This was because in this room there were two distinct scents and this time the blood only belonged to that of two people. One of them was a witch. And the other was what I was looking down at now. The agonising sight of large droplets of blood lay nestled in the sand in my hand,

The blood of my Chosen One.

I felt every muscle in my body turn to stone, and one glance at the top of the altar to find the Eye missing and my hand fisted. Black sand poured from between my fingers just before I hammered that fist into the altar next to me, twisting my torso into the punch with a roar,

"RRRAAHHH!" The pearlescent figures of Gods crumbled on impact as I cursed every fucking one of them! Because the horror of what had happened hit my mind in nothing short of an attack! A rage that destroyed not only the altar but the archway when my demonic form erupted through it!

Whoever had taken my girl would pay and, unlike the McBain brothers, this time they wouldn't just hear my rage, they would feel it.

They would...

Pay with their life!

CHAPTER NINE

AMELIA

ANOTHER DRAVEN DAMNING

PRESENT DAY IN HELL

I walked into my apartment after what felt like a long shift at the museum, with only one thing on my mind, Pj's and food, in that order. This bra was coming off and getting flung across the bedroom in protest the second I stripped off. And as for the trousers, I mean who wanted to stuff themselves stupid with frozen pizza whilst wearing a tight waistband…no one that's who. I let the door slam behind me, knowing that Ben would be out at this time on a Friday night.

I also had a Firefly marathon with my name on it, thank you Aunty Pip for that boxset in the mail. I threw my bag to my shabby sofa and went straight to the kitchen to grab the pizza, so it could be cooking while all this stripping was going on. Then the nightmare thing happened to any single, hungry girl who lived alone, the freezer was empty. My usual back up pizza was gone, along with the back up to my back up. Great, crunchy nut it was then.

I grabbed the box and strangely the second I pulled it from the shelf the box disappeared, and I saw myself somewhere else. I was now staring at shelves filled with cereal boxes instead of my bare cupboards and I was also no longer alone.

"What seems to be the dilemma?" Lucius suddenly asked me, startling me when his voice suddenly hummed next to my ear. I turned to find him stood behind me. I looked down at my empty hand and frowned.

"They are all out of Crunchy Nut, Chocolate Clusters Cereal," I whispered in confusion as if I were suddenly playing a part in some strange play and didn't need to think of the script. I heard him chuckling and when I looked up, I found myself asking him,

"What?"

"It's nothing," he answered with a shake of his head, done in such a way, it was as though he didn't know what to do with me. But again, I found history pouring out of my mouth,

"No, go on, what's so funny?"

"Alright, it's just that you had three men show up and try to kidnap you. Then you had a Hex try to claim you after which you collapsed in my arms, then only days later for you to be taken, and now you are here with me, having a conversation about cereal..." Lucius paused a moment with that handsome smirk playing at the corner of his mouth. Then he leant down so his face was next to mine and those perfect lips were now smiling at my ear. Then I heard him say,

"So, don't you think you should wake up now and deal with that?" At this I swallowed hard, feeling it push down my throat as if I was pushing down a piece of hot lava.

Then I asked fearfully,

"Deal with what?" This was when his voice got hard and unyielding. It was one that commanded Hell and did so as a demon. It was one that was furious and spoke only of revenge. It was one that was a threat and warning all wrapped into one. And more importantly, it also turned out to be one that had the power to...

Save me.

"The fact that you're tied up in a fucking cell about to die?" I immediately woke up, snapping from my dream and instantly moving into action the second I saw the threat coming towards me. A blade flashed in a demon's hand and I yanked my hands down with little result. This forced me to glance up, quickly noting that they were shackled above me.

Well, that was just great, I thought with a grimace. So, with no other option at my disposal, I curled my fingers around the chains, gripped on tight, and lifted my whole body the second the unknown enemy lunged. I kicked both my legs out hitting them hard enough in the chest that they fell backwards and against the bars of what looked like my cell. Thankfully, her weapon also slipped from her grasp and went flying across the room with a clatter.

What happened next was like someone clicking a survival switch, for my actions barely felt like my own. So, with my enemy still dazed on the other side of the room, it gave me enough time to turn around and face the wooden post I was shackled to. A quick look up at the rusting bolt my chains were connected to, and what seemed like my natural abilities took over.

I jumped a little to get a better hold on the chain links above the cuffs, that were secured tightly around my wrists and I started to run up the post, gaining more length of the chain the higher I got. Then when I reached the top of where it was bolted I used every ounce of strength I had to flip backwards, kicking off the wood and therefore snapping the link with the force as I went over. I landed still facing the wood and looked down at my hands that were now only linked together by the chain between them.

Now this I could work with.

I spun around the second I heard a noise, seeing the threat coming back at me for another go. The winged creature was closer than I thought, and my instincts took over once more as I ducked under the swing of what looked like a serrated sword coming at me. It was one that looked so dirty that a simple nick would have most likely killed me from blood poisoning.

I spun around whilst still in a crouched position and elbowed the creature in the back and kicked out at the side of its knee. Then its wings expanded outwards, doing so with enough force that it knocked me back into the wooden post, so I ended up hugging the damn thing!

But this also meant that the creature staggered forward enough for me to push off the post and run back towards it. Then, just at the right time, I jumped with one leg forward, so I was now running up its back whilst its body was still hunched over. I ran up its webbed spine that connected its wings together and before it could throw me off, I hooked the chain between my shackles under its chin.

Then I jumped off its shoulders and off to the side, so it crossed the chain over around its neck. Doing this meant I had it chained around the neck and could then use my weight to strangle the fucking thing!

"Okay, time to die now." I wheezed out as I yanked even harder but still feeling the thing fighting me, I decided to use a different tactic. I rolled forward and took the creature to the ground with me, making sure to keep the chain around its neck tight. This meant that I could swing once more to its back and use my feet to pin each wing down so it couldn't knock me off with them again. Then, with a surge of energy and rage, I screamed as I lifted my arms up as if I was doing a power lift. My bellowing anger somehow aiding my strength as I did so, finally ending in snapping its neck. The sickening sound was only one indication that it was safe to let go, the other was when the body beneath my control went limp.

I let go and once the danger was over and my adrenaline was spent, I staggered back a step, staring at the creature I had just killed. I looked back at the wooden post I had been chained to and started to ask myself what the fuck had just happened? How the hell had I managed to free myself, and kill a fucking demon at that?!

And I was happy to report without the aid of a piss pot… or shelving unit, or bed sheets, or…well, I think I made my point. But I swear, it had almost been as if I had been possessed or something. Like a deeper part of me had snapped or broken free and once that switch had been flipped, someone else had taken over. I mean, yeah, I had always been able to handle myself but being able to do so in Hell was another thing entirely. Especially seeing as I was still mortal, despite my stolen birthright. Not that it had been Lucius' fault, but still, my abilities as a human in Hell were limited at best…or at least, *they should have been*.

But then what else was there for me to think when the proof of what disproved that mortal fact was right in front of me, lying dead on the floor of what looked to be my cell.

I took in more of my surroundings to see that it looked like some kind of cave with a stone block wall that rose higher at the back than the front of the cell where the bars were. They also looked crudely made, just like the chains that still hung loose in between the two-inch-thick cuffs that were rubbing my skin raw.

I looked over to the dead demon, who was still face down in the dirt floor, and it took half a second to see that there weren't any keys on the thing, or clothes for that matter. I decided to take a closer look and started to kick the body over, asking aloud,

"So, let's see what you are then…whoa, well shit me!" I said the second the thing rolled to its back and its jaw flopped open to the side as if death had made it go slack. Its elongated jaw stretched further to allow all the rows of teeth to be seen. I shivered at the thought of the damage one bite out of me could have caused had I not reacted quickly enough.

Its hideous wings creased and folded at a strange angle due to the sagging skin that was void of feathers. Pitted marks in the skin looked like a plucked chicken in between long finger bones and its naked body was covered in withered, paper thin skin. However, its protruding ribcage, over pronounced bone structure, and a pair of pitiful sagging naked breasts told me exactly what creature this had been.

Which is why I uttered two words that I could have sworn had been said by a Draven once before…

"Damn Harpies."

CHAPTER TEN

HARPY QUEEN

Now what the fuck a bunch of Harpies would want with me, I had no clue. But one thing was for sure, I wasn't going to stand around and wait for the opportunity to ask them. So, with escape firmly on my mind, I walked over to the cell's bars and looked to see if there were any more Harpies on guard.

I also had to ask myself what had gotten into this one? Had she been given the order to kill me or gone against orders not to? Most likely the latter seeing as I doubted they would go to all this trouble to get me here, when they could have just killed me alongside...

"Oh no...Nero," I whispered in horror as my hands flew to my mouth and my legs gave way underneath me. I barely even felt the pain as my knees hit the ground for the pain at knowing I had got her killed was all that consumed me. Granted, I didn't know her well, but what I did know was of her kindness shown to strangers in need and of her love for a cheeky Wyvern shifter.

And now she was gone.

I opened my eyes, ignoring the tears rolling down my cheeks and instead focused on the watery sight of my hand as it turned into a fist, doing so the moment anger penetrated my grief. I pounded it into the ground before looking over my shoulder and narrowing my eyes on the dead Harpy.

They would pay for this.

They would all fucking pay!

I rose to my feet and looked for the weapon I had seen the dead bitch attack me with, finding it in the corner next to an empty wooden bucket. No ten guesses needed for what that was supposed to be used for and taking a shit right now was the last thing on my mind. What was on my mind, however, was busting out of this place and killing myself some Harpies, mainly the one I had seen standing over Nero's dead body back in the Eye's cave. If nothing else, I wouldn't leave here until I saw that bitch dead at my feet just like this one.

Meaning, it was time to leave a message.

I flipped the large curved blade in my hand, before catching it and going to work, starting with cutting this bitch's head off!

By the time I had finished introducing myself with my slightly overkill bloody message on the wall, I severed one of the Harpy's talons and used that to pick the lock on my cuffs before breaking out of my cell. I picked both locks with ease when using the sharp tip and decided to keep it, seeing how handy it seemed to be. For starters, I had already used three others I had ripped off her bird like feet to nail her head to the wooden beams I had been attached to. It was gruesome, I knew that, but then how else were they going to take the threat of me seriously.

Now, of course, I just had to pray that whatever had happened on that field when I was angry at Trice and Lucius for fighting, would happen again. Or really, that bloody threat I left on the wall would have been an empty one.

I slipped from the cell once the door was open and I looked both ways to find that I seemed to be in some crumbling cell block that looked half ruined by age. In fact, the cell I had been put in looked to be one of the only secure ones left, making me question where exactly in Hell I was?

I followed the cracked stone floor holding the dripping blade in a death grip by the handle, knowing I would most likely be needing it again soon. I also had slipped the curled razor tipped talon into the waistband of my now dirt colour trousers. Let's face it, wearing white in Hell was never going to last...Poor Nero, I thought with a grimace. She had been the one to dress me and help take care of me after I had passed out on Lucius.

I closed my eyes, holding back the tears as a pained expression swept over my face. I just couldn't get the memory of it out of my head. I kept seeing my hand reaching out to her, my fingertips blurring as her dead white eyes came in to focus. All that blood, soaking up the white tips of her hair and that beauty shining through, even in the face of death.

I gritted my teeth and tapped the edge of my blade on the stone walls of the cell block a few times. The echoing sound soothed my nerves, telling me I could do this.

I would do this.

I straightened my frame along with my resolve and continued through the dimly lit space that I could only barely see from the few torches that were lit. It seemed Harpies had far better eyesight than humans did.

I continued to walk around in what seemed like a maze

with no purpose until I came to a broken set of stairs that finally led above and out of this madness. The staircase was made of wood with a lot of the steps either rotten or missing completely. This then meant that when my foot went through one, I screamed anyway despite not being surprised. Thankfully, it was a sound that didn't travel far, or if it did, then no one had been around to hear it.

I carefully pulled my foot up and out of the hole, gripping on to whatever wood I could find that looked strong enough to hold my weight. Doing all this while trying not to lose my weapon in the process. Once back on my feet, I continued up the stairs with more determination and admittedly, more care. Damn, but now was not the time to be clumsy and well, looking down the centre of the spiral staircase, I knew it was a long way to the bottom. Not only that but falling through one of the treads would no doubt mean falling through them all. Gods, by the sounds this wood was making I felt as if I were walking over thin ice on a frozen lake.

The moment the staircase started to narrow further I knew that I must have been climbing some sort of tower and now it wasn't just the steps that had been left to ruin. But then again, what did Harpies need with steps?

"Duh, Fae," I muttered to myself, already out of breath and in need of about six pints of water! Well, at the very least I had healed from my injuries, ones sustained from when I was knocked out and kicked in the ribs...thank you Harpy bitch but more sincerely, thank you Lucius for your magical blood.

"Oh Gods," I hissed, pausing to lean against the stone wall, covering my mouth with my hands. Shamefully, I hadn't even thought of Lucius until now. Of course, it wasn't as if I hadn't been a little preoccupied, what with killing things and dissecting them for slightly insane and sinister reasons. Which also meant that I hadn't thought of the shit storm that was going to come from his wrath at finding me missing yet again! Fuck, but I was going to find myself locked up for good this time! First the McBain brothers and now fucking Harpies…I mean what the Hell was wrong with me! Was I seriously a magnet for this shit, talk about a chip off the old block…*thanks Mum,* I thought wryly, being aware of only some of the times she managed to get herself kidnapped and needed her ass saving.

"You're in Hell, that's what, idiot!" I scorned myself, and speaking of which,

"Time to get this shit over with!" I said with a snarl of my own whilst looking up to realise I was near the top as I could see more natural rays of light reflecting off the stone. Of course, I soon discovered why when I reached the last few steps. The tower looked as if a giant boulder had catapulted through the air and had taken it out. In fact, the second I breached the crumbling stone and looked out to the view in front of me, I realised it wasn't just the tower.

"It's the whole castle," I muttered in awe as I took it all in. To be honest, all that was left of the place were crumbling battlements and towers surrounding a bailey that was filled with broken stone from the castle and thick clusters of soul weed. I couldn't tell if the castle had been attacked or it had just been left to ruin. Its walls almost looked so deteriorated it gave it a sense from up here as if pieces of it had simply melted away. Grey stone matched that of both the soul weed below and the dead landscape I could barely see past the fog. And like this, I could also see arched doorways to nowhere and windows that had long been without glass. Few features remained of what it once was, but one thing I was certain, before its ruin it would have been spectacular and beautiful.

Of course, that was minus all the Harpies that now

occupied its space below, with a few of them I could see perched at the different levels of broken stone walls. The main group, however, seemed to be circling something below, snapping out at it making me wonder if I had just been about to interrupt their evening meal? Well, whatever it was, something was obviously keeping their attention and with their large bat like wings stretched out, it was something I couldn't yet see.

What I could see, however, was the lack of Harpies at this level, which gave me an advantage and time to make a plan. It also awarded me a view of the two larger Harpies, who admittedly stood out from the rest, not just for their size but for their difference in features also. Their hair for example was different shades, although styles were obviously a thing of the past and long gone. No now, each of them wore it long and hanging down in knotted waves.

One had larger, more pointed ears than the other, and one had black spots mottled on its skin. This one also had a red tinge to her hair making me wonder if she used to be a redhead before being cursed and sent down here? Either way, she was an ugly creature now, and her overly large jaw was one filled with rows of long, thin, pointed teeth. It also made her narrow chin jut out further than it needed to be, which was made more prominent with the superior way she kept lifting and nodding her head as she clicked her jaw.

It was an unnerving sound, even from way up here. The two were currently sat in the largest empty arch that looked as if it once belonged to some broken church window or something. Underneath it was another arch that was made dark by the remaining part of the building behind it. One that had me wondering if this was the main part of their lair?

It was obvious that they had stolen this place, being known as the scavengers of the sky and well, the two fuglies, as Aunty Pip would say, looked to be the leaders of these hairless rodents with wings. Now all I needed to do was figure out a way to tap back into the power that had come out before, and I knew it would give me the edge in this fight I was looking for. Oh, who was I kidding, it was one I needed, well past the point of borderline desperation, *I was just plain desperate!* Because I knew I wasn't getting out of here without it...*whatever it was.*

Keeping low, I emerged from the tower and made my way along the battlements, being careful of both where I stood and where the broken stone was. However, my foot slipped, and the stone crumbled beneath me enough that it went rolling down the side. This meant that I had to save myself quickly from going down with it and drop to my belly so they wouldn't see me.

I heard one of the two Harpies snarl up at my direction, but when I heard nothing more, I lifted my head to have a sneaky peek. They had turned back to the swarm at the centre, making me realise that having parts of the castle crumbling around them was most likely a regular occurrence.

But then movement overhead quickly had me reacting once more as I suddenly found myself ducking again. I also had to roll this time so the half wall around the battlements could hide me from above. This was so I couldn't be seen by the largest Harpy of them all, who was flying over the edge of the castle walls. Thankfully, a big enough crack in the wall I was curled up against allowed me a good view of below.

The Harpy swooped low, making all the smaller minions below call out to her in some high-pitched cry. She circled the bailey, with her green toned wings glinting off the few fires that were dotted around the space in cast iron grills. The large Harpy, then circled back towards the biggest arch and after her wings batted her back enough to stop mid-air, she lifted her skirt and reached out with her bird feet to grab the edge. The other two made room for her instantly, each moving to their sides so she could perch in the middle.

Then she started to speak, and I recognised instantly that same malevolent voice that had taken me. She also wore the same headpiece made of shadowy fingers that hissed like snakes and reached out like dead souls trying to grasp back at life. Her eyes were also different, slanted snake eyes of crimson pools of hatred. However, her face and body weren't like the other Harpies.

No, amazingly, she was in a scary way, *beautiful*. I couldn't understand how she was, for what I knew of Harpies, being beautiful was far from how one would be described. Yet here was this radiant, if not bat shit crazy, beauty that had dirty white wings with tips of emerald green.

She was even dressed in a regal medieval dress that was most definitely what you would call form fitting. Her dress was made of dark green satin that looked almost as black as her coiled dark hair. It was a style she wore twisted and curled up around the headdress she wore, pinned in such a way it became hard to distinguish between what was hair or not. It reminded me of a traditional Japanese headdress cross between a helmet of a samurai warrior. The front of which came down low and covered her forehead in a V shape, with the point touching the bridge of her nose. Her eyes, which had once been slanted and that of a crimson snake, were now as a human's was. Well, if that human had dark green eyes and looked menacing to the point of murderous that was.

She had slim features that admittedly gave her a regal edge, with a thin nose, high cheekbones and distinct jawline that lent its way to a graceful neck. Her body was also all that of a woman and not at all like the painful flash bag of bones like the rest of her hideous race. Her tight bodice was embroidered with swirls of roses and thorns that framed the lines of her body, mirroring the V shape of her headdress as it finished at a harsh point at her navel.

Long bell-shaped sleeves were tight around her slender shoulders and tops of her arms before flaring out at the elbow, making her hands appear swallowed up by swathes of material. The skirt was the same, being a full skirt making her look like some dark medieval Queen out for killing all that threatened to take her crown. Basically, she was your typical looking fairy tale baddie, other than the fact she had wings and feathered bird's feet hidden underneath her skirt, legs that you only saw when she lifted the material enough to aid in her landing.

In short, she didn't look like a Harpy at all, which made me question...*was this their Queen?*

Whether she was or she wasn't, it didn't matter. She was the one that brought me here and she was the one that needed to pay! A flash of that same image assaulted me, with my fingertips reaching out to Nero only to blur again before haunting me with those dead eyes. In the end, this was all it took for that rage to ignite something in me and I could feel it happening again, only this time more slowly.

I looked down at my hands to find them twitching uncontrollably, as if I was casting spells or commanding something invisible just beyond my fingertips. That's when I saw it seeping up through the cracks and gaps in the stone. Small lines of blood appeared like red grout between the blocks before it overflowed and turned into pools of crimson. Each one started to join up until suddenly I found myself lying surrounded by a small moat of blood, as if protecting me in some way.

I had no idea how I was summoning this blood or how I knew that I could summon a lot more than that. I didn't even know where it had come from, I only knew that it seemed to be linked to my anger. Linked to the very hatred I could feel burning inside me as if it would soon burst and when it did, I knew exactly where I wanted it aimed at!

So, I rolled to my front, mindful of the blood and once my knees were under me, I got to my feet, looking out to the Harpies below and getting ready to unleash the fury that was building inside me.

I would kill them all!

I started to lift my arms out wide, as if this was all instinct kicking in and knew that it would cause more damage this way. When suddenly I heard a muffled scream just as the Harpy Queen laughed. Then she raised a slender hand, flicking it aside and giving a command for the swarm to separate. I also knew that my time for getting them all was now or never, as I needed them in a large group like this. Because I didn't know how hard it would be directing this power at any should they decide to take flight and attack me from above.

But then something in me couldn't seem to go through with it. As though I was being held back and it was a feeling only explained the moment when enough of the Harpies parted, that I knew why.

Because I wasn't their only prisoner.

And death had not been delivered like I thought it had. Suddenly those fingers in my memory curled back into a fist as those dead milky eyes flickered back to life.

A sight my mind had missed before unconsciousness had taken me.

"Thank the Gods..." I muttered closing my eyes before whispering her name like a prayer that had been answered...

"Nero."

CHAPTER ELEVEN

BACK FROM THE DEAD

"*She's alive!*" I muttered in utter shock at what I was now seeing!

Nero was currently chained to a wooden post like I had been down in the dungeon, only for her it looked as though it was one that was part of some contraption. A large H shaped frame stood over what looked like an old well of some kind, with a large crank at the side which was obviously used to lower and raise the large bucket I could see hanging over the opening.

The relief I felt at seeing her alive was only soured by the sight of how bloody and beaten she was. She definitely looked as if she had seen better days, especially with the way the swarm of Harpies had obviously been toying with her.

I narrowed my eyes at the sight, feeling myself getting angrier by the second at who I considered a friend, tied up and picked at like fucking meat for these bitches! I looked down at my hands seeing the thin streams of red particles snaking from my fingertips. They each looked like some miniature Milky Way amongst the darkening sky that was rolling in from all sides.

It was a power that I knew if I wanted to, I could unleash like a plague, destroying all those it touched by ridding them of their life force, controlling the very blood that ran through their veins! But then one look back at Nero and I was pulling back that dangerous power, knowing that I couldn't risk it. I didn't have enough control on it yet...and like I said... *whatever 'it' was.*

No, I needed to know more about this power before just throwing it out there. Because Nero wasn't like Lucius or the McBain brothers. She didn't have their strength and means to fight against it. And accidentally killing her just to take them all out wasn't a risk I was willing to take. No, what I needed to do was be smart and sneaky, if such a thing were possible for my stumbling ass.

So, I decided I would wait until they all slithered their grey asses back underground to sleep, as I had read somewhere they were like bats, only they weren't nocturnal. They preferred the cover of darkness and slept in large groups, which meant I hoped the moment night started to take hold that they would piss off. Because, like this, with so many of them down there, well, I had no hope of getting Nero out of here. Which was why I lowered back down, leaning my back against part of the wall that hadn't fallen to ruin.

"Come on and think, Fae!" I snapped at myself banging my head on the back of the stone in my frustration. So, not only did I have to potentially kill a load of Harpies and then find my way out of whatever level of Hell this was, I now had to break out Nero without getting caught. Because either way I looked at this, I needed to protect her before unleashing the bat shit crazy version of myself on these bitches!

"Okay, so new plan, save the girl, get her somewhere

safe, come back, kick ass, find the bloody Eye of Crimson that started this whole holy fucked up thing and then try and find a fucking map out of this place...oh yeah, piece of fucking cake, Fae...*idiot."* I ended this scorning myself by slapping a palm to my forehead as I lowered my head in frustration. Because the likelihood of this actually happening was like pissing in the wind and hoping not to get soaked. Of course, there was always the option to make a break for it with Nero and not look back. But then my biggest fear was losing the opportunity to kill them all, doing so when they least expected it. And with those bitches still alive then they would most likely just come and hunt us down when they realised we were gone.

Gods, but I swear if I ever ended up making stupid decisions and coming to Hell again then I was doing so dressed like Arnold Schwarzenegger in Commando after robbing that gun shop. Of course, I would first have to learn how to use most of that shit, as I was more of a 'fighting with a sword' kind of girl. Which reminded me to pick up the weapon I had dropped when seeing Nero.

Speaking of which, I glanced over the top of the stone to see what was happening now. The poor girl looked half ready to give up and half ready to die trying to kill every last one of them. Her head hung limp between her arms that were pulled up above her the way mine had. Her clothes were covered in dirt as if she had been half dragged along the floor, and blood stains edged the parts of the fabric wherever it was torn.

"Just hang on a little longer, Nero," I whispered as if she could hear me. Then, as if she were subconsciously answering me, her spark of power ignited when one of the Harpies got closer and tried to take a menacing swipe at her. She muttered something I couldn't hear, which I gathered to be some kind of spell as a blue flame grew in her fist and

when she opened her fingers the flaming orb shot from her hand above and hit the Harpy square in the face.

It screamed a high pitch wail before falling back with its head on fire. The other Harpies screeched all around it like a pack of birds fighting, making me realise they mustn't like the fire despite obviously needing it to see. The Queen barked an order in some other language making the dark spotted one next to her push off her perch. She swooped low and grabbed the one on fire by its legs before carrying her off into the air. I then watched as she heartlessly flung the flaming Harpy over the Castle wall and away from the rest of the swarm. The whole time it was screaming as the blue flames were melting its skin and hair, filling the air with the horrid stench of burnt flesh.

I watched it fall out of sight and the second the screaming stopped I knew it was dead.

"Well, that's one down," I muttered with a grin.

I don't know how long I had to wait until they finally started to piss off for the night, but it was dark with a strange red hue in the sky. Some of the surrounding torches still flickered but from the look of things, it wouldn't be for long as two of them had died out about fifteen minutes ago. The night was also eerily still, with the two Harpies put on guard duty dozing where they perched. One was positioned on higher ground and the other closer to where Nero was still hanging by her wrists. Her head had fallen lower now, telling me she was either asleep or passed out.

I also knew that to take out two Harpies without them making a sound was going to be tricky and cutting their throats was going to be my only option. To be perfectly honest, I was winging it from this point onwards. Because without being able to use these strange bloody powers (yes, pun totally intended with that one) then I was taking this each step as it came.

For starters, I didn't even have a clue where the Eye was or where we were for that matter. I knew from what I had read about Harpies that at one time they had occupied parts of Tartarus but seeing as most of it had been destroyed in the war, then who the Hell knew. Not me that was for damn sure!

Gods, for all I knew we were on a fucking island surrounded by demonic looking starving sharks with twenty extra rows of teeth that could shoot lava from their ass and fire fins like throwing stars. Or simply put, we were surround by an impenetrable wall and were basically fucked. Either way, I was holding out for the 'getting out' part of this plan to be the easy part.

What wouldn't be easy, however, was making my way down these battlements without being heard. I swear, but if I ever managed to get my ass back to Earths' realm, then I was taking ninja classes! Fuck, but at this rate I was willing to learn how to drive a damn tank if it meant living a semi normal life. Because I was pretty sure that was the only way Lucius would let me leave to go shopping…okay, so maybe just a drive through, I thought with a smirk.

"Seriously?" I muttered to myself, shaking my head at my random thoughts.

"Get your head in the game, Fae," I added, rolling my eyes at myself. Then, after this unoriginal pep talk, I crept along the top of the battlements hoping that the next tower along had a staircase. Only one that actually led to the lower levels where the first Harpy was dozing.

"Bingo," I muttered the second I saw that it did and thankfully it was more intact. Well, for the most part it was as

the further down I travelled, the more of my next problem started to present itself. This being a huge hole I could now see that had taken out about seven steps. It looked like a boulder had taken out a good section by a catapult or a trebuchet. This being a medieval machine that worked by a counterweight dropping on the end of a pivoted beam and launching a payload into the air from a sling.

Gods, I could be a bigger geek than Sheldon from The Big Bang Theory!

Well, despite that title of geekhood, it didn't take away from the fact that whatever it was that had happened here, it was obvious the other side had won, as most of this castle had been utterly obliterated. In fact, it looked as though all that remained were parts of the ramparts and curtain walls that connected the three towers. The one on the side of the large arch was only half the size of the other two, due to being caved in on itself and inaccessible.

The usual Keep found inside the castle walls was down to its foundations and was nothing more than a metre-high shell, reminding me of some architectural plans laid on the floor. There was also a pointless part left of what would have at one time been the gatehouse, with its only use now being nothing more than a crumbing entrance into the bailey.

This meant that I had no choice but to put the blade between my teeth. I was near gagging on the bitter metallic taste that I knew wasn't all down to the blade but also the smears of Harpy blood that remained. Then, I got to my knees before holding on to the ledge and lowering myself down to the next set of steps below hoping that when I landed on them, they didn't just collapse under my sudden weight. Because I wasn't only sure that something like that would wake everyone up, I was also sure that it would in all likelihood kill me in the process.

I landed with a creaking of wood and with my arms held out wide as I froze in place waiting for the fall. But when nothing happened, I let out a relieved breath, which ended being premature the second I heard movement outside.

Fuck, but I had…

Woken up the Harpy!

CHAPTER TWELVE

ESCAPE PLAN

Fuck, but I had...*Woken up the Harpy!*

I knew this when I saw the shadow of wings entering the opening before the creature did. This meant I had no other choice but to improvise. I did this by dropping my blade in a place she would see it, placing it directly in front of the archway that would have led onto the level she had been sleeping on.

I sank back into the shadows and waited, with my hand curling around the large talon, pulling it from my waistband. I was positioned next to the arch she would be walking through and as I predicted, the moment the Harpy entered, she focused solely on the blade. It was one that was glinting in the light and stole her attention instead of looking around the space to find me there hiding.

Then, when she bent down onto one of her bird like legs to pick it up, she sniffed the blade and obviously scented the death of one of her own on it. She started snarling but it was too late, I was already upon her. Because before she knew what was happening, I jumped on her back and said,

"Smell anything you like?" Then I slit her throat to prevent another sound coming from her, making her slump forward, with a resounding crack. Then, whilst still on her back, I finished the job, knowing she wasn't dead yet...not if the twitching body beneath me was anything to go by. So, I grabbed a handful of her hair, yanked back her face and this time when I slit through her throat, I very nearly took her head off. Well, I guess it was my day for beheading Harpies...jeez, wouldn't Mum and Dad be proud. Well, maybe my dad would be, *he hated Harpies.*

"I'll take that," I said, reaching under the dead Harpy to retrieve the blade she had fallen on top of. I also wiped as much of her blood off the blade as I could, using the grotesque folded baggy skin at her wing to do so, along with the talon that admittedly was my new favourite weapon.

"Seriously, when did my life get so fucking complicated?" I asked myself when standing back up, remembering simpler days when all I had to deal with was running late for work, finding dried toothpaste on the corner of my mouth and spilling tea down my shirt. Not wiping the blood off my weapon by using the body of my latest victim and doing this so I wouldn't taste its blood in my mouth the next the time arose that I had to scale down a broken staircase, needing both my hands.

"Fuck, but I miss my boring life," I muttered before flipping the blade and catching the handle, admittedly feeling like a badass. Then I continued on, ready for taking down my next Harpy and trying to ignore missing my small flat in Twickenham, takeout Fridays and lazy Star Wars Sundays. Damn but my Netflix account most likely thought I had died or something!

I snuck my head around the side of the arched doorway, one that had one time most likely lead down an ornate corridor to another part of the castle. I saw that the Harpy closest to Nero was thankfully still asleep. This was good, seeing as I needed to continue down the staircase, reach the bottom and then make my way across the open space to stab another Harpy in the throat.

Always good to have a plan, Fae.

I crept back down the staircase, only stopping when I could see that any lower and I would be heading underground and most likely back into the dungeons from the other side. But then I froze the minute I swear I thought I could hear a growl of some kind. I looked down the centre of the spiral but couldn't see anything other than black, so put it down to whatever else these bitches had locked up down there.

I shuddered at the thought.

After this I strengthened my nerve and made my way out of the door that lead into the bailey. Most of the doorways had thankfully been cleared of the falling stone blocks that had made up the castle. These had been moved to the sides and piled in mounds that were now overgrown with Soul Weed.

One look up, told me both Nero and the Harpy guard were still asleep, so I crept over to them, dodging anything on the ground that could potentially trip me up and wake up the entire swarm. But then, the second I got closer, Nero moaned a little as she lifted her head and I knew the second she opened up her eyes some reflex action might kick in, like her shouting my name in surprise. So, as quickly as I could I ran towards her, stepping up the wall surrounding the well so it put me face to face with her. Then I slapped a hand over her mouth the second it started to open.

Her wide eyes took in the sight of me before relief washed over them making tears appear. I gave her a grin and mouthed the question,

'Are you okay?' She nodded as I removed my hand and placed a finger to my lips telling her to stay quiet. Then I cocked my head towards the sleeping guard, silently explaining why. Her dried, cracked and bleeding lips then mouthed the question,

'What are you going to do?' I jumped down to the ground, pulled out my weapon from my back, waved it at her and mouthed back,

'Watch.' This was before I made the creepy and sinister sign for slitting her throat by drawing the tip of my blade inches away from across my own throat. Her startled eyes stared back at me as if asking herself where had this deadly version of me come from?

In the end I gave her a wink and crept around to where the Harpy was leaning back against the well. It was only when I was in front of her crouched to her level that I positioned the blade at her throat, and the second her eyes flickered open I asked,

"Good dreams?" Then before she could open her mouth to scream to the others, I grabbed a fist full of hair by her forehead and slit her throat, turning my face away and closing my eyes just as I felt its blood spray out over me. Once I knew she was most definitely dead, I let her go, wiped the side of my face with my sleeve and stood, watching as the body slid down to one side.

"Tut, tut, that's what you get for sleeping on the job," I told her before running to free Nero from the chains.

"Okay, that was both badass and utterly disturbing...oh shit, tell me you're not like some ridiculously trained assassin back topside, are you?" I smirked at her question and told her honestly,

"Nope, but I do work with dead bodies and once killed a

guy with a pencil." I finished this with another wink before pulling the pin from the cuffs and letting her free.

"Right, well in that case remind me to really not piss you off then."

"Noted, now come on, time to get out of here," I said, putting her arm around my neck and holding on to her waist to help her walk. At least until she got the feeling back in her legs. After this, my first priority was to get her somewhere safe and then come back to try and find the Eye…oh yeah, and then try and kill them all…*piece of red velvet cake, Fae.*

We started to head towards the ruined gatehouse, that seemed to be the only way in or out of this place, when Nero's whispered croaky voice drew my attention from my shitty plan making.

"Do you think we will make it?" Nero asked me in a strained voice that spoke of both her pain and her anxiety. I was just about to give her the optimistic answer when suddenly four Harpies dropped from the sky and were now standing in our way.

"Erm…*that would be a no,"* I muttered the second I heard the rush of flight and swarm of wings all battling for the air around us. We stopped dead before starting to walk backwards, only stopping again when we were back in the centre near the well.

"Ah, I guess they found my little leaving present down in my cell then," I told her making her shoot me an incredulous look.

"Do I wanna know?" she asked, making me reply truthfully,

"No, probably not." She released a sigh in return and muttered what sounded like a prayer to some 'mother goddess'.

"Just answer me this, was it as bloody as that?" she asked

after kicking the dead guard on the ground that was now surrounded by an impressive amount of blood for such a skinny, grey body. She definitely had looked healthier on the inside, that was for damn sure.

"No, no...it was bloodier," I told her making her reply,

"Okay, I am starting to see why you are down in Hell now." I laughed at this, wondering what she would think had she seen my life before Lucius had stepped back into it and painted it blood red.

It had certainly been a far cry from the sight that surrounded us now, as each Harpy began to land with a resounding thud. As for the three biggest, they were now back at their high arched perch with the Queen in the middle. Another Harpy flew over to her and handed her something round, hairy, and dripping, and it only took me a second to figure out what it was. The Queen took it in her hand holding it out as far away from her as she could and listened to what the other Harpy had to say. Seconds later she was snarling and hissing down at me in her response to it. I grinned, gave her a two finger salute, then I lent my head slightly into Nero.

"I think she just got my message," I said through gritted teeth that were still smiling at the winged bitch.

"Your message?" Nero asked in a tone that said she was almost afraid to.

I looked side on and leaning further into her this time said,

"I kinda, might of, just a little bit, painted a threat on my cell wall."

"Wait, what did you use for paint...oh okay, never mind, don't answer that." She paused her question the second I gave her an 'isn't it obvious' look. So, she asked me something else instead,

"What was the message?" This time she whispered this

and I laughed through those same gritted teeth, whilst not taking my eyes from the Queen as I told her,

"That her head was next." Then, the Queen threw the bloodied mass towards us, making Nero scream. Only after she had taken a step back and shivered in revulsion did she speak.

"Yep, you weren't kiddin', definitely bloodier," she said in response to the severed head of the Harpy I had killed as it rolled to our feet. I nudged her shoulder and said,

"In my defence, this was done before I knew you were still alive."

"Oh, that makes me feel so much better," she said sarcastically making me play along,

"Really?"

"No, of course not, you pretty cute psycho!" she hissed making me giggle.

"Can I just ask at this point, because I feel like I need to, what with my life currently hanging in the balance and all… what were you planning exactly if I hadn't been here?" I laughed once and said,

"That's easy…*To kill them all."* Then I stepped forward to the sound of Nero hissing behind me in a strained voice,

"Oh right, but of course, silly me…And exactly how were you planning on doing that…got more than a talon in your knickers, do you?" I chuckled again and looked back over my shoulder to tell her,

"Like I said, you haven't seen what I can do with a pencil," I joked making her sigh and say,

"Gods' assholes, but you and the King really are made for each other." I smirked at her and delivered the classic Hans Solo line before addressing the fact we were surrounded by snarling Harpies that wanted to tear us both limb from limb…

"I know."

"You will die at my feet, mortal!" The Harpy Queen said, making me hold open my arms and say,

"Why not let the girl go and you and I can go one on one." She snarled in response, morphing her features for a short time and flashing those Crimson Eyes I would never forget.

Then, I held up my weapon, pointing it at her and said,

"Time I take another head, and this time…

"It's yours, Bitch!"

CHAPTER THIRTEEN

STORY OF THE BLUE HAIRED DAMNSEL

"Well, this is nice," Nero said making me grant her a wry look before holding up a finger and saying,

"It should be noted that this wasn't part of the plan." She shrugged, swatted a hand in front of her and said,

"Nah, don't sweat it." I raised a brow making her hold up her wrists before giving them a shake and adding,

"At least I am no longer impersonating a piece of meat in a butcher's window…baby steps." I laughed at this and replied,

"Glad I could be of assistance."

"Hey, gold star for completing phase one of this rescue." She smirked back at me and I think chatting like this was obviously keeping us both sane and able to ignore the fact we were now in a large cage that looked like a holding cell for those ready to be executed.

The cage was at the far wall of the bailey and against one that had been heavily damaged because it had no doubt been facing the army that had conquered this place. Shortly after they had found my bloody reminder of what I had done, having it literally fall at our feet, was when we were grabbed, dragged and thrown inside here. At the time I'd had to force myself to calm my ass down or I would have ended up getting Nero hurt and not by the Harpies, but by me. I didn't know what it was, but it was like the longer I was down here the harder it was to stop my temper from blowing up and manifesting into the bringer of death. I felt like some ticking time bomb and I knew I had to get my shit together before Nero got caught in the crossfire. She had already been put through so much and all because of me.

"I am sorry you got caught up in all of this," I told her making her nudge me and feign a,

"Who me? Are you kidding, I live for this shit...genuine adrenaline junkie here."

"Really?" I fell for it.

"Fuck no, I am normally in bed by ten." I laughed at her reply and knew she was joking around just to make me feel better. Then when we were silent a moment, she released a sigh and said,

"Look, none of this is your fault, you know." I gave her a raised brow of disbelief.

"I am serious...I mean do I look like I ask anyone for permission in my decision making?"

"It's not the same thing," I muttered.

"Yeah, it is. Look Fae, Faith, Amelia, or spring chicken, whatever it is you wanna be called, Princess, just as long as you listen to me. I was the one who let my heart rule my head that day you all walked into my shop. I let that cocky bastard flash his handsome smile at me and knew the second he did I would end up doing anything he asked," she admitted, making me ignore the spring chicken part.

"You would have?"

"Shocking huh, I guess my badass act is a good one?" Her reply didn't surprise me.

"You got it that bad, huh?" I asked making her drop her head to her bent knees, at the same time running both hands over her hair, pushing it back with her fingers combing through it.

"Hey, I am not judging here and trust me when I say I know the feeling." At this she lifted her head and looked at me, silently prompting me to say more.

"This may seem hard to believe seeing as Lucius is just known as some tyrant king without a heart to you, but to me…oh Gods, he was always so much more." Her eyes widened in surprise before admitting,

"Well shit, I always thought he kinda just found you one day and then stole you away to be his queen." I laughed and admitted,

"I wish."

"You do?" Her shocked disbelief was clear.

"Oh yeah," I said in that dreamy way that couldn't be taken any other way.

"Look, you think you have it bad for Vern, only ask yourself how bad would that obsession be now if it had lasted over ten years?"

"Ah, I see," she said nodding, finally getting it.

"When I first met Lucius, it was when he saved my life and after that point, well let's just say, he wasn't exactly nice to me," I told her making her laugh and say,

"Sorry, but now this is the part of the story I can see." I flicked her arm and said,

"Oi, I am kinda bleeding my heart out here…do you mind?" She smirked and said,

"Seriously, I get it…When I first met Vern, he saved me

too…well after making the trouble that got me into trouble in the first place, that was."

"Ah, now this is the part of the story *I can see*," I said throwing her words back at her and making her laugh.

"So why don't you tell me about it." She raised her eyes and looked around before saying,

"What here?" I laughed once and replied,

"It's not like we don't have time or anything." She shrugged her shoulders obviously agreeing with me before starting her story.

"I first saw him when I was in this crappy pub near my shop, you remember, the Devil's Cup?"

"Oh, that fine establishment, yeah I think I remember," I said making us both laugh.

"Yeah, that shit hole. Anyway, I was doing a house call, delivering some cure for hoof fungus when I first noticed the notorious McBain brothers." I smirked and asked,

"Notorious, huh?"

"Are you kiddin', those three are bloody famous for the shit they get up to. In fact, they have never lost a bounty and claimed coin for every one. They are about three harrowing stories away from reaching legendary status," she informed me making me agree,

"Oh, I can believe it," I said because just thinking back to the way they had torn that Spider Queen apart and saved me that day, I would have said they hit legendary level with that one alone.

"Anyway, this was the first time I had seen them, not long having my shop open, before me it was a fucking florist, can you believe it? Some stupid pixie thinking she could actually sell flowers in that shit stain of a town. Anyway, after that lasted all of five minutes before making her broke, I bought the place for a steal." I chuckled as I could literally see it being played out for myself. A naïve, blue haired Nero turning up with nothing but a bag and a mind full of hope at starting her new life, even if like she said, it was in some shit old town.

"Thank the Gods romance is dead in Hell, eh?" I said making her laugh in response to the flower shop dying a wilting death.

"Yeah, well that may be true but there were enough bloody females ready to lay down a pathway of rose petals to get one of the McBains into bed, man sluts every one of them." This only half surprised me.

"What even Gryph?" I asked shocked, because, yeah I could totally see it from the other two.

"Especially Gryph...hello, have you seen those muscles? Besides it's all about hot Vikings nowadays, and as long as he keeps his Scottish mouth shut, then they would be all over that Viking man candy." I laughed at this not exactly picturing it, even though, yeah it had to be said, all three of them were hot enough to burn down parts of Hell and that's without it coming from a fire breathing Wyvern.

"So, where was I...oh yeah, so there I was stood at the bar waiting for the barman to finish his order and not gonna lie, I was enjoying the view from my spot when suddenly I felt a flunkin hit my foot."

"What's a flunkin?" I asked getting her off track.

"It's used in a pub game called Aimitin."

"That's a weird name for a pub game...oh, I get it, Aim. It. In."

"And there it is...anyway a flunkin is a spiked ball that you throw at a target to gain points, a bit like Earth's dartboard only square but there's a hole in the middle that's only just big enough for the ball," she explained making it easy to picture.

"What happens if you get it in the middle?" I asked truly interested to know.

"Then you automatically win the game, despite how many points your opponent has accumulated."

"Okay, so that sounds easy enough...so you were saying one hit your foot?" I said, steering her back now the importance of a flunkin and Aimitin were fully explained.

"Yeah it did, but not before first hitting Kellen, a big pissed off bastard who is known as a Mephistopheles." This was a name I hadn't heard before so naturally had to ask her what one was.

"Just think of your worst nightmare and then the guy who is your nightmare's worst nightmare and you get the picture, but if not then think a winged demon with tusks protruding out of his cheeks, with his skin stitched together with the skin of his victims like some patchwork quilt your grandma would make...that was if your grandma was a murdering psychopath that was Godmother to Ted Bundy and Hannibal Lector's love child." I winced and said,

"Geez, okay, okay getting the picture, the guy is ugly and in a 'I ate the ugly stick for breakfast' kind of way."

"Yeah, after first beating other people to death with it and making a coat out of them...anyway, the flunkin bounced off Kellen, before rolling into my foot. Meaning that when I picked it up, I was left holding the bloody thing when Kellen turned around and saw the cause of his now bloody face held in my hand," she said making my eyes grow wide before whispering,

"Oh shit."

"Yeah, oh shit indeed," she agreed with a shake of her head as if she were seeing it all play out in front of her.

"So, what happened next?"

"You mean after the bastard lifted me up by the throat and started strangling me?"

"Okay, so that's another oh shit moment," I added with a nod of my head, asking myself now how she had survived as long as she had in that town. Oh, right...*magic.*

"It was, but then let's just say it was worth the pain when a hand landed on the arm that held me and a sexy Scottish voice ordered to let the pretty girl go." I couldn't help it, I actually girly sighed making her say,

"I know right...anyway, when Kellen refused, that same hand became inflamed and the scent of burning skin kinda ruined the moment for a while there. But after punching a flaming fist into Kellen's face and knocking him out cold, he bought me a drink and led me over to where his brothers were still playing. No doubt still having their brother's back from a distance...they are cool like that," she added with a chuckle.

"And then what happened?" This was when Nero frowned and started to look uncomfortable. *I soon knew why.*

"Oh, that was when he spent about five minutes with me, before snagging one of the waitresses around the waist, whispering something in her ear before disappearing with her upstairs into the room he was staying in for the night." I winced at that, put a comforting hand on her shoulder and said,

"That's sucks, I am sorry, Nero...Gods, but what an asshole," I said because I knew it would make her feel better. She shrugged and said,

"Ah, but it is what it is, Vern just sees me as a friend and that's it, once he told me he thought of me as a little sister or something, which was after I questioned why he broke some demon's hand for touching me." I frowned at this wondering if there wasn't more to it than she was obviously seeing. I had a feeling Vern was hiding how he truly felt and let's face it, I knew what that felt like too. But I didn't say any of this, as I didn't think it fair to get her hopes up when that might not be true.

"So that's why you give him a hard time, to hide how you truly feel?" She tensed her shoulders a little and said,

"What can I say, defence mechanism 101, baby." Yep, I knew all about that one too. After all, it was a game Lucius played with me for years. I went on to tell her a little about my own experience with Lucius, explaining how he treated me in his nightclub the first time I sneaked in.

Of course, she did the classic girls stick together mate thing, which was basically call him a bastard and dub him an asshole for treating me like that. But then I went on to tell her a little of why, and how mainly it was to protect me. That in the end none of it really mattered anymore because he loved me and I loved him, which was all that really counted.

Naturally, she was also curious to know what it was like, dating the Tyrant King of blood and death, ending my explanation with her stunned reply,

"You're shitting me?!" This was of course, after I told her how sweet he was and how he even watched geeky programs with me. That he was romantic and caring, protective and even at times, a gentleman. Nero's reaction ended up getting us some attention when one of the Harpy guards hit her mace type weapon against the bars, snarling at us to be quiet.

I would have said something equally as threatening as it was funny in return had my attention not been rooted elsewhere. This was because the Queen was now on the ground and barking orders at her minions to have something covered in a deep red material brought forward, for their master was coming to claim his prize.

Meaning that when the object was being placed on a

plinth at the centre of the open space and the material was pulled back to reveal the Eye of Crimson, I had to question,

What prize was that exactly?

The Eye or…

A Vampire King's Chosen One?

CHAPTER FOURTEEN

A HARPY'S REVENGE

"Okay, so I take back all previous oh shits and reserve the right to use it now…oh shit," Nero said at the sight of the Eye being displayed like some crown jewel. Another bang on the front of the cage made us both jump this time and again I would have reacted differently. That was if I wasn't doing a guppy impression whilst watching the show unfold in front of us.

The Harpies were crowded around a black plinth that held the Eye of Crimson at its centre like a jewel on an ostentatious crown. It had long fingers of gold that were steepled up like the decorative parts on a cathedral's roof. But it wasn't the site of the Eye that struck me silent and without a witty comeback, it was the Harpies strange reaction to it.

The way they circled it, whilst clicking their tongues on the roof of their mouths before hissing out words I couldn't understand. Even their wings spread out and shuddered as if they couldn't contain themselves at the sight of the power presented to them. From what I could gather from Nero's reaction back down in the temple and before we were attacked, was that before this point in time the Eye had been little more than just a myth. And now, watching the way the Harpies reacted to it, I had to question just how far that myth had travelled down in Hell. Because to watch them now and you would have thought the God Janus himself had been sat upon a throne in the centre of their world. Not just a representation of his bleeding heart for mankind.

"I don't know about you, but I've got a bad feeling about this," Nero said, without taking her enamoured gaze from the Eye of Crimson. But with this comment I couldn't help but turn to ask her,

"And you're only now getting this bad feeling? Because unless kidnapping is a regular occurrence for you, then I think time for bad feelings was when you were knocked unconscious and presumed dead…which was not fun for me by the way." My sarcastic response got me a raised brow in return before she admitted,

"Okay, so I see your point because being knocked out and bleeding on the floor wasn't fun for me either."

"It never is," I commented dryly, and her look said it all.

"Seriously, girl, do you have a normal life or anything because I live in Hell and even I don't go through this much shit on a regular basis?" Nero said making me laugh before telling her,

"Would you believe me if I told you my life was pretty boring before I met Lucius." She started nodding and agreed,

"Actually yeah, I would…damn men, eh?" It was my turn to nod.

"You got that right. Although it does have to be said that since meeting him, I equally get myself in this much shit without his help," I admitted, feeling guilty daily for what Lucius had to deal with. Hell, but trying to keep me safe was almost a pointless endeavour these days. Because you could lead a horse to water but making it drink was another thing or in my case making it stay in its bloody stable until it was ready to be ridden was another thing. And well, Lucius was one hell of a rider!

"No, Princess, that really does not surprise me." I gave her a coy look and questioned,

"No?"

"No offence, but I smelled trouble on you the second you walked in my shop...well, after the walking, talking, troublemaking, sex on a red Scottish stick, Wyvern...that was, oh but damn that hot blooded male sent from the Gods to ravish..." I swear I started choking before holding up my hands and saying,

"Okay, okay, getting a pretty clear yet steamy, overly hot picture here." She laughed before shrugging her shoulders unapologetically and despite what was happening all around us, every time either of us did laugh, it only managed to ease the tension of our unknown fate.

"What do you think they're going to do with it?" Nero asked after a few moments of silence.

"Well, whatever it is, I don't think they're going to play dodgeball with it. *Look, here comes the Queen,"* I said whispering this last part as she walked across the bailey dragging behind her the long silk tail of her dress. Now doing so as if she had been born into royalty. But strangely this thought led into one that had no reasoning behind it and for purposes I couldn't explain, I knew that she had been granted or gifted the life she now possessed.

Not only did she not look like the others, now that she had the body of a beautiful woman, with only her legs resembling that of a bird like creature. But it was also her wings and although not as full and glorious as the feathers of an Angel, they were there nevertheless, if not lacking in lustre and magnificence the Gods readily provided.

Now, as for the rest of her body, there were no protruding bones or paper-thin sickly grey skin over her feminine frame. Even her breasts looked voluptuous and held high in the bodice of her tight dress. Seeing such beauty made me question the origins of the larger Harpies. I also wondered if this was how she'd looked before falling from Zeus' good grace and plummeting straight to Hell? But out of all my questions what I wanted to know the most was what little left of her soul did she bargain with? What did she offer to gain back this beauty and more importantly, who was the one that had the power to grant it to her?

These thoughts brought me back to what the Eye had shown me before this bitch had turned up and knocked me to the ground. Could this really be the work of the one she called Master? A master that Lucius didn't yet know was in fact his brother.

The broken pieces of both past and future the Eye had shown me was like trying to make sense of a picture on a broken vase. I didn't know what had happened or what was still yet to come, but I knew one thing and that was Lucius had a brother and that brother utterly...

Hated him.

"So, what's the plan, just sit here and wait for the cavalry, 'cause, I'm sure that boyfriend of yours is gonna be tearing the place apart and no doubt cursing me to damnation?" Nero asked looking around the cage as if to look for weaknesses, although I have to confess our chances of getting out of here surrounded by half crazed Harpies wasn't looking good. In fact, it was looking the opposite of good and little did I know, it was about to get a whole lot worse.

Which prompted my change of subject.

"Tell me about the Harpies," I said, trying to get both of our minds off the situation unfolding in front of us.

"Why, you planning on writing a book?" she asked in a sceptical tone.

"No, but I am a firm believer that knowledge is power and the more I know about these bitches, the better prepared I'll be." At this she shrugged her shoulders and said,

"Why the hell not, it's not like I have anything better to do and no doubt singing kumbaya will just get little miss stick bang happy over there too excited." I had to laugh at this.

"Tell me about the three, starting with the Queen," I suggested, for what I knew of Harpies was very little, other than being damned and punished by Zeus. Most of which I had read in Greek mythology books.

"Okay, so the quick and easy version of it is that Harpies, when first created, were known to be the hounds of Zeus, with the sole purpose of stealing whatever he wanted."

"It's starting to sound like Oliver Twist, minus the wanting more gruel part." Nero smirked and carried on,

"Yeah, well, every supernatural being with a brain and ears knows about Zeus being the most egotistical of the Gods. So then it's not surprising that he would create four sisters, each one being as beautiful as the next."

"Must have been one Hell of an aviary," I mused making her chuckle again.

"And knowing Zeus, most likely looked like a caged sex club with feathers, or maybe he just had a thing for birds... who knows, as he certainly had a thing for women, and lots of them. Anyway, over time it seemed that the oldest sister must have gotten bolder or some shit, because this one in particular didn't really take too kindly to being forgotten about." Looking at the Queen now as she strutted her importance around the Eye and I couldn't say that it surprised me.

"Think of it as a naughty child trying to get the attention of their parent."

"Did she throw her little birdy mirror and bell out of the pram?" Nero replied,

"Needy bitches, eh…yeah they started making life difficult for Zeus and not surprisingly really, I mean how many women does one man need…anyway…"

"…this is the part where he banishes them and punishes them to Hell and all that?" I interrupted making her scoff,

"Hey, I thought I was telling the story." I laughed, holding up my hands in surrender and said in the words of my Aunty Pip,

"My bad."

"So yeah, it's pretty much that part…anyway, the story goes that on their fall to Hell they were stripped of both their feathers and of any beauty they once possessed. Meaning, pretty soon they landed and were soon known as nothing more than the scavengers of Tartarus, like vultures fighting over whatever rotting corpse they could find." I made a face that looked as if I was smelling bad cheese but asked anyway,

"What happened next, because it looks like they have come on a long way since then?"

"A long way?" she questioned sceptically raising her brows.

"Okay, so not so much of a long way that I think they eat their food at a dinner table with a good use of a knife and fork…I just mean in a more, I know how to share my pound of man flesh with my sisters, type of way," I said making her grin.

"So come on, what happened?" I asked steering her back to the conversation,

"Only that it was your grandfather, the one and only, dishy Prince of Lust that took pity on them…" My eyes widened and my mouth dropped before I replied drily,

"But of course it was."

"Yeah, something about the beauty that they once had or some crap. Anyway, he gave them purpose and naturally being the Prince of Lust, that purpose was of a sexual nature."

"Shocker," I joked making her grin, which ended up looking painful due to the split in her lip. But then I looked at the Harpies and shuddered at the thought of being forced to lie with a creature so hideous.

"So, it's true then, they actually force themselves onto…" Nero cut me off,

"Anything that moves, that's got a dick…yeah, that's pretty much their gig."

"And suddenly, periods once a month and not being able to pee standing up are not so much of a problem anymore." Now she really laughed and who Nero had dubbed as little miss stick bang happy once again got a hard on for banging on the bars, hissing at us like a wet cat.

"But then it's not exactly about just getting their rocks off either," Nero added lowering her voice a little so we could continue to talk.

"I'm almost scared to ask, but it's not?"

"No, their obsession is born from the offspring that they can produce. The continuation of their race means everything to them. And from what I heard years ago, something happened that not only drastically depleted their numbers, but it also killed one of the sisters." The moment I heard this part of the story I couldn't help but tense, hoping that Nero didn't notice. Thankfully, instead of focusing too much on me, she continued on with her Harpies' dark tale of woe.

"Ever since that, there has been rumours, secrets whispered in the dark."

"What kind of secrets?" I asked whispering and taking a quick glance at our guard. Nero scooted closer and told me,

"Secrets about a Harpy army being built somewhere on the ruined outskirts of Tartarus. Of course, no one really believes it, almost like ghost stories told to small children around a campfire in the mortal realm, these were stories told to lesser demons, becoming a step up from just your usual gossip whispered on street corners and boasted about in Taverns...that was until..."

"Until what?" I asked following her gaze directly on the Harpy Queen.

"Until a Queen emerged as if being reborn into her once Angelic form. I don't know the ins and outs of it, or whatever piece of her soul was left to sell but it is rumoured that the two things that she wanted she received."

"To rebirth the children she lost, gaining back her army and as an extra, that of her beauty," I finished off for her.

"Yep, that pretty much sums up the crazy bitch," Nero said with a roll of her hand in the direction of said crazy bitch.

"Well, looking around at this lot I would say she received both, along with a new wardrobe of dresses fit for a Queen... really gives new meaning to the whole 'Devil wears Prada' film."

"Huh?" Nero asked, making me wave my hand and say,

"Nothing important, just human ramblings." But whether that might be true or not, I couldn't help but look at her now, dressed in all her finery. Included in this was that creepy head dress, one that looked half alive and connected with the darkness of her soul. The black shadowy serpents wavered in and out of existence, disappearing with her sudden movements as she circled the Eye, still not daring to touch it. But this surprised me, as I would have thought it was the first thing she would have done. Especially given all the trouble she went to in getting it in the first place.

Unless of course, it was forbidden?

If not, then what was she waiting for...or should I say, *who?*

"So, you think she did all this just so she could get revenge on whoever it was that killed her sister?" I asked Nero, who was looking at the other two sisters, a pair who were still high up on their perch. It was obvious that they had not received the same deal their sister had, making me wonder if they had even been in her thoughts when making this bargain.

"Honestly, but who knows what the bitch is thinking, but one thing's for sure, she's definitely not working alone," Nero said with a shake of her head.

"What makes you say that?" I asked because I was curious to find out how much she knew.

"Harpies don't do magic and that summoning Hex you have on your back is the work of a witch, and a powerful one at that." Nero nodded to emphasise her words. Of course, I knew this already, Especially, after what the Harpy Queen had said to me down in the temple. Her Master wanted me, and it wasn't a stretch to assume this Master was Lucius' brother and the witch that had been behind the scenes making this all happen was just another one of his lackies.

"Tell me more about the Queen," I said after a moment of silence stretched between us.

"The Queen is called Celaeno, and being the older sister she was also the one who led the other three to ruin and got them kicked out of Heaven as well as far from Zeusy boy's good graces as she could get...but don't quote me on the details because they are sketchy. But this is the reason I'm not exactly surprised that she was the only one to be granted beauty in this bargain...As I don't think she's going to win any sister of the year awards, do you?" I had to agree on that one.

After this Nero went on to tell me about the other two, who were the twins, Aello and Ocypete. Nero also said that supposedly they were born with their wings entwined with one another and that was also how they arrived in Hell, landing together as one. She also went on to speak of their skills in the air and how their speed could not be matched. Although, it also had to be said that intelligence was not their strong point, hence being lackeys overshadowed by their sister.

I then asked about the sister that had been killed, again trying to discover what she knew and if the 'gossip' hymn sheet she was singing from mentioned a certain someone. She told me her name had been Podarge, a Harpy, who had been quicker on her feet than in flight.

But then Nero surprised me when I asked who it was that had killed her.

"That's the odd thing, no one knows her name but the only thing that is confirmed is that whoever killed their sister, unbelievably, was mortal." Nero took a glance at my worried face and grinned a little before nudging me on my shoulder and telling me,

"Oh, don't worry. After all, they should know it was well before your time." I gave her what I knew was a strained smile in return before evading her concerned gaze. Because she didn't know what I knew. She didn't know who that mortal was...*but I did.*

Which meant that if I did, it also meant that the Harpy

Queen did too. That was why she told me back in that Temple that she had been waiting a long time for this.

She had meant her revenge.

Well, as if shit couldn't get any more convoluted. Meaning this little escape plan of mine just got a whole lot more complicated. Because this was no longer a snatch and grab type of gig for these winged bitches. They hadn't kidnapped me solely to hand me over to their master.

No this was all about a bargain made. It was all about their revenge for a sister's death.

A sister who was killed by...

My mother.

CHAPTER FIFTEEN

THE MASTER ARRIVES

This conversation ended abruptly, and this wasn't just down to the secrets I was keeping. Of course, it wasn't ever confirmed that the death of this Harpy was indeed my mother's fault, but seeing as she was the only mortal known to be down here before me, then who else could it have been. And besides, the reason the Harpy Queen had wanted me was for revenge, meaning it didn't take a genius to add these two together and have it equal one dead Harpy, and three pissed off sisters.

The moment a hush fell amongst the Harpy swarm, I knew the time had come…*the Puppet Master had arrived.*

"Who is that?" Nero's question was one I couldn't yet answer even though I had seen his cloaked form before. I also knew the face of the man hiding underneath the large folds of his hood, just as I had heard him speak of his hatred for his brother.

In the end I didn't get chance to tell Nero this, because the moment he was seen a silence swept through the bailey like a wave of doom, forcing all the Harpies to place their heads to the ground. Even the Queen bowed to the shadowed figure, one who had seemingly created a tear in the realm and simply stepped through it.

This was the only way to describe it, as he seemed to have arrived out of nowhere, creating a portal from nothing. In all honesty, I didn't think there was a being powerful enough to do such a thing. For someone to have the ability to go anywhere was a scary thought indeed but mostly, I had to wonder how could you defeat a being such as this? How would you be able to contain him once he was even caught? Such a feat just didn't seem possible.

The portal he created had been higher up on one of the only levels left with an arched walkway. I could just imagine that at one time it would have made for a decorative part of the castle. But for now, well, its beauty was long gone and with it a large chunk of the balustrades and arches, having been lost to the war won against its residing Lord.

However, enough of the ledge remained for the cloaked figure of Lucius' brother to stand upon as he addressed his adoring Harpy Queen and her minions.

"My Master, I have completed my task and did as you commanded, I brought you not only the Eye of Crimson but also the Chosen One of your enemy. All I ask is that when you are done with her, I am to be awarded the honour of delivering her death," The Queen said after rising up, sweeping the length of her skirt out to the side as she did. I couldn't help but wonder if these actions were part of an old soul who, until her change back to a heavenly beauty, had resided in her as a dormant part of her past and was in fact how she used to address the Gods when in their presence.

"You will have your revenge, make no mistake for our bargain is intact until the end. But trouble yourself not, for her life will be of little worth once I am through with her.

However, for now it is the Eye I want." I had to admit that the voice of Lucius' brother terrified me. Even Nero shuddered next to me, telling me I wasn't the only one affected by the depth of evil I could hear coming from his demon side.

Neither of us were strangers to the demonic nature that surrounded us on a daily basis, but his voice was something else entirely. It was one of pure poison that was fuelled by a river of hate. Oh, but the Harpy Queen may have thought she was on the road to revenge but this man, this demon, was the one who paved that road for all of the others. A road taken by those that held nothing but hatred in their hearts, for his own brand of hatred knew no bounds.

The Queen bowed her head once more, answering in what I knew was a more angelic voice than before this bargain for her soul was ever made. As no other Harpy sounded this way, not even those of her sisters.

"But of course, my Master." She walked towards the plinth where the Eye sat like a beacon for all malicious intentions. She then reached out ready to take possession of it, when suddenly the booming voice of her Master ceased her actions. Moments later and I knew that I would be wishing that he had been too late in his warning.

"STOP!"

"Master?" she questioned, after bringing her hand back to her chest, as if it were a wounded animal in need of the comfort of her bosom.

"Have one of your children bring it to me," he ordered making Nero and I frown at each other. He motioned with his gloved hand, one that matched the harsh hard lines of his armour-plated body, you could just see beneath the swallowing folds of the strange shadowy cloak. It almost looked like a separate entity encasing itself around every inch of him, being that of half material, half creature. This eerie movement could be seen whenever he raised a hand or shifted his stance, as its darkness seamlessly shifted around his movements.

The Harpy Queen, who I now knew was named Celaeno, looked uneasy for the first time. You could see this as she gazed around at her children as if trying to decide whose fate would be first tested and at the mercy of the Eye. Her obvious reluctance was forced to the back of her mind with only a simple action from her Master when he folded his arms across his chest. This provided us with more than just a glimpse of the scaled armour beneath, and it was one that looked as if it was made from the hide of a dragon. I couldn't say I was surprised when she hurried on with her task of choosing.

She motioned one Harpy forward and if there was any way to describe the creature, then it would have been classed as the runt of the litter. This, or the reason it was smaller was due to its young age, either way it made its way through the rest of the swarm coming to the front to bow before its mother Queen.

"Take the Eye to our Master, youngling," the Queen demanded answering my silent question. The youngling as she had named it, lifted its head and clicked her tongue on the roof of her mouth three times, reminding me of the sound of a cricket in the summer grass. The sunken hollows of her cheeks dipped even further when making this sound and her little breasts shook as her small wings vibrated.

She then straightened her back, thrusting out what little chest she had, as she made her way towards the plinth. The moment she got there her wings spread out and they fluttered once again. Only this time they shivered like a nervous bird waiting to take flight at the first sense of danger.

"Oh, this is gonna be bad," Nero commented and before I could ask why, the smaller Harpy reached out and grabbed the Eye, one that was now glowing a brighter crimson. For a few seconds, it was as if all that was happening to her was that she was receiving some glimpse of the future. I let a held breath out only to end up sucking it back in through my teeth. This was because the moment a certain image must have penetrated her mind, she opened her mouth and let out a horrified scream. This was the last sound she would ever make, for the scream lasted only a few seconds before it stopped.

This wasn't because she had asserted the will and right to stop it herself. No, the sound stopped when it became stuck in her throat when her air supply had been cut off abruptly. Her entire body followed as the rest of her became imprisoned by the power of the Eye.

It was as if she couldn't move, as if she couldn't speak and more importantly for her, she couldn't do anything to free herself. Her eyes were frozen wide with fear but even then, they could not move beyond staring at the Eye. I didn't have to wonder long as to what the Eye had shown her, as it took about three seconds until she suddenly burst into a cloud of black sand before floating away.

The haunting image she had been shown, had been that of her death. The rest of the swarm let out a wailing cry at the loss of their kin. Even the twins cried out at this loss, as they were still sat up high and perched with the bird's-eye view of their young offspring's death. Their echoing pain was by far the loudest and continued on until the Queen demanded silence.

"I'm sorry, my Master, but my offspring are clearly not worthy, perhaps if you were to…" His hand went up demanding silence and this I knew was so he could issue another order. I was right when he spoke without an ounce of feeling,

"Pick another one." The Queen baulked, recoiling back a step before saying,

"But Master it will only mean the death of one of my..." He raised a hand to stop her and demanded again, in a deadly voice,

"I. Said. Pick...*another one!*" At this the Queen's shoulders slumped and the panicked looks between the twins were witnessed by the older sister's silent devastation as she glanced up at them.

It was clear, if nothing else, that the Harpy sisters cared for their offspring. But in the hands of their Master, they had all become nothing more than expendable puppets to use for his gain. So, with little else to do and no other option, the Queen motioned for another one to step forward, only this time they knew what awaited them. This meant that they had to be forced to do the Queen's bidding and the whining and hissing sounds became louder as they fought for freedom.

"Okay, so I don't particularly like these bitches, but even I think that this is brutal," Nero exclaimed with a shake of her head, with the same disgust written all over her face that was mirrored on my own. But yet, one by one we were all forced to witness as Harpy after Harpy sacrificed themselves for no gain at all. In fact, by the seventh death, the twins Aello and Ocypete were holding each other's hands as tears freely ran down their deathly skin. Yet during this willing massacre the Mother Queen did nothing to spare her children from this horrific ordeal.

Finally, just after the last Harpy had burst into black sand their Master held his hand up and ceased the order for another one to be brought forward. I think that if the Harpies had the ability to sigh, they would have all released an echoing sound of relief at the same time. As it stood, it was only Nero and I who made such a sound.

But during this whole horrific moment, I couldn't help question why the same hadn't happened to me? Had it been because it had called to me, starting with a dream? Had I been chosen or trusted with the secrets of the Fates for a reason?

Unfortunately, it seemed as if I wasn't the only one having these thoughts, because now who they named their Master was staring my way.

"Oh no, that oh shit moment just came back, *big time,*" Nero said, obviously observing the Masters' shift of attention as I had done. This was confirmed when the next order out of his mouth was directed my way.

"The Vampire's Chosen One, she had possession of the Eye when you found her, yes?" His question may have been aimed at the Queen but as it was said, his gaze was solely on my own. The demonic red glow ringed by an abyss of darkness was the only feature that could be seen through the low hood covering most of his face.

"Yes, my Master, she had possession of the Eye." In that moment if I could have hissed and made it sound half as effective as the way they did, I would have done so, directing it solely at the Queen bitch!

"I've got another bad feeling about this," Nero muttered between clenched teeth, and I had to confess, I wasn't feeling too great about it either. This feeling was only cemented when the Queen stepped up to our cage and ordered me to do as her Master commanded.

"Yeah no, I don't feel like bursting into a cloud of black sand today, thanks…but hey, you go right ahead, pretty sure it's your turn anyway" I said making her hiss at me and like I said, she had it mastered hands down, complete with a spray of spit and everything. At this rate I was starting to think that Zeus had a thing for cats as well.

"Very well, bring me the witch!" Lucius' brother commanded, making the blood in my veins turn to ice.

"No wait, you can't...!" My calls of protest were cut off the second the door swung open and both of us started to fight. Unfortunately, the Harpies were too strong for us and Nero was still too close for me to unleash the blood power that was inside of me. At this point I questioned everything, where it came from, why it only arose when I was angry and most of all, how to control it. Because if I knew this and understood it better, then maybe I would have the ability to direct it at my enemies and not that of my friends. But until that happened I couldn't risk Nero's life.

I tried once more to fight and kick my way through the Harpies that stood in my way, preventing me from getting to a screaming Nero. I was pinned back against the bars and held there until their Masters' orders had been fulfilled. I knew what he was doing, they were going to use Nero as a pawn to get me to do what they wanted.

"Let me go!" I shouted but it was no use as my face was slammed against the bars and I gritted my teeth against the pain, not wanting to give them the satisfaction of how much it rattled my jaw. I was forced to watch as they dragged a struggling Nero over to the well. I sighed in relief when their intentions didn't mean Nero was next in line for being forced to hold the Eye. Meaning that she wasn't going to become the next sacrificial lamb stepping up for the slaughter.

No, instead her body was lifted and positioned in the well bucket with her hands tied once more over her head. The length of rope was then looped over the hook the swinging bucket was attached to. At least her feet had something to stand on so she wasn't just hanging there by her arms over the sheer drop of the well. Naturally, she looked utterly terrified and I couldn't say I blamed her. Her eyes kept snapping between looking down at the death that awaited her at the bottom of the well and back up to mine, silently questioning what was coming next.

It was only once she was in place that I was also dragged from the cage before being pulled and pushed until I was before Lucius' brother. I was quickly forced to my knees and the bastard in front of me clapped his hands once, as if the sight pleased him.

"You won't be laughing soon, asshole," I muttered between clenched teeth. I could feel the rage, the hatred and the anger all directed at this man and the creatures he commanded. I could feel it like a sickness sweeping across my skin. Like an infection I wanted out of my body knowing that when it did, it would become a destructive force eradicating my enemies that surrounded me.

"You will touch the Eye and reveal to me what you see of the future." I released a deep sigh already knowing how this was going to play out.

"And if I don't?" I asked needing to know what they would do if I didn't comply. Lucius' brother simply shrugged his large shoulders and said in a nonchalant tone,

"Then the witch dies." He stated this in a simple, matter of fact way before raising his hand and silently commanding them to drop the bucket. Nero and I both screamed at the same time, but hers was only one that echoed down the well before tailing off, the further underground she went.

NO!" I screamed when I heard the splash of water and my heart sank with her. The cranking sound of the mechanism that had been released for a quick drop had stopped and the deadly silence of her cries was deafening.

"Alright, alright! I'll do it! I'll do whatever the fuck you say, just pull her up...come on pull her up, for fuck sake, do it quickly!" I shouted desperately hoping that the fall hadn't killed her. Lucius' brother nodded to the Harpy that had been stood next to the crank, someone who started to turn it far too slowly and I could only breathe again when I heard her body emerging out of the water. However, I still needed to know she was alright, so only ended up holding my breath again as the rope thickened in the giant cog, until it was coiled around like a nestled snake.

I felt as if my heart had stopped and only started to beat again, the moment I saw her defeated form still attached to that bucket. Water gushed out over the bucket's edge as her feet and ankles fully emerged. Her wet, dripping hair hung limp to one side where her head seemed too heavy for her body.

"Come on Nero, just give me a sign you're still alive," I muttered to myself, because from all accounts it looked as if she was dead. Then as if she had heard me and my prayers, she suddenly gasped for air, her swinging movements making more water spill over and splash up her legs. I released a heavy breath and felt like crying with relief.

"Now, do as I ask, or next time your little friend won't be coming back up." I felt my lip curl in revulsion and bitter loathing, as I sneered back up at him, but his threat was one I knew wasn't empty. I looked back to Nero to find her eyes on me, her blue lips quivered and even with her body shivering, she was telling me not to do it. I ignored her, then silently closed my eyes before I told the bastard,

"I will do it."

"Then by all means get on with it, after all, your friend doesn't have all day and neither do I."

I had to wonder at this and whether it had been said because Lucius knew where I was? Had he somehow discovered who it was that had taken me and was now on his way here with the cavalry, as Nero had put it?

In the end, this hope became a moot point because time was not on my side and trying to stall him was not an option as it could only end up getting Nero killed. This meant that I had no other choice. I had to do what he said and if my plan worked like I hoped it would, I would touch the Eye and in doing so hold on to the comforting thought that in the end, it wouldn't be the outcome he was expecting.

But first, it was time to step up to the Eye and take possession of the future it would show me once again.

The haunting image of my own sacrifice.

A price paid with…

My Stolen Heart.

CHAPTER SIXTEEN

PAST BRUTAL BEAUTIES

The moment I touched the Eye this time I knew it had taken me back to the past, not the future. I also knew the second I saw my mother that the reason for that was to show me what really happened to the Harpies' sister.

I naturally questioned who the tall beautiful blonde was who walked with my mother, doing so almost as if she was escorting her through Hell. They had just entered a corridor that looked like a wide gallery you would find in a castle or English manor house. It made me wonder about the castle we were in now and if it had anything to do with it?

I watched like a ghost seeping out of the wall as I followed them. It was a very similar experience to when the Keepers of Three had taken me down a journey of Lucius' past. I had felt like some silent witness following hopelessly through his own flickering of time.

But as for now, well I had to say that the sight of my mother made me smile, for she didn't look much different than she does now. I found myself wondering at her mind by being in this place. Yes, she was mortal like I am but as I was beginning to understand, being down here made me something different.

It made me something more.

But what had my mother been like back then? I knew for a fact that she certainly wasn't as capable at fighting and hadn't been trained on how to protect herself by my father as I was. She also didn't have the same knowledge of Hell and its demons that I did. She hadn't grown up in my Father's world and therefore wasn't used to the brutality it had to offer.

Although didn't this fact only end up making her more fearless, more courageous? Coming down to Hell with nothing but your wits about you and the strength of your bravery to drive you, well, you didn't get more gallant than that.

But it also made me realise just how little I really knew about my parents and their own history. Puzzle pieces of a picture I would never see was all that had been offered to me growing up. Small snippets of stories told by my aunties and uncles or muffled nostalgic tales heard by small ears of a child with her cheek pressed to the door. Of course, I'd always known that their story was one on a more epic scale than what they first proclaimed it to be, even to me, their daughter. But I knew they did this to protect me, my father especially, as he always had. However, there was no protecting me now and seeing scenes like this one, only meant that I had so many questions. Questions that unfortunately I might never have the answer to.

I watched as both my mother and this unknown person came to a wooden door at the end of the corridor. Above it sat what must have first looked like a gargoyle of sorts being some hideous stone figure. But now, having dealt with these creatures for the last day, then I knew otherwise.

It was a Harpy.

"Wow, that is one ugly looking Gargoyle. I mean I have seen scary at Afterlife but this one takes the biscuit." I had to chuckle at my mother's humour, as we obviously had this in common. A humour used as a weapon to ease the tension during stressful situations. She said this after catching up to the woman who was obviously leading her through Hell for whatever reason I was still yet to discover. The beautiful blonde looked up at the Harpy who was sat statue still but still watching with a keen eye. Then she informed her,

"That's no Gargoyle."

"Eosss!" the creature hissed after leaning forward and spitting this name down at them...no not them, just at the woman next to my mother. I frowned to myself asking where it was I had heard this name before, and then I looked back to the woman I believed the Harpy had called Eos. She looked disgusted in return and with a curled lip, addressed her,

"Podarge."

Moments after speaking her name, it made me realise that I was about to witness the true murderer of the Harpy sister and let's just say, I really doubted it was going to be my mother. But once again I found myself ignoring this name, insight of another, remembering now that Eos was Latin for Aurora. I felt my features twist into my own look of disgust as this was a name I had heard before. And well, let's just say that it wasn't ever spoken about in a good light. In fact, I think my mother hated her just as much as she hated Layla, which made me question now what she was doing with the bitch?

Had this been a moment in time before the cause for that hatred had happened? It would seem so.

"Why are you *here?*" the Harpy demanded, hissing the last word. The Harpy then jumped down from its perch and whereas my mother took a step back, Aurora did not.

"That is none of your business Harpy, you know who I am so you would be wise to have respect when speaking to me!" the bitch Aurora replied, straightening her spine with an arrogant air when staring down at the Harpy as though she was scum beneath her feet.

"Oh, I know who you are and of your traitorous ways," Podarge said, sneering at who she obviously classed as being a small threat before her.

"What is she talking about?" This question came from my mother who turned to face Aurora with distrust in her eyes. This then confirmed to me that whatever had happened between them must have been after this point and perhaps what I was witnessing now was simply the start of it.

"Nothing!" Aurora snapped making the Harpy laugh in a high-pitched cackle.

"You call betraying your Master nothing?" The Harpy threw back at her in challenge, but it was my mother's reaction to this I focused on,

"Draven...? Why you..." I could feel my mother's anger rising in a way that was similar to that of my own down here. And although I couldn't see what I had started to see in myself when it happened, the power I felt coming from her was still there. It was like an invisible wall knocking into me and passing through me like a ghost. However, it only evaporated and released its hold on me when Aurora answered,

"She's talking about Zeus." My mother released a visibly relieved sigh before saying,

"Oh...well, that's alright then I...uh..." Then she paused when the Harpy took a menacing step closer to her and in a comical way, after taking note of the Harpy's annoyance, changed her tune and added,

"I mean, how could you do that?" Aurora simply rolled her eyes in annoyance before addressing the Harpy once more, obviously choosing to ignore my mother's comment.

"My business with that ruthless bastard is my own and does not concern the likes of you and your abhorrent kind." In response to this the Harpy became furious and crouched low, at same time opening her wings. This was in preparation, as if ready to pounce and attack the one who had insulted her entire kind.

"Erm…yeah, good one," my mother muttered sarcastically before Aurora released a frustrated sigh, as if she didn't have time for any of this and it was all so very taxing.

"You die traitor and with it I will cook the flesh of your mortal over your burning corpse to share with my sisters!" the Harpy threatened, painting a gruesome picture and making my mother's face wince as if she could see it herself. Then in another comical and classic way of my mother's nature, she asked the woman next to her,

"Seriously though, do you have any friends?" However, Aurora ignored her and instead focused on enraging the Harpy further, basically goading her into attacking.

"Zeus should have killed you!" Aurora said making Podarge charge at both of them instantly. However, in a surprising twist of events Aurora pushed my mother out of the way just before the Harpy could use her talon tipped feet to rip into my mother's form.

And with my mother now out of the fray, they both ran at each other. A vision I had to confess made for an odd sight to witness, especially when one of them looked like they had just come out of a business meeting from a New York office board room. But then, it wasn't just the business suit that looked out of place, but that of the bladed weapon she pulled from her back and used to slash out at the Harpy. And she certainly hit her mark, first to her back and then one to the neck that had the Harpy stumbling backwards. She tragically did this whilst trying to hold together the gash that almost certainly meant her death.

However, as she went stumbling backwards, she tripped to the floor, which meant now being forced to look up helplessly into the face of her killer. It certainly made for a pitying sight, when seeing her now silently begging for her life to be spared.

And what did Aurora do in sight of this but pull her knee up and hammer down a foot, quickly impaling a stiletto heel in the eye of the Harpy. Podarge's body seemed to curl up around the impact reminding me of a dead spider on its back, before all her limbs and wings relaxed back flat to the floor. My mother looked in total shock at the ruthless cold glint in Aurora's eyes, who instead of looking affected simply pulled her foot from the Harpy's head. Then she pulled down on her jacket and smoothed back her hair before walking past my mother saying,

"Fucking Harpies."

The moment I was slammed back into reality, I dropped the Eye and stumbled backwards. The moment the Crimson orb touched the ground it turned everything around it to black sand being that of a reminiscent representation of its own past. The Harpies all saw this and quickly retreated backwards to the circumference of ground that still remained part of the castle.

As for me, I had fallen onto my backside and my body

shuddered with the strength it took to breathe. I lifted my hands in front of my face and looked at them shaking uncontrollably. And there, travelling down my arms, were the tentacles of crimson snakes slithering under my skin, reaching up through my pores like an overload of power was trying to escape me. Because what no one knew yet was this time, I had been granted a lot more than just a glimpse of the past or that of the future.

A lot more than Lucius' brother was expecting, that was for damn sure! Because this time I had been granted some of its power, like a lingering essence of a God. So much of it in fact, it was buzzing inside me and so desperate to get out that it felt as though it was clawing at my skin. It forced me to question whether this was what it felt like for those like my father or Lucius whose demons felt trapped inside their own vessel. This untapped power desperate to get out and believing that its vessel was the cage that prevented it.

It was of little wonder why then those like Lucius and my father spoke about their demon side like a different entity. As if they were carrying around with them some internal twin, one that was the darker side of their soul who was constantly trying to consume them. It meant that for once, I finally understood the true nature of Hell's beings and the daily battle they had to win, in order to suppress a terrifying side of themselves. But as for now, well...

I didn't have to suppress the thing.

"Now tell me, what did it show you? Where is the Tartarus gate?!" The one they called Master roared down at me. But I closed my eyes and at a mere thought, I could see it. I could see exactly what he wanted to know. Hell, but I could have fucking walked there! It was almost as if I had opened a door of secrets, having just instantaneously absorbed all the knowledge of Hell that I shouldn't have known. I knew it wouldn't last, fading the moment the power was spent but for now, I could see what he spoke of.

The gate led to a crumbling pyramid, a temple that had been destroyed in yet another battle against the Titans. In fact, it barely even existed anymore as all that could be seen amongst the rubble was a Keystone and an opening below it. There were details around the image that I just couldn't make out yet and right now I didn't have the time to try.

Because I was consumed.

I took in a deep breath and knew what I had to do, starting with a little acting. Because I still had one problem to take care of. So, I rose to my feet and continued to stumble backwards as though I could barely stand my ground. I managed to do this muttering in a fearful pathetic way,

"Please I…Gods, but it was so strong I can barely… even…breathe." Granted my acting wasn't going to win any awards, but it didn't have to. No, all it needed to do was fool them long enough to get me where I needed to be. Meaning that I only stopped walking backwards when I felt the well was behind me.

"Fae, are you okay, what happened?" Nero asked me clearly concerned but she didn't need to be. Not when I had everything in hand, one I felt turn into a fist by my side. This was because the anticipation of what was to be an eruption of power was nearly all too much to bear. It felt as if my blood was humming and my heart was beating far too quickly than what should have been physically possible.

"Tell me or your friend dies!" Lucius' brother threatened and my reply was not the one he was expecting,

"I will tell you…When Persians grow hair on the palms of their hands before battle!" I said what was my father's favourite response to those that believed his armies could be defeated.

"Then you watch as your friend drowns!" he said, before nodding to one of the Harpies to do his bidding.

This was when without looking I asked Nero,

"Do you trust me?"

"Erm, not when your eyes look all crazy and shit, not really, no," was her amusing answer, and that was when I first realised that my eyes must have changed with the power surging inside me. This was when I turned to wink at her and said,

"Then I suggest this is the part you...*hold the fuck on!*" I shouted this last part at the same time reaching for the release on the crank, letting Nero once more go plummeting down the well. Then I grabbed the Harpy that had been charged with doing the same thing and threw her into the mechanism, all to the sound of Nero screaming.

But it was a sound that only stopped when the Harpy's body got caught in the turning cog. Because this managed to stop Nero from falling any further and reaching the water, putting her at a safe distance away from what was about to happen. Now her echoing cry of my name was lost due to the furious bellows of rage coming from the Master as he ordered all the Harpies to attack me at once.

I looked up at him with a sinister grin and motioned with my hands for them all to come closer if they dared.

"Let's do this!" I roared back at him, letting them close in around me until I took a deep breath and called forth that surge of rage.

Finally, able to release…

A Crimson wave of Death.

CHAPTER SEVENTEEN

AFTER DEATH COMES TRUTH

The moment I started to hear a voice, one that sounded like my name was being echoed through a tunnel, I started to come around. It took my mind a few blurry seconds to start piecing together what had happened.

Or should I say…

What I had done.

I knew that if I focused hard enough it would all play back and come to me with perfect clarity, but for the moment it was Nero's voice that I focused on.

This forced me to open my eyes and staring back at me was a beach of golden sands. I strained my ears trying to listen out for the ocean lapping its gentle waves upon the shore close by, but there was nothing but the calling of my name. I heard myself groan as I started to move my body, feeling the ache when pushing myself from the ground, which was when I realised, I wasn't on a beach at all. I was simply surrounded by golden sands the Eye had given me.

My name was now becoming a desperate call as I could

hear the tremble in her voice. As it was obvious, she most likely thought I was dead. But then, one glance around me proved that it was everyone else who had been robbed of life and as for my role...

I had been the thief.

I closed my eyes at the sight of so much death at my hands and muttered an incredulous,

"Fuck."

This was because the entire space of the bailey had been turned into a mass grave site, where the bodies and remains of Harpies lay littered among the ground like a bomb had gone off in the centre. The different state of the bodies that I could now see would be a way of tapping into the memory of how they got to be that way. Memories, admittedly, I didn't yet have the bravery to access. However, a pile of bodies that formed a mound told me exactly what I would find inside...*the Harpy Queen*.

This was one particular memory I pushed for, seeing it play out with the start of her desperate cries calling for her minions to help her. It was a desperate plea that was answered when her offspring sacrificed themselves to save her as they had shielded her from the wave of my power. My Crimson painted soul that had sucked each one dry of their very essence and the pools of blood that I had extracted from them, now lay around them like an abandoned island in the middle of an ocean of their own blood. And what would I find at its core but none other than their mother, one who cared more about her life above all others.

"FAE!" Having Nero screaming my name paused my steps when going towards the hidden Queen, making me now run back to the well instead. I looked over the side to find her a small shadow swinging in the centre of the stone.

"Nero! Are you okay?" I asked, making her release a relieved breath before saying,

"Holy shit, am I okay...? No, no I'm not okay...nothing is okay! In fact, I'm not sure I will ever be okay again and that I'm not dead!" she exclaimed dramatically.

"It's okay, I can confirm you're not dead," I told her with a grin.

"Well, that's good then but next question...how are *you* not dead...actually scrap that, I'm swapping it for, why the Hell am I still down here and why are we having this conversation with you up there?"

"I promise I will get you out of there soon," I told her making her shout back,

"As in...as soon as the time it takes you to crank the wheel and pull me up?" she questioned, and I looked back at the mound of dead Harpies and told her,

"No, that is, as soon as the time it takes me to kill a Harpy Queen."

"Oh fuck...Okay, yeah you go and do that and I will just be here hanging...*Literally!*" she muttered this last part making me grin.

"Thanks," I said giving her a salute she could barely see from above her.

"Good luck and remember to break her legs!" This I heard echoing up after I had started to walk back towards the pile of corpses. A sight that looked more like skeletal remains that were hundreds of years old not minutes. It also looked as if most of them had even turned to stone, with only the skin between the long-boned fingers of their wings that remained. It looked like dried, withered skin or paper-thin leather that had been left to burn in the sun.

By the time I made my way over there I was forced to face what I had done. This was because everything that happened after the point of asking Nero to trust me, I had unconsciously allowed to come back to me. It started with raising my arms up and out to my sides as I unleashed the same wave of destruction I had the first time when back in the field.

I also remembered seeing Lucius' brother quickly creating a portal before stepping through it and slipping into another realm. This was naturally and unfortunately done before any of my power could touch him. The first stretch of my power had obliterated the Harpies closest to me, meaning little was left other than grey dust and particles still floating in the air.

The ones beyond this radius had managed to escape this instant death, but in the end, it was a mercy they had missed out on. This was because my power didn't stop at just the first wave, but instead it continued, and I found myself with the ability to control elements of it.

In one instance, I had lifted a hand and pointed to where I wanted it to travel and then watched as tentacles and curled streams of red essence shot from my fingertips. It then lassoed itself onto the Harpies like some beast from the sea. Once it had hold of them, I closed my fist and drew back my power, unsure of what had prompted me to do this. It was as if a natural instinct had taken over my entire vessel, and what my actions became were second nature. Because clawing back on that power had meant draining the Harpies of their blood, leaving nothing behind but fleshless crusts of dead husks.

I watched again as at the time I must have felt the presence of one sneaking up behind me. No doubt believing with my back turned I could be taken down. I suppose at the sight of her entire race dying all around her then what choice did she have but to try. After all, desperation can lead to desperate actions that more likely than not, got you killed.

Which was the case with this one, as at the time I had continued to test the limits of these new abilities using her as target practice. So, this time instead of extracting the blood from her, as I had done with the others, I turned it around and pushed the tentacles and streams of blood I had taken, now into her. And doing so with so much force, that this time it made her explode, unable to contain much more blood that her body was capable of. It literally ripped her skin apart like the seams of an overstuffed doll and in the depths of my fury, I didn't even flinch.

I watched as a few fortunate Harpies decided to save themselves and take flight, but it was the Queen I was most concerned about. For it was the Queen that I had sworn an oath to kill. That same need for revenge was what was still fuelling this untamed power inside of me.

I called to the Eye, lifting it with my mind and bringing it to me, and the second another Harpy got close and tried her chance of bringing me down, I forcefully thrust it into her chest so she would have no choice but to touch it. Taking unwanted hold of what wasn't rightfully hers to take. The same thing happened that Lucius' brother had demanded the Harpy Queen do to her offspring. It tested her worth and found it lacking.

The Harpy's face froze in horror, as would anyone's if seconds before their death, they were shown it. Needless to say, that when she burst into a cloud of black sand, the dangerous and cruel darkness inside of me grinned at the sight.

Once the power of the Eye was finished recapping back all that I had done and forcing me to see it, I found myself bent over gasping for breath. It was of little wonder once this power was spent that I had passed out. I was just thankful that I hadn't needed to sleep for as long as I did last time. But then again, at the moment I was not afflicted by the Hex on my back, which had most likely caused the damage.

I finally gained my breath and locked back on my target as I saw the Harpy Queen now trying to dig her way out of the corpses of her offspring that were mounded on top of her. The moment she was free, she saw me coming for her and it was the first time I saw real fear in her eyes. But then she now knew what I was capable of, although I had to admit, trying to call forth that same power was no longer happening.

I knew then what I must do, which was reach the Eye and try to reclaim the power it had given me. This, of course, was easier said than done, for the second I made a move towards it, I was suddenly plucked from the ground and in the grasp of one of the Harpies.

My leg swung uselessly as I was clasped in the tight hold of two bird's feet circled around the tops of my arms. I knew at any second all she had to do was drop me and I would be a goner, never surviving the fall. However, like every bad guy in a movie that wanted to talk before just killing the hero, she didn't do this. So, I quickly took advantage of her lack of brain power and her unwilling ability to use what little she had. Meaning I swung my legs, doing so until gaining enough momentum so I could pull myself up until they were partially vertical over my head and shoulders, like I was doing a lazy handstand. I then hooked my ankles at the back of her neck and tugged her head down, making her flight uneven. She then had no choice but to let go, however this was something I was ready for.

Now with my hold still on her neck, the moment my arms were free I grabbed onto her scrawny ankles. Then I let my legs fall, using them to swing again, only this time to the battlements the moment that we were close enough. The second I dropped everything in my body hurt as though my bones had been rattled and organs misplaced. But hey, at least I managed to roll into the fall, now ignoring the pain.

I sprang back into action and looked over the broken wall to see the Harpy Queen below ripping one of the wings off one of her dead offspring, making me question what she intended to do with it. I didn't have to question this for long as she started to make her way over to the Eye, telling me this was how she intended to pick it up. Then again, she had obviously been smart enough to do this the first time when kidnapping Nero and I, so it made sense.

This meant that that once she had it in her possession, she was going to make a run for it and take the Eye with her.

"Not on my watch, bitch," I said, watching as the Harpy was coming back round again and obviously intent on trying a second time to take me out. I took a few seconds to weigh up my options and came back with the craziest one yet. Then with a quick scan of the ground for a weapon it suddenly hit me that I still had one on me! A weapon I had made sure to keep hidden when being shoved in a cage...it was my trusty talon still in my waistband.

"Well, that's convenient," I muttered to myself getting ready to do the next crazy ass thing. I took a couple of steps back readying myself to make my move, hoping my timing was on mark or I was so screwed, cartoon pancake style! Then when the Harpy was just in the right position for me to do something potentially suicidal, I said

"Come on Fae, you jumped out of a damn helicopter before, this should be a piece of cake...NOT FUCKING LIKELYYYYY!" I shouted, letting the last word continue on as I took a running jump before landing on the back of the flying Harpy. Then with no time for a 'phew, good job you're not dead congratulatory, victory salute' at myself, I quickly grabbed her neck. Then she was forced to concentrate on levelling herself out, making her wings adjust for the added weight of having me clinging to her back. This was when I acted quickly before she could buck me off, I put the talon to her neck and told her,

"I will slit your throat unless you take me down to your Queen!"

The Harpy hissed at me before trying to throw me off, forcing me to take action by digging the tip of the talon into her skin. She howled in both rage and pain, but it was enough to get her to do as I ordered. However, when she started to take me down, the Queen noticed us and soon had other ideas.

I watched as she kicked up a spear that had been in the grasp of a dried-up severed arm. Then, after only taking a moment to take aim, she threw it through the air, only just giving me enough time to react. It flew straight at us making a humming sound as it cut across the space. Then I was jerked, as it hit its intended target, being the chest of her offspring. Thanks to my knowledge of these weapons I grabbed a handful of her hair and dropped my shoulder back out of the way so I too wouldn't be skewered by the same rusted tip. It just barely grazed my collar bone making me hiss in anger.

However, my next problem soon became an obvious one as I was now riding on the back of a dead Harpy and there was only one place we were headed…

We were going down.

"Fuck, but how I wish you were a plane right now!" I complained as the only thing I could think to do was reach out and grab the tops of her wings and whilst holding steady, I gained my feet on her back like she was a fucking surfboard!

"Oh shit, oh shit…fuck me, this is…fuck!" I yanked back

hard so at least the air was pushed up against her wings like sails on a boat!

"Oh shit, its fucking working!" I shouted amazed as it started to slow our fall enough that I ended up turning this corpse of a Harpy into a damn glider!

I quickly pulled back hard the moment we were a metre from the ground, braced for impact and made the body beneath my feet skip to a stop once it hit black sand. I most definitely had to class this among one of my successes and when telling this story back to Lucius I would have to remind him that this was one occasion where I hadn't shot the pilot!

Someone else had and speaking of the Queen, well that bitch was all mine. In fact, when seeing this epic landing (thank you very much) her mouth had literally fallen open in utter shock as she was struck dumb at the sight. Not that I blamed her for her reaction, I just blamed her for everything else.

I then used her astonished state to my advantage, yanking the now broken spear from my demonic glider after first kicking it over to do so. Then I threw what was left of it at the Queen, catching the tail of her skirt and pinning her to the ground. Doing this gave me just enough time to get to her and prevent her from getting to the Eye.

Which meant that by the time I got to her, she was trying to tug her way free tearing at her skirt and stumbling to stay on her birdlike feet. I quickly found my own weapon, which ended up being a spiked mace residing amongst a heap of ash and I couldn't help but mutter to myself,

"At least it's not bloody this time…nope, just fucking heavy." I was just taking my first swing at her when she ducked, tearing an even larger section of her skirt in the process.

"Quite honestly, I think it looks better as a mini skirt," I said with an evil grin down at her bird legs, adding,

"The scrawny chicken look is so in this season." At this she sneered back at me and soon found her own weapon, meaning that the fight had really begun.

"What's the matter, that power of yours all gone?" she taunted back, and I had to admit I wished in that moment I could have proved her wrong and shot her with blast from my palm. Instead I had to use what the Gods and my father had given me before coming to this place, which was proven when I said,

"I don't need anything extra to beat your chicken ass!" Then my fist connected with her jaw. Admittedly this wasn't as effective as the power the Eye had given me, but it was enough to have her stumbling to one side with a bleeding lip.

I used the opportunity to swing the heavy weapon down at her, a move she counteracted by rolling out of the way so my mace hit the ground. Her own weapon was a long sword that looked one hit away from cracking. It seemed that these Harpies had robbed the armoury of this Castle, for everything they used to fight with was old and rusted and barely worth the handle it was mounted in. Yet despite this, when she swung her sword, the tip of it still managed to catch me in the arm making me hiss with the bite of pain before snarling back at her with anger.

After she had caught me with her blade, she spun on a heel and started to run back towards the Eye, which was when I decided to throw my Mace, knowing it didn't have to travel far.

"RRRAHHH!" I screamed, aiding my throw and making it spin sideways before hitting its target square in the back and knocking her off her ugly birdy feet. I heard her whimpering in pain as she tried to get up, but it must have been too much for her as her hands and her knees gave out from under her.

It was only when I approached that I realised why this was, as the damage caused to her back was definitely not something she could sleep off and feel better in the morning. Not when I had cracked her spine.

She tried again to get up, only this time attempting to flap her wings, but they also were too damaged and wouldn't work properly. They only managed to lift her off the ground and gain her about four feet in height. Her body steered off to one side due to it becoming lopsided when one wing gave out completely. This made it easy for me to reach up and grab her foot before yanking her down hard back to the floor.

"No! You...you can't do this to me! I was promised my revenge!" she said, as she scrambled backwards like a wounded crab searching desperately for the protection of its shell. I picked up her fallen sword and stalked towards her, finding her broken and bleeding form close to one of the mounds of stone that was covered with soul weed. It was time to teach her a lesson in revenge.

I stalked over to my prey and in response, she started to drag herself back quicker, meaning that by the time I had reached her she was closer to the soul weed. Then when she started to try and get up, I made my final move and kicked her chest, making her fall backwards, pinning herself against the large thorns. She screamed as each one pierced through her body and wings. She reminded me of a butterfly pinned on the wall of some eccentric Entomologist's office.

"My Master, he will have your head for this!" she threatened, making me roll my wrist around, swinging the sword and telling her,

"I would like to see him try, for what I remember of him, he was the one running away like a coward and leaving you alone to endure my wrath." She snarled at this but I could see in her eyes she knew it was true.

"Your Master has forsaken you and all of your kind. You were nothing more than a puppet to him to use and now he has cut those strings leaving you for dead." She turned her head away as if she couldn't bear the truth coming from me any longer, but I wasn't done. I put a foot to one of the branches of soul weed and rested my bent forearm to it, to lean in closer, telling her,

"So, tell me, Bird Queen of a dead flock..." I ignored her snarl and snap of teeth, continuing,

"...You really think he cares for your life and all for a revenge you seek when it is sourly misplaced?"

"Your mother killed my sister!" she screamed back at me making me shake my head, now with a look of pity on my face. I straightened back up knowing what I had left to do.

"You're just a mortal, you couldn't understand my pain!" she said with tears of hatred in her eyes. She was a creature lost to her own self-absorbed bitterness and mortal loathing, and it was time to end both.

"No? Well, in the words of Buffy the Vampire slayer... then I will just have to settle with causing it!" I said as I raised my sword and sliced through her right wing. She screamed in such agony it must have travelled for miles, for it was an echoing sound that rang in my ears.

"I hope my Master kills everyone you hold dear to you, I hope he tears them limb from limb and you are forced to watch as everyone you love dies at his feet...Ahhhh!" This ended in another agonising scream as I severed her left wing from her body knowing that this was the ultimate price for a being such as her to pay.

Losing your wings was like mourning the death of your own life when you were forced to face an eternity of living without them. After she could no longer say anything more I got close and told her,

"My mother didn't kill your sister." Her lips curled up and when she opened them to speak, I told her the truth,

"The daughter of a Titan did...but just in case you don't believe me, I think it's time for you to see for yourself." I said before slamming my hand over her face and forcing that same memory from my mind into hers. And like most things that had to do with the power that came from the Eye, I had no idea how I was able to do these things...

I just knew that I could.

I only took my hand away when I knew it was done, forcing myself to ignore the tears that coated my hand as the Harpy Queen had wept for the death of her sister.

The roots of her rage that had consumed her, had been that of her undoing.

I turned my back on her, after watching her head slump forward in utter defeat. I expected nothing else from her, nor did I expect her to admit that she had been wrong. So, all that was left of her now was for her to wallow in the bitterness of her mistakes by herself, for there had been many. Starting with taking me from one pissed off King that would have seen them all burn for the crime.

As for me, well I had delivered my revenge despite not taking her head as I said I would.

No, instead, I thought it better to let her live with the knowledge that she had done all of this for nothing.

Now as for Lucius...

His Demon knew no such Mercy.

CHAPTER EIGHTEEN

THE LAST SOUND OF REVENGE

I left the Harpy Queen to her wingless, pity party and walked back over to the well. I looked over the side to see an exhausted looking Nero staring back up at me.

"You good? I asked, making her shrug her shoulders and wince after saying,

"Not gonna lie, I could be better." I smirked before telling her,

"I'm gonna get you out of there, just give me a minute."

"Why, you got any more bitter bitches you've got to kill?" I had to laugh at this before replying with,

"Oh honey, at this rate I will have enough enemies to send a bumper pack of Christmas cards to." She scoffed and made me chuckle when she commented drily,

"Now why does this not surprise me."

After this I turned the crank enough to free the dead Harpy that had been pinned to the well wall with a cog lodged in its broken back. I was then free to turn the crank, doing so until I could see Nero's dirty blue hair coming to view. Then, after raising her to the right height, I reached over to untie her hands and helped her step onto the well's wall before down onto the black sand.

She was in the middle of thanking me when her sentence trailed off because now she was taking in the carnage all around her.

"Seriously, like who the fuck are you?" Nero asked in astonishment, looking at me as though she was seeing me for the first time. So, I answered honestly,

"I'm a Draven." Of course, she already knew this after discovering who my Grandfather was, hence why she had been calling me Princess this entire time.

"Okay, yeah...so that makes sense," she admitted with a shrug of her shoulders and in reply I winked. She rolled her arms cracking her joints as she did this trying to alleviate what I knew would be the pain and ache in them.

"At this rate I'm going to need to come topside just to get myself a good chiropractor...you don't know anyone by any chance, do you?"

"Sorry, not my field." She then paused and looked around the space mumbling to herself,

"No, I don't suppose it is."

To be honest, she wasn't the only one surprised that I had been capable of doing such things. I mean sure, I had always been trained to fight but admittedly never doing much of it before I met Lucius. But this hadn't been just fighting. What had happened here, had been more like a bloody bomb going off!

Then again, I couldn't find myself being sorry, not seeing as I had done everything I had wanted to achieve. Nero was safe, I had made it impossible for the Harpies to follow us, and I'd also been able to retrieve the Eye of Crimson. Now all that was left was for us to walk out of here and try and find our way home.

ROOTS OF RAGE

Nero walked over to one dead Harpy and kicked out its remains making it sink in on itself as it was nothing but ash inside. She sucked a startled breath through her teeth before telling me,

"Gods, you're fucking brutal."

"You think it's too much?" I questioned with a wince,

"Oh, don't get me wrong, these bitches totally had it coming, and trust me, I bloody love you for it, but just remind me not to piss you off...yeah." After this I decided it was best to inform her,

"I am actually a very easy-going person...erm...*usually.*" Her look said it all, but what followed only added words to her scepticism,

"Um, sure, okay, whatever, Princess." I frowned and pointed out what she had said only a minute before,

"Hey, what about all that about not pissing me off." Her look said it all and I laughed, nudged her and said,

I will make you a deal, stop calling me Princess and call me Fae, and all is forgiven," I said reassuring her, making her joke after looking around all the destruction,

"Fuck honey, I will call you Julia Roberts, or the Queen of bloody England if you want me to." This time we both laughed.

After this we both looked round for any weapons that looked half decent and the least rusted. Then I walked over to the piece of spear that was still stuck in a large section of the Queen's dress before pulling it out of the ground and freeing the material.

"Not sure now is the time for a change in outfit," Nero commented, making me smirk before holding it up against myself and saying,

"Do you not think it suits me?"

"Oh sure, the blood stains go with the murderous glint in

your eyes." I laughed at her joke before telling her the real purpose for it,

"I think it's best we put this destructive baby to sleep." Then I used the material to gather up the Eye of Crimson, that started to glow brighter the moment I was near. It was like it was reacting to my presence and trying to pull me into touching it once more.

"Hey, I think it likes you," Nero said, and even though she joked I couldn't help noticing that Nero was staying well away from it. And well, after what we had seen when being in the cage together, then I couldn't say I was surprised or that I blamed her.

If I didn't already know that touching the Eye wouldn't kill me then I would have been wary also. But this did make me wonder why it called to me in the first place. What exactly was it about me that had made me worthy enough to survive its touch? Had I been chosen, or had it been drawn to the strange powers I seem to have? It was true that after touching the Eye my powers had increased, by not only lasting longer but also allowing me to be able to control elements of it, whereas I hadn't before.

I then thought back to the first time my powers had manifested. It had been back in my father's vault when I had been tricked by the witch into believing she had been Lucius. It was back when she had needed the box or more like the map inside it. It was strange to think that it all led back to that one day my father had brought me the box. All of it leading to the Tree of Souls, which in turn led me here…into Hell.

Every step of this journey was seemingly taking me closer to discovering the truth. The witch wasn't working alone as we once thought, that much was now clear and now I think it was also safe to assume that Lucius' brother was the one in charge of it all. And thanks to the Eye, the only reason I knew that he was Lucius' brother was because of a conversation the Eye had shown me. All in that one fleeting moment when Lucius had his demonic hand wrapped tightly around his throat. Back when his hood had fallen back and revealed who he was. Someone he knew well and had trusted with far more than he ever should have.

In my vision Lucius had gasped at the sight of him, knowing exactly what this meant. Another person Lucius had trusted only to be betrayed. I knew this because I too had felt how Lucius felt in that single moment of time. The deep level of betrayal had taken him straight back to that day of the crucifixion and back to the time of his rebirth.

In that one moment he had questioned everything.

Everything he had ever known about his brother.

In that split second I had been shown this, my heart had bled for him. I also wished that this had just been meant as another metaphor and not as a sign of things to come…

But I would have been lying to myself.

The one thing I was most certain of and that was I would take the image shown to me to my grave, without ever telling a soul. Even if it meant the rest of my life was to be a short one, I would live every second of it to its fullest. And to do that meant first getting the Hell out of here and getting back to Lucius!

"God, you're fucking brutal." I heard Nero say again, this time whilst pulling a curved blade from the chest cavity of one shrivelled up Harpy.

"You said that already," I reminded her, as I wrapped up the Eye without touching it. I didn't exactly feel up to getting zapped by its powers again or experiencing another trip down memory lane. Oh, and I most certainly didn't want to see the future again!

"I know but I feel like I have to say it again…Gods, I

can't believe I'm saying this but I'm actually happy you threw me down a well." I had to laugh at this, which was why I replied with a chuckle and a wink,

"Me too."

"Here, let me help you," Nero said, after wiping the ash from the blade by using her thigh and coming back towards me. She then helped me tie the material in such a way that it acted like a backpack so it would be easier to carry, along with my new weapon I let hang from it.

"Better you than me," she commented eyeing up my back in a wary way.

"Yeah, well let's just say the sooner we get this back to Lucius, the better we will both feel."

"Speaking about your boyfriend, he must be having demonic kittens right about now!" she said, making me wince at the thought.

"Well, he most certainly will when he finds out who their master was," I commented, prompting Nero to give me a questioning look.

"You know who it was?" she asked clearly shocked.

"Yeah, it was Lucius' brother." After this I told her snippets of what the Eye had shown me, surprising her with the knowledge that Lucius had a brother. She asked me the obvious question, which was…did he know? In all honesty it wasn't one I could answer with certainty. As it was one I had been asking myself since we had first been taken. Had Lucius known he had a brother and kept it from me and if so, why?

"Yikes, but I think I'm starting to feel sorry for this boyfriend of yours," she teased, but I tensed knowing that she was right, and I hated that. I hated knowing that Lucius was yet again forced to worry for my life. In all honesty, that seemed to be all he had ever done since being together. It had been one thing happening after another, leaving Lucius forced to deal with it. Lucius, who admittedly was a control freak, having no other choice but to endure my continual disappearances.

I think at this point I was ready for him to lock me in a bloody cage and throw away the key. For starters I felt like I could sleep for a month and as long as he was in there with me what else did I need...well, other than the obvious basics like food, drink, most definitely some alcohol, and yeah... Netflix wouldn't go amiss.

To say that I was ready to go home was an understatement.

I thought about my parents and how they must be going crazy with worry wondering where Lucius and me were. I thought about my friend Wendy, as the last time I spoke to her was when I had been in Jerusalem. It had also been done via email with technology to scramble my computers whereabouts so no one would know where it came from. I had told her I was okay that I was happy and that for the time being, I had just needed to walk away from life. I never read her reply, I had been almost too afraid to, knowing how much having me disappear and be so cagey about it all must have been hurting her.

I thought about everyone else that I cared about, including those in Lucius' council. People that I hadn't seen in a long time. Hell, but it felt like an age ago, and I knew that time was different down here, depending on which realm you were in. It was like travelling the world and not knowing what the time difference was. It felt longer and I was starting to miss everything.

"Hey, you okay?" Nero asked, placing her hand on my arm to get my attention. I thought for a moment knowing that having Nero with me in all this was a comfort I should have felt guilty for feeling. But a comfort it was all the same and one she would probably never realise. I didn't want to do this alone, Gods, but I wasn't even sure that I could have. This was why I answered her truthfully,

"I know this may seem like a really awful thing to say, but I'm really glad you're here, I don't think I could have done this without you." She looked thoughtful for a moment as if fully digesting my words and then with a slight smirk she said,

"You're right, that is a really shitty thing to say, but you know what, I'm glad you said it. Not that I think I've helped in any way shape or form, you know, since you have been doing all of the killing and all, but I am glad that you're not doing this alone...and of course you did save my life, so you're not that bad of a friend." She joked making me laugh and once again easing that tension that I needed to let go of.

"Let's try this again shall we...let's get out of here," I said, knowing I had repeated these same words the last time, just before we had been discovered.

"Yes please," she agreed, and just as we started walking off a sinister laughter coming from behind us made us both take pause. We both turned our heads at the same time to look to see what type of crazy the Harpy Queen had sunk to next, neither of us liking the sound.

"Hey, where do you suppose she's trying to get to?" Nero questioned the second she saw the Queen dragging her broken body closer to the tower. It was the same one I had emerged from when trying to save Nero.

Her back was covered in blood from the deep lacerations the soul weed had caused, along with me crushing her bones with my mace. The brutal end of the V shape of bone coming out of her spine was bloody and covered with matted feathers from where I had cut her wings off.

I started to narrow my eyes, questioning like Nero had, as

to where it was she thought she was going. Was she trying to get underground, potentially trying to find a place where she could heal? Personally, I thought the damage inflicted to her body looked too great and I didn't think it would be long before she ultimately bled to death. I believed her end was near and it was a mercy I could not grant for making that death a swift one. Not after knowing what she had been prepared to do to me. She would have seen me tortured over and over again along with Nero just to amuse herself. No, she didn't deserve a swift death, far from it.

I took a step closer and frowned having a bad feeling about the determination in the way she dragged herself across the floor. Doing so in what looked to be a painful endeavour and for what looked to be little gained. It didn't make sense, that was until I saw her reach for something.

"What is she doing?" Nero asked, watching her and obviously having the same concern as I, that the horror we had had endured was not yet over. That was when I remembered something from earlier. It had been before I'd walked out into the bailey to rescue Nero. A deadly sound I had heard coming from the depths below in the tower.

This was when dread filled my veins.

"Fuck!" I swore as I started running towards the Queen, hoping to prevent whatever it was she was trying to do. But then her evil cackle grew louder until it became like nails scratching the edges of my soul.

"You're too late! Nothing can save you now! Nothing!" The Harpy Queen started laughing hysterically as if the thought of our deaths was one that brought her great joy and even if she did die in the next few minutes, she would now do so happy in that knowledge.

"What the hell is she smoking now!" Nero shouted over to me, but the second I saw her grab the hidden lever, I knew

I was too late. I skidded to a halt and started running back to her and before Nero could question why, she said,

"What the...oh wait, never mind." This last part was in response to the thunderous demonic roar that ripped through the air as it echoed up the tower. The beastly snarling sound combined with that of the thundering footsteps of whatever it was she had released was now running up the staircase.

I turned to Nero with panic in my eyes and said the very last thing that I wanted to as the Hellhounds finally emerged ...

"RUN!"

CHAPTER NINETEEN

NICE DOGGY

After shouting this, neither of us needed to be told twice as we left these gruesome memories behind when running through what was left of the gatehouse. Of course, the speed we both ran at had everything to do with the beasts that were chasing after us, meaning that we didn't stop, not even when crossing the precarious looking drawbridge.

It was one that had a large section missing from its centre and was merely held together by the beams either side of the hole that stretched to the land on the other side. I told myself the whole way across not to look down, but then again, we had no choice because if we didn't, then one wrong move and we would find ourselves falling into an abyss. The drop below could have been anything from ten feet to a hundred, if not more. I also doubted that you would have landed in any water usually found in a moat but instead through a cloud of fog, and one that could have covered up an endless drop. Either way, neither of us wanted to find out any time soon, hence our caution.

I felt as though I could only breathe the second I made it across. I also noticed that Nero was a lot nimbler than I was, making it across first. But once both of us were on the other side, this was when we got our first break. Because in the end, that giant hole where the missing beams of wood were, was a means of slowing down the beasts. We knew this after they had finally burst through the castle gate and had been forced to a stop, by digging their razor claws in the wood and gouging deep grooves in the planks, pealing it away like skin.

"Holy shit, you've got to be kidding me...seriously, Hellhounds!" I shouted, slapping out a hand in their direction as the demonic dogs snapped and growled on the drawbridge, with its damage preventing them from going any further.

"Oh, they're not just any Hellhounds," Nero said giving me a bad feeling.

"But of course they're not, because some psycho Harpy Queen wouldn't keep normal pets in her basement, no, no, these ones have to be special Hellhounds," I muttered sarcastically throwing up my hands.

"Yep, pretty much," Nero agreed with my mocking reply.

I quickly thought back to that night in the silent garden on the roof of Lucius' German castle and the Hellhounds I had encountered there. But then looking at these now and I could definitely see the differences. Not only were they bigger but that cracked flesh seemed to glow with lava blood in between the broken skin. They reminded me of a cross between a panther and a Doberman, having pointed ears and long snouts. Their tongues whipped out like thin snakes and their glowing red eyes burned with hunger, burrowing into us. Spikes ran down the length of their arched spines, all the way to the tips of their tails that were complete with the largest and most deadly spike. Their hind legs were shorter than their front ones, lending all its menacing appearance to the front of their bodies. I just hoped that meant their bodies weren't particularly good when it came to jumping, or we were so unbelievably screwed.

"Just a quick and terrifying question I know I am going to regret asking but what's that under their skin?" I asked, referring to the glowing veins covering their bodies.

"Oh that, yeah, that's lava." I shot her an incredulous look before she said,

"I think we should still be running."

"Yeah, that sounds like a good plan right now." I agreed, as it looked like the three Hellhounds weren't giving up and kept trying to look for a way across. In reaction to this, we both turned around and started running down what looked like an overgrown road. We both continued to look behind us becoming more nervous by the second. Because even with the growing distance between us, we could still see the Hellhounds trying to make their way across.

So, we ran.

And we ran.

And then we ran some more until we could no longer see them.

"Where do you think we are?" I asked Nero after we both needed to stop to catch our breaths before passing out. Like me, Nero had her palms to the tops of her knees as she bent over taking deep breaths but at this question she straightened and looked around. To be honest I didn't think there was much of the landscape to be able to tell us wherever we were, but she still said,

"My guess, somewhere on the outskirts of Tartarus." At this I sucked in a startled breath, because this is what Lucius' brother had been wanting to find out. He had wanted to know where this gate was and the place I knew from my future. I also knew it was the only way to stop the plague that was killing Lucius' people and one that would eventually reach me and my mother at the top of the Tree of Souls.

"What...what is it?" Nero asked, no doubt after seeing my face drop. I shook my head a little and told her it was nothing, when in actual fact, *it was everything.*

I knew that being in Tartarus and potentially this close to finding the gate he was looking for could be my only shot at stopping this. But I was torn because I also knew that I couldn't do this alone. However, this in itself presented a problem, as the person I needed was also the last person that would ever help me. This was because as soon as I made it back to Lucius, then it was doubtful I would be allowed to go even a few feet away from him. And let's just say that I didn't think my powers of persuasion were good enough to get Lucius to believe that Tartarus would make for a nice romantic weekend away.

Nero and I continued to run, stopping for only a few minutes to catch our breaths before we were off again. From the looks of things, then neither of us was in the best of shapes and at our fittest. But then having Hellhounds chasing after you was a heck of an incentive to get your ass moving. The only time we started to slow down was when the vast open space was no more and instead the view in front of us now, was that of a looming, dark forest. A forest, I should mention, that held nothing growing but giant soul weed.

The seemingly never-ending bush, if that was what it could be called, rose higher than trees in the forests back home. Their roots were pushed up from the ground as thick as tree trunks, and the way they arched made them look like giant grey snakes trying to hide in the dirt. It also reminded me of the scene from Sleeping Beauty where Maleficent surrounded the castle with thorns. Only in this forest the thorns were the length of VW Beetles and looked big enough to spear elephants!

"Well, this looks like a happy place," I commented, making Nero reply,

"You're in Hell, sweetheart, what did you expect, A fairy tale forest with talking rodents?" Nero asked dryly whilst looking uneasy.

"Hey at this rate I'll take the Bates Motel even if it was situated on Elm Street!" I replied making her frown.

"Yeah, I don't know what any of that means," Nero confessed.

"Tell me you've seen a horror movie before?" I asked, clearly shocked, well that was until she pointed out the obvious.

"What do I need to see horror movies for, I live in Hell, all I gotta do is step outside and I'm in a damn horror movie!" Okay, so granted she had a good point with that one, although I also thought it fair to make my own in return,

"And in what part of the movie do you come across three hot Scottish shifters huh?" She smirked, wagged her eyebrows and said,

"The part where the female lead gets laid."

"Yeah, I think you will find that's just called porn," I told her.

"Ah potato, patato." I laughed and to be honest this weird conversation we were having was currently the only thing keeping me sane as we walked down the centre of these creepy woods. It was formed in such a way that it looked as if the centre had been tunnelled out giving us at the very least a place to walk through it. Of course, we still didn't have a single clue where we were going.

"I wonder what's at the end," I said referring to the end of the tunnel of twisted soul weed.

"More creepy shit probably," Nero said dryly making us both laugh, a sound that ended abruptly the second the demonic growls could be heard from behind us not too far away in the distance.

"Well, whatever it is, it's not gonna be as bad as what's coming for us...run!" I shouted, and once again we found ourselves running for our lives. Looking behind us now and we could see the Hellhounds emerge, looking vicious with red drool falling from their open mouths, pooling in their jaws and overflowing their teeth. I don't think I had ever seen a creature looking so hungry before. I knew we had to do something because there was no way we could outrun such beasts.

I suddenly stopped in the centre, turned to face them and pulled at the material over my shoulder.

"What are you doing?! Come on!" Nero shouted in an understandably panicked tone.

"I am going to use the Eye," I told her fishing around and trying to touch it.

"Erm, is that wise?"

"Probably not, but here goes!" I shouted, before bracing myself and slapping a palm to the cold sphere. But then... nothing happened.

"What the...?" My question trailed off as I smacked it this time, trying to make the connection. But once again, nothing happened and now, here I was, in the middle of this new Hell, having a stand-off with three of its Hellhounds.

This was when I could think of only one thing to say...

"There, there...nice Doggy."

CHAPTER TWENTY

TEMPLES LOST IN TIME

"What's wrong?!" Nero shouted, ignoring my comment about nice doggies.

"I don't know, it seems to be out of juice or something!" I told her and her navy eyes nearly popped out of her head.

"Out of fucking juice, it's not a fucking car!" Nero said, hysterically this time. And it was justifiable panic considering the Hellhounds were getting closer by the second! I looked around frantically trying to think of what to do and really there was only one other option left.

"Come on! We're going to have to go into the soul weed!" I told her, grabbing her by the arm and dragging her with me.

"Are you crazy, how would we make our way through something like that?!"

"I don't know, but if we struggle then they most definitely will and right now, it's the only way, because let's face it we're not going to outrun them!" I told her making her see my point.

"Come on, I think I see a break." I pointed to what

seemed like a small tear in the thicket of the soul weed branches and we ran for it. But then just as Nero was pulling her foot through the gap, she got herself caught. Thinking fast, I grabbed her blade hooked inside her belt, and started chopping at the part that had her caught. It was tough stuff, but I managed to break it enough for her to wiggle her foot free. This was just in time too, as we both screamed falling backwards against the branches, as the face of the Hellhound snapped its jaws through the gap. We both scrambled back over each other, trying to free ourselves from the tangle of our bodies before breaking free enough to start climbing through it.

It was tough going but we made our way through far enough away that we no longer felt the threat of the Hellhounds making it through. Unfortunately, we also had no other choice but to continue on as we climbed and crawled and squeezed our bodies through the tightly entwined roots. Scraping our skin on the rough texture covering the branches and the smaller thorns snagged our clothes. Although with most thorns at this level being the length of my shoe they were easy to avoid. But on looking up these thorns also ranged from a foot long, all the way up to the length of school buses.

I couldn't help being thankful for this as I knew if they'd have been smaller then we would have been cut to pieces. Thankfully, having bigger thorns meant they were easier to navigate around. The downside to this of course was that one wrong move and we could easily find ourselves impaled.

However, it was a risk we were willing to take considering the alternative was being ripped apart by Hellhounds. And I wasn't surprised when they stopped following us as the large beasts were five times that of a Great Dane and would find it difficult getting through such tight spaces. For a large part of the journey through, Nero and I had no other option but to crawl down on our bellies and drag ourselves over the smoother roots that covered the forest floor.

But it was worth it when, not long after starting, we could hear their whining and the growls of frustration, sounds that only died down the further we went. All we had to hope for was that there wasn't another way through for them to find.

"Okay, I'm getting real sick of commando training," Nero complained, and I couldn't say that I blamed her. I opened my mouth just about to add to her complaints with those of my own, when I saw in front of us an opening. I could not explain the utter relief I felt when seeing this, making me grab out to shake her arm,

"What?" she said, looking down at my grip on her instead of looking in front.

"Look...LOOK! We made it through, we made it!" I shouted after what it seemed like crawling for days. Of course, in reality it could only have been an hour or two but that was definitely enough, as I didn't think I had ever felt so tired in all my life!

"Thank the Gods!" Nero let this out in a whisper as if her prayers had been answered. This also managed to entice us to use that last shred of energy we had left for there was finally light at the end of the brutal tunnel. Or should I say, a wide-open space, one void of any brutal forest.

Once through to the other side, the bare landscape showcased a broken temple. It looked as if it had fallen from the Heavens and landed here, right back before mankind even truly existed. Back to a time where the only wars fought were those between the Gods. It was incredible but there was still something so haunting about it. Taking in all the details, all that was left to do then was close your eyes and think for a moment before suddenly you could see it as it once was.

The temple looked very similar to how I imagined the Temple of Olympian Zeus before it had fallen into ruin. However, this particular temple was one of Earth's creations and it was situated in the centre of the Greek capital, Athens. Its construction began in the 6th century BC during the rule of the Athenian tyrants.

They were certainly ambitious and envisioned building the greatest temple in the ancient world. However, it was not completed until a different reign of Roman Emperor, one whose name was Hadrian being now in the 2nd century AD, which was an astounding six hundred and thirty-eight years after the project had begun.

Once finally finished it was known to be the largest temple in Greece, being made with an impressive one hundred and four colossal columns. But the temple's life was short-lived, as after being pillaged during a barbarian invasion in 267 AD it fell into disuse, only a century after its completion. It was never repaired and was reduced to ruins after this point.

Centuries after it merely became a useful place to be quarried for building materials after the fall of the Roman Empire. For a historian like myself I found this soul destroying, that such a marvel of history and a triumph of man was picked at like vultures tearing whatever flesh was left from a dead carcass. However, despite this disappointing end, a substantial part of the temple still remained today, although only sixteen of the original columns survived. Naturally, this is still classed as a very important archaeological site of Greece.

Now as for this temple, its large columns looked in better shape, even if only half were still standing. The pristine white marble looked incredibly maintained although this couldn't possibly be the case. Not when some lay vertical on the floor, broken and with large slices rolled away, like giant wheels on a cart. These missing links split the columns in two or three pieces and now flat they looked as if they could become foundations for a house, they were that wide. Surprisingly, most of the inner columns seemed to remain, which was why parts of the domed roof were still in place. You could tell that the pure white unmarred marble at one time would have been pristine and gleaming like a white jewel, as most of it still shone now.

"Gods almighty, it's the Lost Temple of Olympia," Nero said in utter awe and astonishment. We both were, as it was said the Lost Temple of Olympia started life on Mount Olympus, being known as a temple of worship in Zeus' realm of Heaven. However, Zeus had no other choice but to sacrifice this temple, creating a lightning bolt so strong that it split the mountain once the Titans were asleep inside. This was the only way he defeated them, as it was said that with Hades' help, the temple fell to the deepest levels of Hell.

I had grown up hearing these stories and being fascinated as a child, which no doubt paved the way to my career choice. Which meant that I knew what I would find inside. My father told me of the time that he'd spent there, not revealing why or the circumstances surrounding it. According to my father, inside would have been a treasure trove of statue remains, anything from giant arms to broken feet the size of a transit van. There were also statues over a hundred-feet tall and from the looks of how large the temple was, even in its ruined state, I could very well believe it.

I once asked my father when I was younger why he didn't have any statues of himself and he told me, 'if I was ever in need of a statue to gaze upon, it would not be of the sight of myself but would be that of your mother'. At the time my mother had heard the tail end of this and snuck up to my father from behind, wrapped her arms around his neck and told him,

"That's it, I now know what I want for my birthday..." and then with a wink directed to me she finished by saying,

"I hope you don't mind staying still for a long time, because I'm looking forward to that gold statue I can hang my coat on." After this I remembered giggling and now being an adult, I no longer wondered what she whispered in his ear after it.

I did, however, always wonder if my mother ever got that statue and if she did where she kept it. Although, knowing my mother's humour I could very well imagine it in some walk-in closet, one where she probably had it decorated with a scarf around his neck, complete with big hat, sunglasses, and wearing a dress.

After all, one of my mother's favourite pastimes was reminding my father of his mortality and that included not taking himself too seriously. Just as my father's favourite pastime was teasing my mother of that mortality that he fell in love with.

This was why, when gazing upon this place, knowing that my father's footsteps had once walked its broken halls, I couldn't help but grin.

Of course, it was also said the only statue with little damage that remained inside was that of Zeus sat on a golden throne. This was said to be an exact replica of the one that once sat in Earth's realm for more fools to worship. At the time it was also known as one of the seven wonders of the ancient world, that was until its eventual loss and destruction during 5th century AD.

I remember at the time asking my father how it had been

destroyed but his reaction was strange as, instead of marvelling at his daughter's inquisitive nature, one for the history of the world he lived in, he had steered the conversation away with the promise of cookies and milk. I later discovered that it was believed to have been the work of Cronus.

Cronus had tried to murder his son Zeus as a child, but such a thing would come back to haunt him. This was because when Zeus was of age and of considerable strength, he came back and defeated his father who had once ruled over the Titans.

Cronus had also been the one who had started the Blood Wars and was a great enemy to my family and all the Kings who aided in the prophecy to win the war and overcome him.

"In all my years I never thought that I would ever see such a sight," Nero confessed, and I had to agree with her, because despite the horrors that had brought us here, I couldn't help but see this as a small shred of a silver lining.

"You know I hear there is a portal inside," Nero said nudging my arm, but I moved away turning my gaze from the impressive heavenly sight of a broken temple. I knew without looking back at her that she was frowning at me in question, so I turned to her and gave her an explanation why I wasn't running towards the temple entrance.

"That portal only leads to one place."

"Yeah, back to Earth's realm, back to the Temple of Janus....So, what are you waiting for, this is your chance to get back and away from this hellish place?" Nero said. But she didn't understand the importance of why I was needed here. Don't get me wrong, her words had strength, but the strength needed to stay was far greater.

"I can't leave."

"Why not, what is keeping you to this place...actually,

better yet, what made you come here?" I frowned at this, now wondering what had been said. I didn't have long to wait,

"The King…he said something about you being impulsive and putting yourself in harm's way for what you believe in…Personally, I was shocked and didn't believe it for a second," she added making a light-hearted joke out of it.

"I bet you could have added a few choice words to that also, knowing how he would have said it," I told her, making her grin sheepishly.

"Yeah, I didn't get the impression that this was one of those added to the 'pro column' type of things." I laughed without humour because I could just picture it for myself.

"Come on, let's keep going, I may not be going to the Earth's realm, but we've still got to find a way out of this level of Hell." I said moving quickly on and away from the reasons I was here or what my future held.

"Now, that I'm totally on board with!" Nero said, giving me a salute and following me closer to the temple. I wanted to go inside, just as I could feel that Nero did, but I also knew to do so would be too much temptation. So, we stayed clear of the entrance and walked around the side, coming across a courtyard of sorts. It was this side that had most of the temple sunken into the ground. Because of it, it looked as though when it had landed into the dirt, it caused an explosion of black quartz to erupt from the ground. The space in between had been cleared so that the wall which surrounded this courtyard was jagged with razor-edged crystal formations. It was only now at this angle I could see that only half of the temple actually remained, for it looked like the other half had continued to fall into a cavernous abyss of darkness below.

"That's when the Titans fell," Nero whispered as she too took in the haunting sight.

"What do you mean?" I asked, curious to hear the rest of

the story and not from books but from someone who lived in Hell.

"The story goes that when the Titans were defeated, they were imprisoned in the temple of worship on the top of Mount Olympus. Then good ole Zeusy boy, split the mountain and the temple fell into Hell, half of which you see now, the other half..." She then made a comical sound like a bomb had been dropped before exploding. She reminded me of my Aunty Pip in that way as she often included sound effects in her stories.

"Let me guess, the other part was where the Titans were imprisoned?"

"It is said that the powers of sleep were needed just long enough to keep the Titans from breaking free. However, once they awakened, they found themselves with the core of Hell shaking around them and it was enough that the impact rocked the core and lava encased their awakened forms. Once cooled it became an unbreakable force imprisoning them until their father Cronus could break them free...well, that had been the prophecy anyway."

"You're talking about the Blood Wars," I said making Nero nod, looking grave.

"Mount Tartarus, where the Titans were imprisoned is no more." After this Nero continue to walk, obviously not wanting to speak of it anymore and I knew when to push and when not to. We crossed over the courtyard and I shuddered as a weird feeling crept over me. It was as if some part of me had already been here once before. I shrugged it off and followed Nero, wondering how far it would be until we eventually came across something useful, like a portal back to where we belonged. Back to the realm of blood and death.

"You know when we get back, I'm really gonna speak to Lucius about changing the name of his realm, it doesn't exactly sound welcoming," I joked cutting the tension between the conversation we'd just had, and it worked as it made Nero start laughing. However, once again that laughter was interrupted by a sound we had both come to dread.

"Oh, you've got to be kidding me!" Nero shouted, throwing her arms up in the air and no doubt wondering, as I was, if we would ever catch a break. The growling and snarling behind us told us that this wasn't likely, and once again we found ourselves running for our lives.

Running once again, from…

"Fucking Hellhounds!"

CHAPTER TWENTY-ONE

DEJA VU DAUGHTER

We continued running until we came to what looked like a vertical tunnel that had been drilled even deeper underground. It was a huge spiral staircase that looked overgrown by the soul weed that was overflowing the edge. This created a grey curtain of twisted roots and deadly thorns. It covered the first few turns of the spiral of steps making it almost impossible to get down from the top, making the first lot of steps unusable but even if they hadn't been, then trying to navigate down quickly enough to outrun the Hellhounds was even more impossible.

I suggested that we could take the steps and possibly hide there, hoping they wouldn't see us. But then, it was like Nero had said, if they'd not given up by now, she didn't see them giving up at all. I had to agree as after all, Hellhounds were just as stubborn and tenacious as their masters, the Hellbeasts.

The centre of the spiralling staircase was so wide you could have dropped a four-bedroomed house down there and still have space either side. The drop was so vast that the bottom seemed no bigger than my thumb.

"Then what are we gonna do?" I questioned nervously looking behind me, knowing that they were going to be here any second, as the growls were travelling across the distance and getting louder the longer we stood here.

"I have an idea, but it might be a bit risky," Nero said making me nod behind us, and point out the obvious,

"Riskier than being eaten alive?" I asked, making her grimace before replying,

"Good point." After she agreed with me, I went on to ask her what she intended to do, wishing one of us had wings and the other the muscle strength to hold the fuck on.

"What's your plan?" I asked, knowing at this point we needed to try anything.

"When you touch the Eye you absorb its power, yes?" I frowned wondering where she could be going with this and said,

"Yes, I think so, but we already know that you can't touch it it's too dangerous." Nero looked down the drop as if trying to weigh up something and I grabbed her arm to get her back to the conversation.

"Yes, but you can touch it," she pointed out, making me question,

"You think I should try and face the Hellhounds again, because the last time…?" She quickly cut me off,

"Gods no! What are you, suicidal!"

"Okay, then I'm confused," I admitted.

"If you touch the Eye and I touch you then I can draw its power through you, like a conduit." I frowned and shook my head a little as if testing if I was hearing her right.

"Oh no, no, no, that's a bad idea…besides, we don't even know if it will work again and the last time…" She cut me off once more.

"Look, I have depleted my power, meaning I have

nothing left in me after using it all to save my own life and stitch my head back together so I wouldn't bleed to death. But with this, well, if I had the barest amount that the Eye could offer, I could get us down there and away from the Hellhounds." I had to admit the louder the growls behind us were getting, then the more I thought this plan had merit. However, I felt I had to say once more,

"I don't know, Nero, this sounds dangerous," I said, clearly uneasy about this whole thing, but then as I had only moments ago she made the point of saying,

"What's more dangerous than being ripped apart? Come on, Fae, I don't like this anymore than you do but what other choice do we have?" Her panicked voice rose to the point of being almost high-pitched telling me that fear was making her desperate. She didn't want to do this anymore than I wanted her to, but what choice did we have?

None.

"Alright, let's do this," I agreed pulling the material from my shoulders ready to use the Eye of Crimson once more and this time, all I could hope for was that instead of showing me my death it would aid us…in preventing it.

"Are you sure you're ready for this?" I asked with the material open at the ready to touch the Eye. Nero rolled her shoulders and answered me truthfully,

"No, not really, but let's do it anyway." After this we both nodded at each other at the same time and just as I touched the Eye, Nero clasped my shoulder. Thankfully, this time something happened, as the reaction was instantaneous. I closed my eyes and sucked in a breath as I drew up the power it offered. It was as if the Eye already knew what we faced and this time gave me what I wanted, without visions of the past or future.

I heard Nero suck in a startled breath before she

whimpered as if the power she was gaining from me was too much. It was a strange feeling as the energy from the Eye went straight into me and then out again, and for once, it didn't stay in me. It was almost as if it was being stolen, even though I, myself was letting it go. Truth be told, it was a conflicting feeling that had me fighting my emotions, as on one side, I was growing angry that it was being taken from me and on the other, I was thankful that it was.

So, I tried to focus more on the feeling of calm and serenity. As if I knew that I was letting it go for a good reason, one other than death and destruction. Either way, I knew when it became too much for Nero and this was what made me sever the connexion. I quickly sucked in more air and the second I could breathe easier again, I turned to check that she was okay.

Her eyes were completely white, making me realise now that when I had seen her on the ground and bleeding in the temple, it hadn't been the face of death as I first thought. Her eyes changed because she was channelling the last of her power into healing herself. Although now there was a slight difference, being that the extra power had manifested itself in her eyes as a crimson ring that circled the white.

I shrugged her off my shoulder breaking yet another part of the connection, then I grabbed her face and shook it a little, dispelling whatever had gripped her. Then I told her,

"Now is not the time to freak out, Nero, now is the time to get your head in the game and do the shit you promised." She shook her head a little when I dropped my hold on her cheeks and seemed to have snapped out of whatever it was that had gripped her.

"You good?" I checked making her nod once before she shook her slight frame and then cracked her knuckles. I looked behind us to see that the Hellhounds would be at us in less than a minute for they were getting bigger by the second.

"Okay then, magic time eh?" I said in a rush of words that were masking ones that should have been…'I think it's time to hurry the fuck up.'

Nero smirked and said nothing more before she cupped her hands together and started to pull them apart showing the tendrils of power between them. It was as if she had a sticky rubber ball that was being stretched and manipulated before it became too big to hold. The glowing blue essence stretched out so far, it became a flat disc in front of her as it grew and grew until it was the circumference of the spiral staircase. I took a premature step forward thinking that this was some sort of platform we were supposed to stand on to lower us to the bottom. Thankfully, one of her hands slapped to my chest preventing me from going any further, then with white and red demonic eyes finding my own she told me in an ethereal voice,

"That's not what this is for." Then before I could ask, the flat glowing blue disc started to spin. my eyes widened at the sight as I no longer had the capability to follow its movements. Seconds later I heard the grinding of stone against stone, a sound so loud it made me believe there was an earthquake beneath us, for the land shook. I looked back over my shoulder to see that we weren't the only ones affected as the hounds of Hell had to contend with some ground they walked on as it split and ruptured.

However, this didn't stop them, it was only a means of slowing them down as they now had to jump over large cracks. I looked back to Nero to find her stood steady whereas I had to have my hands out and my knees slightly bent trying to stay on my feet and gain back my balance. I watched as the bottom of the staircase started getting closer and closer like the whole spiral of stairs now acted like a giant corkscrew. She was unwinding the staircase until eventually the blue spinning disk stopped and the bottom became level with the rest of the land and was one we could now step onto.

But first she raised the large flat disc of glowing blue light enough for us to walk under it. I followed her as she stepped into the centre before making the glowing disc start to spin again only this time in the other direction. This was when the staircase started to go back down, unscrewing itself from where it had been raised up.

I had to admit the motion of this made me feel slightly sick and I found myself having to close my eyes against the dizziness it caused me. As for Nero, she seemed unaffected and completely unfazed by the motion, concentrating instead on the spinning flat surface above us that she continued to keep in motion until we reached the ground.

Once we did she sucked back the power making it form back into how it was first made. First it started to shrink back into a smaller disk until forming that of the ball that she had started off with. One that she eventually could cup between her hands before absorbing it back into her skin. Her eyes slowly morphed back to normal and she took a deep staggering breath making me catch her as she started to fall. I caught her under the armpits, and said,

"Whoa, easy there." This made her giggle as if she was slightly drunk.

"Are you okay?" I asked helping her back to her feet.

"Oh, hell yeah, I feel great," She said with a ridiculously big grin.

"Well, I don't know what that was, but it was bloody brilliant!" I shouted, looking back up making her smirk and she granted me a wink telling me,

"That was my game face for magic time." I had to laugh at the words used, but then looking around the large space I found myself questioning what we were seeing. I bent down to pick up a little gold shell I recognised as a bullet casing.

"Now what could this do be doing down in Hell?" I questioned before scanning the area and seeing that the floor was littered with them. But that was not all to be found scattered around the large circular space.

"Wow, it looks like a lot of things died here," Nero commented, kicking over one of the bones that looked decades old. I held up the bullet casing and told her,

"Yeah, and I think I know how. Look, you can see all the bullet holes in the walls too." Nero glanced at what I was looking at and then back down at the bodies before picking up one of the long thin bones that looked more like grey sticks with a sharp end.

"I think these are Harpy bones," she told me, making me look at the bone again in a different light and seeing that yes, its light curve would lend itself to being that of a wing.

"Hey, you don't think this is where your mum could have…?" That sentence died in her throat the second we heard the demonic roar above us. we both looked up in time to see one of the Hellhounds hadn't stopped in time and had literally run and leapt off the edge of the staircase. We then watched as it fell down the centre, scrambling with its legs trying to reach the sides so it could stop itself. This was to no avail as it landed with an echoing thud that kicked up dust and broke the bones of the dead Harpies it had landed it on.

The Hellhound whimpered as it wasn't yet dead, but it was wounded enough that it still moved but couldn't get up. The glowing lava in between its cracked skin was also starting to extinguish, telling me it didn't have long. A howling haunting sound from above made us both look up to see the other two hadn't made the same mistake and were now circling the edge while snapping down at us.

"It won't take them long before they discover a way to get down here," Nero said, and I knew this was true as I could see them testing ways through the drapery of the soul weed trying to get through. then suddenly one of them took a brave leap and landed on the lower levels of the staircase having only one hind leg get tangled in the thickest of the thorns.

It snarled angrily back at its leg, chomping at the soul weed trying to free itself whereas its brother had decided to make the same jump also. Only this time it managed to go that little bit further, so it missed not only the soul weed but also his trapped brother. After this he pounded down the staircase, telling Nero and I it was time again to be on the run.

"We haven't got long before they'll be down here, and it seems to me like there's only one way out," Nero said nodding to the broken door that looked as if it had been opened with a battering ram. I felt Nero taking the last of our weapons from behind my back and before I could ask what she intended to do with it, she gave me her obvious answer by thrusting the sword down into the Hellhound's head.

I raised a brow in question, making her hand the sword back to me as she walked past telling me,

"Just in case." I had to agree because in this place you couldn't be sure if anything was really dead. We both ran through the doorway and along the corridor, making me wonder what would face us on the other side this time. Of course, when we finally made it through, I could barely believe my eyes.

What faced us the moment we were through was literally a river of fire, cutting off all means of escape. We also looked to be in the belly of some mountain that's only purpose seemed to be where this raging river of blue fire cut through the tunnel. It started at one end and disappeared through the other as it crossed the space like a flaming blue snake.

"At least it's not lava," Nero commented and she was right, it was black water with a blueish flame flickering on the surface, as if there had been an oil spill and this had been set alight, creating the unusual colour of flame due to some chemical giving it that blueish green tinge. This in turn reflected off the cave walls giving the appearance of being under a blue moon. There were also holes in the rock that created flaming waterfalls as this strange liquid was gushing from the top and feeding this river to Gods only knew where.

Basically, this also meant we were screwed because there was nowhere to go, and stranger yet was the weirdest feeling of déjà vu. It was the same feeling I had felt when seeing the Lost Temple of Olympus. Was it because Nero had been right…had my mother been here before? Was I now walking in the footsteps my parents had?

It almost seemed too unreal to actually believe, but then what else could have caused such a deep sense of feeling?

"Oh, come on, where is it?" Nero said, looking left and right before suddenly she found something attached to the side of the rock. It was a large black, shining round disc that hung from chains held by a wrought iron demonic hand.

"Hey, help me swing this," she said, motioning me over and as she took one side, I mirrored her action by taking the other. This meant the large round disc, that on closer inspection was deeply pitted and was the size of a bed, was in between us,

"Ready?"

"Yeah, but for what I don't know," I admitted, before doing as she did when lifting the Gong up and letting it crash down so it swung back into the rock. It hit against what I could now see was a jagged piece of rock big enough to hit its centre. When this happened, the sound it created was almost like a haunting roar, that gained in strength the further it travelled. The cave also acted like an amplifier, and became so loud that both Nero and I had to cover our ears as it sounded like the souls of the dead were screaming.

After this I heard the cranking of a gate I couldn't see, and seconds later the tip of a strange black boat could be seen emerging. It barely looked like one that was able to float let alone exist at all, because the closer it got the more horrifying it became.

"Oh, thank the Gods."

"Seriously, you're thanking the Gods for this?" She ignored my comment and instead walked over to the point which was made obvious as to what its purpose was, especially when the boat stopped next to a protruding ledge over the flames…a dock. As for the boat, it looked as if it was made from iron held together with crude strips of twisted metal with charred wood on the inside. The shape was a long wide rowing boat that was being powered by six bodies, all mutilated for the sole purpose of rowing. Where they'd once had limbs, these had been replaced by oars in the water for propelling the boat forward. Not that any of them could complain or even look to see what level of Hell they had been doomed to, not considering their eyes and mouths had been sewn shut. I wasn't ashamed to say that I felt like gagging and this was only made more so when I looked at who was charged with controlling the boat.

The female demon at the stern of the boat was also missing her limbs and had a large portion of her body mounted in an iron contraption. Her arms had been replaced with long whips meant for lashing out at the tortured creatures that rowed the boat. Her large breasts were encased in crude metal cups that looked to be connected to the hooks in the bottom of her chin.

She was terrifying, with missing lips permanently forced into a grimace of teeth but when turned your way, she looked as if she was smiling at you. She, too, had had her eyes removed and thin hair displayed large patches of her scalp and floated around her as if she were underwater. She was utterly horrifying.

"Well, it ain't no Mississippi river boat," I muttered, wondering where the thought had come from as if I had heard it being spoken before. Or was this place merely echoing the past, making me pick up on parts of it.

"No, it isn't, but it is our ticket out of here, so get your ass on the boat, Chickadee!" Nero said making me go first. I did as she asked, stepping off the ledge and down onto the deck that was only a step below. There was a strange worn Chesterfield couch that looked oversized, with a high back that curled around the top like a scroll of paper. The old leather looked cracked and well used over Gods only knew how many years this ferry of the flames had been travelling for.

I stumbled forward the moment the roaring of the Hellhounds could be heard echoing through the tunnel we had travelled through, and it brought me face to face with one of the mutilated souls chained to the boat. It turned its head in my direction slowly, before it sniffed for this was the only sense it had left. Its skin looked burnt and puckered, and it was also stitched in ways that didn't make sense, especially when parts of its cheek had caught up in the stitching, forcing it to lift closer to the eyes. It moved its head around in quick little movements reminding me of old black and white movies where actors flickered across the screen. I quickly scrambled back to the centre, making sure I was well away from either side. Then I looked to see Nero who hadn't yet got on the boat but instead was staring at the opening as if waiting to take on the Hellhounds by herself.

"What are you doing, come on!?" This seemed to draw her into action as she followed me onto the boat. Then she blew on the palm of her hand and a coin suddenly appeared, after which she threw it towards the ferry keeper who caught it in her mouth and swallowed it whole. It was only then that the boat moved away from the stone dock to start its journey.

We both started to breathe a sigh of relief, that was until the first of the Hellhounds broke through the entrance with a leap. One snarl our way and it didn't take long for it to realise its prey was floating away. I thought that this would have been the end of it, that it would have had to have given up the kill and go back to the dying Harpy Queen without its prize. But then something unexpected happened as it leapt into the water and instead of going under, each step it made formed a black crust like cooling molten lava after it had started to roll down the mountain side. It began to stalk towards us, letting us now realise that even on this boat escape was not going to be an option.

We were dead in the water

I watched as Nero closed her eyes, at the same time she grabbed my hand and then she told me,

"Tell Vern I love his annoying ass and that I'm sorry I never kissed him that day," she said, before standing up and just as I opened my mouth to ask what she was doing she ran the length of the boat and flung herself off the edge barely just making it back to the cave's floor.

"NERO!" I screamed her name in horror realizing what she had done. She was sacrificing herself to draw the beast away and save me!

"It's been fun, Princess," she said, calling me the name I'd asked her not to but giving me a wink and even from the boat I could see her eyes glistened with unshed tears.

"No!" The whispered plea came through my quivering lips, that I had to bite to stop from bursting into tears. We'd come so far and to lose her at this point was unbearable. Unbearable and utterly heart-breaking. But then the Hellhound turned its head away from the boat, now seeing easier prey stood waiting. It turned its back to me and then again to her, as if weighing up its options. A sob broke free the moment it made its decision and slowly stalked back to Nero's side of the River.

I looked back to see that we were nearly at the other end and would soon disappear through an arched tunnel. So, with nothing else to do, I called her name and threw my weapon through the air, swinging it as hard as I could so it would reach the other side. It fell with a clatter on the stone floor a few feet away, meaning the last sight I had of my friend was as she rolled on the ground to retrieve the sword, at the same time that the Hellhound pounced.

I closed my eyes as the darkness of the tunnel overwhelmed me and I could only breathe again when I finally heard the whining sound of death coming from the Hellhound,

Not of that of my friend.

CHAPTER TWENTY-TWO

A BOAT TO NOWHERE

For a good while after this I found I could do nothing but hang my head in shame. I couldn't believe I had come all this way just to lose Nero. It was a bitter blow and all I could hope for was that she'd managed to kill the two beasts that were after us. After that I had no idea how she was going to get back home.

I went through every possibility in my mind. Asking myself how many coins she had, and if there would be another boat headed her way. If not, would she be able to make her way back up the spiral staircase and find another way out? I wondered if there were any portals and if not, whether she would brave using the gateway in the Lost Temple of Olympus and enter the mortal realm.

I don't know how long I sat on this old Chesterfield with my head in my hands trying to ignore everything around me, like the haunting sounds of two whips lashing out and cutting through the air before hitting the flesh of those that powered the boat. I wanted to drown it all out, every single minute of it. Simply put, *I wanted to go home.*

But the truth of the matter remained that I had no idea where I was going, and I had nothing to guide me. It wasn't as though anyone on this boat was going to start being chatty anytime soon. And well, the one who seemed to be in charge of whipping people didn't exactly look like the approachable type, despite the eternally creepy smile. No, my only hope was that this boat was headed to another dock somewhere and where there was another dock then surely there would, hopefully, be a point to it, meaning a town of some sort.

Of course, another hope I had was that I didn't starve to death or die of dehydration before I actually got there because for all I knew, I could be on this boat for weeks. After all, it wasn't as though there were many mortals in Hell who required basic needs and when you were dead, you didn't really need to eat. Embarrassingly enough I was also desperate for a pee and was regretting not using the wooden bucket in the cell after killing the Harpy.

Gods, but it had been one fuck up after another and now being on this boat I wasn't even sure if Lucius had any way to track me, even if he did discover that the Harpies were the ones that took me. The only saving grace for this thought process was that if Lucius did turn up at the ruined castle, then he might be able to track our scent enough to find Nero, if she was still alive. After all, I had to pray for something and what better than the life of my friend.

I lifted my head when I heard a different noise ahead, other than the brandishing of leather on skin. it seemed as if we were heading through a wasteland of some kind. It was a swampy landmass of black lakes and brown moss-covered stone. The river snaked through it, a flickering blue flame as far as the eye could see, telling me that we had a long way to go. The boat wasn't exactly fast, which surprised me considering the motivation was pain. Hell, but by the time I got to wherever it was we were going, I would have tortured myself from my bitter thoughts and these guys would be sick of me.

I didn't know how long it was until the scenery started to change and we left the swampy wastelands behind us. The sky had started to darken, no longer a red hue to dust the clouds. this time it was all dark greys seeming as if there was a storm about to roll in, which was when my day went from bad to worse as the rain started.

"Well, at least it will wash the blood from my clothes... small pleasure and all...not that you guys know anything about pleasure anymore...*poor bastards.*" I muttered this last part as I lifted my hood up to at least make a slight attempt to keep my face dry. Something that lasted all of about ten minutes due to the heavy downpour. Forget about starving to death, I was going to freeze to death before that happened.

As darkness started to overtake the grey, the mottled glass lanterns suddenly lit as if someone had clicked their fingers. These were situated around the boat, dangling over the water from foot long poles. What encased the glass of each lantern was a wrought iron snarling mouth with the teeth holding the glass square in place, making it look as though a snarling dragon was breathing fire.

As for the front of the boat, there was one I could see that was the largest of the design and that too had its mouth wide open, only with the flames deep inside it looked as if its head was on fire. As if this boat couldn't be menacing enough, I thought wryly.

But then, if I thought this boat was bad, then the one that passed us took creepy to a whole new level and I found myself quite comfortable on the one that I was sat in. The one that passed us was much bigger than this one, although it looked to be made of the same material, making me wonder if it was something that could protect the boat from the everlasting flames. At the bow of the boat was a giant winged demon who was actually part of the boat itself. His spine arched down the centre and all the way under the water and up the other side where it ended in a spiked tail that held a large lantern at the other end. The large skeletal creature had two giant oars in its hands and it singlehandedly propelled the vessel forward being that it was the height of a building. Its bat shaped wings were stretched out like giant sails with each point roped to the edges of the boat, making them curl inwards to catch the wind. The only part that had any flesh was the thick meaty arms that obviously needed the muscle to complete this particularly strenuous task.

Its face had barely any flesh beneath the skin, it looked like wet paper had been placed directly over the bone for he had no nose to speak of just a gaping hole. His eyes didn't move from the centre point facing the direction in which he was headed. Eyes that sat deep into his skull and if it hadn't been for the reflection of the flames in the lantern, I wouldn't have even known they were there.

But this wasn't the most horrifying part, no that came from his payload sat on the opposite side of the boat, closer to his spine's tail. It was a cage with every single inch cram packed full of desperate crying souls. Each one trying to reach out to me as it went past, as if they all recognised life and were trying to cling on to it.

I didn't want to know where he was taking them exactly, as all I wanted to do was rid the memory from my mind the second it passed. At this rate it was going to cost my father a fortune in therapy, that or my credit card was going to get a hammering.

The river continued on, but then the moment it started to get wider, was when I realised that we were coming to an end, for it started to open out into a lake. It was one that was surrounded by little lights, telling me there was a town there. The closer we got the more I could see, like the other boats that were dotted here and there. They were floating on the water that I quickly noticed was no longer flaming.

As for the other boats, for the most part they were unoccupied and left to create moving shadows from a distance. Multiple docking stations curved around the landscape, framing the large lake and I couldn't help but notice that we were heading towards the biggest one.

Thankfully, my journey was at an end.

After we approached the dock, the boat rocked to a halt just where I could step off and as I stood, I felt strangely weird about leaving without saying anything, even though up until this point I had barely said a word.

"Okay, well thanks for the lift...erm...happy boating and all," I said in a strained voice before giving them a salute and wondering quite frankly what the hell I was doing!

Naturally, I stepped off the boat muttering to myself,

"Really, Fae...happy, fucking boating?"

CHAPTER TWENTY-THREE

BOUNTY CLAIMED

After walking along the dock, I realised that the prospects of seeing a town weren't as hopeful as they seemed when back on the boat. Of course, it didn't help that I couldn't actually get into what I'm sure was a town, not considering it was situated behind a towering wall that looked as if it had been made from mud.

It was still raining, making the whole thing slick and wet, surprising me that it wasn't actually crumbling away to nothing but sludge. The houses that I'd seen situated around the lake only belonged to those who owned boats, and not one of them was open to the idea of taking me to the Realm of Blood and Death, not even with the promise of a truck full of treasure that Lucius no doubt possessed and would have paid. A few harmless looking demons had asked me what was behind my back and I told them nothing but clothes.

This was when I decided that to try to beg for a lift from strangers probably wasn't the best of ideas, not especially considering what I was carrying. The Eye of Crimson was most likely classed as one of the most wanted objects in all of Hell. Meaning that for anybody powerful enough, or stupid enough to want to use it, then it meant I had a large target on my back.

Lucius' brother had obviously believed that anyone could use it, unless watching Harpies explode into black sand was how he got his kicks. Either way I believed the outcome was still a shock to him. But that did mean that if he had been under this dangerous assumption, then, in all likelihood, this would be everyone else's assumption too. Needless to say, that me possessing it was not actually a good thing, making me now very wary about even speaking to anyone.

Of course, those I had spoken to were curious to know why a mortal was in Hell, one of which asked if it was even possible. At least that's what I think he said considering he had a mouthful of protruding teeth that gave him a considerable slur. Another one had been drunk off his ass and having a merry old time with a female demon that had six breasts. She was laying naked on the bed and it looked as though her main job was to be milked or she was getting ready to feed her litter. Either way the second he suggested I join them was when I was on my own merry way.

In fact, it was the small demon after this who was only the size of a dwarf and had the horns of a bull, that actually offered any help. And after stepping sideways out of his door (on account of the big horns) he pointed to the gated keep that was the entrance to the main part of the town. I thanked him after receiving a grunt in return and for some reason, he then butted the side of his house three times before walking back inside…sideways of course.

"Ooookay," I said, wondering if this had been some sort of 'good luck' thing. Like when someone sees a magpie or throws salt over their shoulder if they spill it. Did Hell have its own version of old wives' tales?

I ended up shaking my head a little as if I hadn't just seen what I had and turned in the direction he'd shown me. I also had a pretty good reason to believe that he was not going to be the last strange thing I saw this night.

Notably, I stuck out like a sore thumb being there, as there weren't that many demons walking around in mortal vessels. But then, as for behind the wall, I was still yet to find out, because after knocking on the door my plan abruptly ended. This was when a little window was opened and a gruesome face full of eyes told me to fuck off. After that the window was slammed shut and I looked up at the sky still pouring with rain, asking anybody up there who would listen to give me a break.

Unsurprisingly, no one answered.

Of course, if I eventually did get inside, I wasn't holding out much hope for a reputable community, as no creature had batted an eyelid at my appearance, where I was covered in blood and dirt and soaking wet. Well, one thing was for sure, and that was I couldn't just sit out here in the rain all night. And as much as I hated to admit it, I most likely had a better chance in finding someone to help me behind those walls, than I did on this side of them. I turned around and leant back against the door before saying,

"Come on, Fae, think damn it, think! There's got to be a way inside!" I shouted, banging my fist against the door and hearing the guard grumbling once more and telling me to fuck off,

"Yes, yes, I heard you…Asshole!" I shouted back when suddenly the door swung open and my body went falling backwards. I was flat on my back in the mud looking up at a huge demon. One, I should add, that currently had all of its six eyes staring down at me. Each one ran in a line down the length of his face and was positioned at the start of where six antlers began. Each antler joined up to form two huge arch shape horns high above the top of its head. It was also hairy, smelled like rotting cabbage, and had a row of large yellow teeth that looked jagged and in desperate need of a dentist. Although, I was also pretty sure if this guy turned up next in line for the chair, then that dentist would run out of the building screaming from looking at his teeth alone. Forget about the creepy bug eyes.

He was as hideous as he was mean, and he looked like the asshole that I had claimed him to be. However, he also looked about two seconds away from being the last face I would ever see before he killed me, meaning that I had to act quickly and hope the big bastard was slow.

His hands were a combination of antlers and bone, so that when I scrambled backwards, his fist connected with the earth and not my face. He tried to reach out and grab me, but my foot was caught in the middle of the two sharp ends of his antlers, thankfully missing my skin. I pulled my foot through the gap quickly got to my feet and ran for it down the muddy path.

"Get back here, mortal scum! Seize the girl!" he bellowed as I continued running, trying not to get my foot stuck in the mud as the rain was making the path difficult. Thankfully though, it was also one that wasn't well lit, which meant that the second I rounded a corner I did the only thing I could think of and that was jump over a small fence before curling up against it.

I pulled the hood over my face hiding myself in the mud and hoped it was enough to camouflage me. I waited as I heard the gatekeeper catch up to where I was lay hidden and heard him barking out orders to his men,

"Find the girl and when you do, crush her skull, for she can't have gone far!" Great, that sounded fun...*not!* Thankfully I still had the Eye strapped to my back and boy didn't I know about it, as I had felt it when I fell backwards, landing on the damn thing! If I finally got back to the mortal realm I could now add a trip to the chiropractor to the list of things I would need to do to get over this ordeal.

I gave it as long as I possibly could lying there shivering in the mud and trying not to gag with the stench, now praying that it was actually mud and not just demon faeces. Well, I was gonna look the pretty picture when Lucius did finally find me, I thought with a groan and a roll of my eyes as I pushed my body up, ignoring the squelch of mud between my fingers.

By the Gods, but what I wouldn't have given in that moment to come across a vacant house that had a bathtub full of steaming hot water, a bottle of wine, and a plate full of food...I would have added pizza, but I didn't want to push my luck with the wishing. Besides, I very much doubted they had an Italian takeaway around these parts.

I got up and looked around to find that if I stuck to the back alleys and in between the houses, I had more chance of finding somewhere or someone without bumping into the guards. I added to my list of wishes and I hoped they got bored of looking for me sooner rather than later.

The town wasn't the same as the one where Nero's shop had been. This one was definitely more of the rustic kind, as the houses were made of mud and some strange netting. The roofs were spiked with bales of dried grass dumped on top of them. It could have been soul weed and the thorns were used to hold the straw like substance in place.

None of the roads or pathways were paved and with the constant downpour, walking through them became like walking through sludgy snow. In fact, after about ten minutes of trying to get to what looked like the centre of the town, my legs were killing me! They felt as if I had weights attached to my ankles every time I lifted up my knees.

Forget about the bath, all I needed was a bed and that was because I felt as though I could sleep for a week. The centre of the town was in the shape of a diamond and at its centre was the gruesome sight of torture. At the very least I could say I was glad that all that was hanging from the noose was the skeleton of a demon without legs, not a fresh-looking corpse. Only one wing remained, telling me that whoever had been hung, had lost parts of its body before being put there.

"Therapy, Fae...lots and lots of therapy," I muttered to myself as I finally came across what I was looking for...*a Tavern.* Now the last time I had been in one of these I'd had three powerful shifters at my back, so I wasn't sure I was making the right choice by walking into an establishment filled with drunken demons that most likely wouldn't give a demonic rat's ass about my problems. But seeing as I hadn't come across anyone other than pissed off guards, then from the sounds of life humming behind its doors, I knew this was my only choice.

I had run out of all my options.

I went to pull the door open, when suddenly it disappeared from my hand as someone had done it for me, making me have to get out of the way quickly so they didn't just bulldoze into me. Thankfully, the big creature looked two sheets to the wind and staggered off without even acknowledging my existence. I crept inside with the door swinging closed behind me. I made sure my hood was up, so I could potentially get away with not looking so obviously human, and I squeezed myself in between all the bodies that were clearly there for a good time.

ROOTS OF RAGE

Some creatures, beasts, and demons were recognisable from books, research, and even stories told by a family member. But I would say these only made up about ten percent of the occupants currently packing out the space. Because as for the rest of them, I had no clue what they were. There were ones that looked more animal than human, and most of these were a combination of more than one.

Some had wings that were folded tightly to their backs due to the lack of space to move, and others had scaley tails wrapped around their waists so they wouldn't get stepped on. There were more horns than in a hunting lodge and each of these ranged in both size and shape. Even skin tones went from albino white to blazing red, to black as night.

Being someone with as much of a curious nature as I always had, then admittedly, it was hard not to stare. But then equally as clumsy as I was, it was also hard not to fall on my ass or get that same ass kicked by first knocking into someone. Thankfully, the one demon I had knocked into already was blind drunk and actually apologised to me thinking it was his fault.

In fact, due to the obvious lack of kindness I would find in a place like this, I homed in on this person thinking that in them I might be able to appeal for their help. Naturally, in this state they were probably too drunk to do much, but at the very least I might get a coin or two to pay some kind of ferryman to take me closer to Lucius' realm.

Of course, this was until a demon, who later turned out to be his lover, grabbed me back by the scruff of my neck and accused me of feeling up his boyfriend. I had to say it was most likely one of the strangest moments of my life and when I tried to explain that I wasn't trying to take advantage of the blue skinned demon who had buck teeth and his large dick on show, I found myself stuttering for the right words.

"I told you to put that away!" The demon, who still had me by my neck, snarled at his boyfriend nodding down at the dick in question, which like I said, was hanging free, and swaying with his movements as it was close to his knees. I swallowed at the thought as the thing looked more like a truncheon and something to batter you with, than something that would give you pleasure. Of course, having me staring at it didn't help matters, meaning that the hairy demon that held me now brought my head closer to his snarling face and said,

"See anything you like, bitch, for I will make you spin on it!" I frowned and despite his threatening hold, I found myself saying,

"I thought you were jealous a second ago, now you want me to ride the damn thing…jeez, make up your mind!" I knew instantly that this was the wrong thing to say the second it came out of my mouth because his hands around my throat tightened and I was suddenly gasping for breath.

"Oh, she's cute, let her go Bubba and let's play with her, not break her," the long schlong demon said, coming to my defence. His boyfriend let me go and I fell to my knees coughing and gasping for air.

"See, she's in the right position now," the blue demon said with his surprisingly high and squeaky voice for such a brute. I quickly gained my feet before giving him any more ideas on how to choke a mortal and his boyfriend chuckled at my quick movements.

"Not so willing now, are you?" he sneered, making me shake my head a little and say,

"I knocked into him by accident, dickhead. What part of that made you think I was coming on to him and wanted to play hide the Pogo stick, huh?" The demon did a double take and I didn't know whether it was the surprise that I was answering back or more about the fact he had no idea what a Pogo stick was. To be honest, I think it was a mixture of both.

Either way the second something penetrated his thick hairy skull, the one named Bubba (which I thought was a fitting name) growled and reacted by lunging for me, making me duck out of the way quickly. However, by doing so I fell into another demon, which in turn made him fall into another demon and so on and so on, until five of them were all piled at the end of the bar covered in whatever ale they were drinking. The music of conversation stopped abruptly, and every demonic head turned my way.

"Okay, well this couldn't have gone any worse..." I said backing away into a corner, and as if the Gods were truly against me, they chose that moment to make things a lot worse. As suddenly the gatekeeper burst through the door, flanked by two guards before all three stormed inside taking all of about two seconds to find me.

"You just had to go and say it didn't you, Fae?" I muttered looking up at the Heavens and wondering if it existed at all or just filled with empty space! I mean hello, were there any Gods up there even paying attention to shit or were the buggers all on vacation?!

The gatekeeper, his guards, and about ten demons I had managed to piss off since being in here, all started to close in around me, making me suddenly bargain with my life in the only way I knew how,

"The Vampire King wants me!" I shouted suddenly, making everyone take pause.

"So, what if he does!"

"Yeah, why would we give a fuck?!" A few more comments were flung my way about not giving a shit and even some that sounded like a cross between a duck and a dog barking.

"He's willing to pay for me, idiots!" I snapped, with a roll of my eyes that really wasn't doing me any favours considering my situation. I received a couple of growls, a few snarls and one weird clucking sound, making me decide it was probably best to rein in on the attitude.

"You have a bounty on your head?" the gatekeeper asked, obviously now very interested in this.

"Yeah and it's a big one but here's the kicker guys, this Vampire King wants me alive...eeek, sorry guys. I guess if you want the money you have to take me there with all my limbs and toes and *everything* intact." I said, emphasising on the 'everything' part and motioning up and down my body with my hands, just to make things extra clear.

"Now that makes things interesting, I claim the bounty!" the gatekeeper said, making another one step forward and declare,

"You already have a job, so go fuck off and do it...I will claim the bounty!"

"And you're pissed on root water mead! I will have her!" another argued.

"Wow, have to say, I've got a lot of good propositions here it's hard to choose." Suddenly the guy who had manhandled me before grabbed me again, this time by my top tearing it slightly as he brought me closer to him telling me,

"Who says you get to choose?"

"I do!" A demonic, rough unyielding voice spoke up from the being that suddenly appeared behind me, before the towering form shifted to step in front of me and pushed the demon back hard on his ass.

"And who the fuck are you?" the gate keeper asked, as others stepped back the second he whipped back his cloak, showing them something I couldn't see. My guess was a weapon and not the kind like the blue schlong demon had.

Then he answered in a way that became unmistakable as to who he was.

"I'm th' one hunting her, 'n' I'm th' one who came tae collect…

Ma bounty."

CHAPTER TWENTY-FOUR

LUCIUS

MY BRUTAL LOVER

The moment I had finished destroying the Eye's tomb, I was in the water and through the other side in seconds. I could barely believe that she had been taken from me yet a-fucking-gain! Only this time the problem I faced was that I had no means left in trying to find her. Fuck! Also, this time I didn't even know who it was that had taken her! There was no evidence left other than her blood in the sand along with the blood belonging to the witch. All that was clear was that both of them had been attacked and taken.

Needless to say, I was killing mad! The rage that consumed me was giving way and giving total control over to my demon. The only thing that would sate his thirst for revenge was the blood of our enemies coating our hands! That, and the feel of our woman back in our arms knowing she was safe.

Because admittedly, the last time she had been taken had

been different. I had known instantly that the three brothers would not have harmed her. The furious rage and anger had been there yes, but the worry and fear for her life had not. No, I could not claim as much now as I had no idea who had her. But even if I could venture a guess and say it was the witch, then I still didn't know what she wanted with her. I also had to question how they had gained access into here in the first place? Because if it had been as simple as the Hex taking her to wherever the witch was, then why was Nero also missing? And not just the girls, but also the Eye of Crimson?

I couldn't even suspect what I had classed as my inner circle because Nero had been the only one inside and she had lost enough blood on that black sand to have died. The moment everyone had left my tower, they would once more need my permission to gain access to it again. It was the way the tower had been built as an impenetrable force to protect the Eye. Even if they have made it through the storm without it ripping them to pieces, they would not have been able to get through those doors without my blood.

So, how had such a thing even been possible?!

Admittedly, I felt helpless, and it was a feeling that gutted me from the inside out. Naturally, it wasn't something I was used to experiencing, for even when I first came here in search of her, I had motions and steps to follow in trying to aid my search. I had things that could be done and places to go but in this...*I literally had nothing.*

I had an entire world to search and even though my connections with the Kings of other realms were vast, even that wasn't enough to stretch over even half of Hell. Amelia could have been anywhere and captured by anyone, and tortured by even more. The thought of this had me staggering to the side of the wall to hold myself up. Parts of the wall crumbled in my grasp as I roared my agony up at any God who would listen to it, hoping they feared my wrath!

I made it to my throne room with the path of destruction left in my wake, for I cared little for any of it! The second I stepped foot inside the vast white stone covered room everyone knew to cower before me as my demonic steps cracked the ground. It looked as though I was walking on the ice of the frozen lake that usually surrounded my German castle Blood Rock.

I could barely believe she was gone again, no longer questioning if I was cursed, but fucking knowing I was! For I seemed forever doomed to lose the woman I loved. It was starting to become an inevitability, an unescapable future that surrounded me whenever I was with her. I was losing count of the number of times she had been ripped from my grasp during moments when I had foolishly thought her to be safe.

"Where is my brother?" I bellowed, with enough force that a crack travelled all the way up to my throne where it split the demonic horns collected there. At this dangerous question asked, it was only one being brave enough to approach and answer me. Carn'reau cut across the distance from the front doors I had just walked through and was in front of me in less time than my patience would allow, which was why I snapped,

"Tell me, he'd better be fucking here!" Carn'reau cleared his throat before admitting with a shake of his head,

"I'm afraid not, my Lord." At this my body twisted suddenly and I went down on one knee as I punched my gauntleted hand into the ground, this time splitting it the length of my throne room.

"SHE'S GONE!" This new information came out in a burst of anger that could no longer be contained. My general closed his eyes a moment as he digested this information.

"And what of the witch?" The second he asked this I started growling at him and was back on my feet in an instant. I was a hair's breadth away from taking hold of his throat before ripping it out for the insult that I should care about one over the other. And shit me, but didn't he know it! His hand snapped up to halt my actions as he quickly added,

"I only ask because she could help if she were here, not because I hold any importance of her over that of your Chosen One." On hearing this I took a calming breath, knowing that he was right, my rage was making me irrational. I took a deep breath trying to calm myself enough to answer,

"The witch was taken also." Carn'reau simply nodded and after this, he didn't need to be told what to do, calling for his second in command instantly. Alvaro appeared out of nowhere, for I was so deep in my rage I could not think straight enough to acknowledge those present around me.

"The witch, she told you how to use the casting spells for tracking down words spoken...yes?" Carn'reau asked, seemingly now taking charge and I couldn't have been more fucking grateful for it! I couldn't think straight, that was fucking obvious!

"She gave me the incantation needed," he replied with a bow of his head. Suddenly, my own head snapped up,

Explain!" I snapped.

"Nero didn't tell you in fear of your wrath in believing such a thing was needed, however she came to me and told me that the cloud spell could also be used in a different way should the need arise and your Chosen One go missing once more." After this I took another breath and nodded for him to continue, knowing that if I did happen upon the witch and she was still alive, I was indebted to give her anything she wished for!

"Everywhere the spell was cast we can go back and by

speaking a different incantation, it will home in on any word spoken of the girls' kidnapping." I closed my eyes and released a sigh, before they snapped open and I admitted,

"It is the best chance we have...send your men out to do it directly and whilst they are there, have any contacts or dealings with anyone with a loose tongue, tell them to loosen them further and find out what they can."

"At once, my Lord," Carn'reau said, nodding to a second for him to go. He bowed to me before he left to do his general's bidding, and just before Carn'reau could do the same, I told him,

"I have another job for you."

"My Lord?" he questioned, making me tell him,

"Get me the Gryphon and the Wyvern. Call them back for I will need them on this also." Carn'reau looked thoughtful for a moment and agreed,

"They are the best bounty hunters around and managed to retrieve her the first time, but what of Trice, I believe he is closing in on his target who can remove the hex."

"Then in that case he can stay, for the other two shifters should suffice and when she is found, she will be in need of this mystery being who can remove the hex," I said, planning for the best and trying not to focus on the worst, so I may continue to function.

"Very well, my Lord, it will be done." My general lingered a moment longer and I jerked up my chin telling him with little patience,

"You have something more to say then I suggest you get on and fucking say it!" I snapped, and he wasn't surprised due to the delicate subject.

"And what of Dariush, my Lord?" His question was one that made me turn my head in the direction of his office and snarl my reply...

"Leave him to me."

Five excruciating hours later and I was practically tearing my hair out waiting for news. At the very least Gryph and Vern had returned, and I found my rage bursting to the surface yet again when I had to go through the events of what had become of Amelia. At the very least I was thankful the bastard Trice was not with them, for if he had been, then it would have taken very little for him to say or do before tearing his head off. This was something I didn't think Amelia would have taken kindly to upon her return, it was also not a death I could have hidden from her, for she was sure to notice.

The two brothers had walked the length of my throne room taking note of the destruction as if an earthquake had cracked the crust of Hell. Instantly they had known something was wrong. But then, as I was in the middle of explaining to them what little of a plan we had in using Nero's spell, it prompted a difficult question from Vern,

"So, Nero, she's out there now reversing…?" I would have winced had I had cared enough at the time, for all of my energy, worry, and anxiety was solely focused on Amelia. So, with no tact at all, I snapped,

"The witch was also taken!" This was when I saw a mirror image of my own reaction, for Vern reacted badly. I simply stood back and let it happen as he found himself surrounded by my guards taking his anger as a threat towards their King. I didn't have fucking time for his own heartbreak, but I was at least sympathetic enough not to let him get killed for it.

I ordered my men to give him space and let his brother

deal with his outrage. I also wanted the Gryphon shifter to do so quickly for my patience at having Vern making demands of me would not last. So, I had warned him of this and Gryph's reply was a simple and effective,

"Aye," before he went on with his task of calming down his brother. It was at this point when I turned my back on them both that something hit me. It also had the strength to knock me to my knees as I grabbed my head with both hands and looked up at the ceiling with my back arched, as the vision gripped my entire being.

At first I thought it was some sort of attack from the witch, for I couldn't understand the power if it. I didn't know what was happening, when suddenly I was assaulted with image after image. And every single one was of what Amelia was going through...or should I say...*had been through.*

It was like a flicker book of time. The last five hours she had been missing started with a painful image of her hanging by her wrists. She was attached to a wooden beam in some fucking cell, but before the pain of this could continue to consume me, I became a witness to the raw and sheer magnificence that was Amelia.

I watched as she kicked out with her legs at the creature that had run at her with a blade in its hand, only to be thrown backwards from the impact. Then I found myself astonished when she freed herself by running up the pole and using the force of her weight to snap her chains. But even as the images continued to hit me in a wave of action, I still had the time to question how the fuck was she able to do these things?

This same question only ended up repeating itself in my mind the second I saw the brutality she was capable of. Not just by killing the creature, one that I was yet unclear as to what it was exactly, but then in the very sinister message she left behind. This was all before watching her picking the lock with nothing other than a bloody talon she had brutally chopped off.

But then as she exited the cell, I was able to focus on the message she had left behind, finally giving me the insight needed as to who it was that took her,

Fucking Harpies!

CHAPTER TWENTY-FIVE

TO KILL ME A HARPY AND CRY ME A RIVER

I could vaguely hear those around me calling something about their Lord, but I switched all my focus on Amelia, blocking all else out as I didn't want to lose sight of the image. It continued with Amelia's clumsiness when nearly falling down a spiral staircase one moment, and the next creeping along the battlements like an assassin waiting for the opportunity to kill. I have seen glimpses of the Harpies and the ruined castle before, knowing it was where they had made their lair.

At one time they had occupied the outskirts of Tartarus around the Lost Temple of Olympia when they tried to keep their connection to Zeus, even though rumour had it that they were forbidden to enter inside the temple itself. Which, seemingly, no longer mattered as from the looks of things they had since moved on.

However, that didn't matter for it was a castle all the same and one I knew I would find in Tartarus. A place where they had been cursed to remain for all of their days. I did then have to question how they had managed to snatch Amelia away, seeing as it was always believed that they were incapable of leaving.

But thinking back to the castle and I knew there weren't many sites to be seen from the sky like this one. I knew after receiving the clues that I needed to help find her, I shouldn't have been wasting time with these visions, but I found myself locked to the sight of her bravery. She was unbelievable and a true master in the art of killing. I watched her dispatch one Harpy in a tower before creeping across a bailey to kill another. That one was done face to face and I swear at the sight, I knew she would have made a formidable demon, for right now there was nothing angelic about her.

But then I suppose that wasn't true, considering she was doing all of this in the hope of saving her friend, for the witch, Nero, was still alive. I felt my hand fist in frustration the second they were caught in their escape and put into a cage after the Harpy Queen had found her little gruesome message. I could barely believe, after witnessing all of this, that my little geek, my little Amelia with her cute pyjamas and her childish hobbies was the same girl. Yet I knew with a certainty I couldn't explain that once I got her back topside and away from all of this brutality that she would revert to being the same. For she didn't have it in her heart to change. I knew this as, still in the face of a seemingly doomed position, she was still making jokes and trying to ease the fear of another.

The Angel inside of her would never leave, not even after all she'd endured thanks to the Hell she had willingly stepped into. After this, parts of what happened next were hazy, and flickered and jumped to parts of the past that didn't follow in order. What happened before this point became clear that it was leading up to what was happening now, and the only thing that made sense to all of this, was that she was being forced to take hold of the Eye. This had been after seeing several Harpies die after being forced to try first.

However, there was one focal point that always remained as a blur. It was as if the Eye itself didn't want me to see this part and withheld the vital bit of information, and that was the one who was obviously pulling all of the strings. I knew this because conversation was always directed to this void in the memory. Of course, the second Amelia had taken hold of the Eye this was when it was connected with me, as its keeper, showing me her recent past. Meaning that the moment it released me was when I knew it had released her too, and we were now back living in real time.

I suddenly fell forward on my hands, slapping my palms against the cracked floor and adding to its destruction. But then I looked up once just in time to see my brother had created a portal and slipped back into this room from wherever he had come from.

But I didn't have time for questioning him on his absence. Not now I knew of all the new events that had taken place. So instead of explaining, I turned my back on him and only stopped long enough to offer hope to one I knew better than most needed it right now. I look down at the Wyvern shifter and said,

"Your witch…she is still alive." Then I released my wings and flew from the throne room ready to take on all of Tartarus once more, if that's what it would take to get back…

My Chosen One.

Entering Tartarus wasn't a problem for me, not when a part of me had become connected to this place after losing my hand and having it sacrificed. This was because when it had grown back, it had done so with the Venom of God.

My blood, at least the infected part in me, had thankfully stayed in the one place on my body and in doing so it meant that it was the only key left to releasing the Titans. Of course, it was also a means of locking them back up again, hence my sacrifice. Thankfully, I had the power within my vessel to manipulate my own blood, making it travel to wherever I wanted it. After biting a certain shit stain upon the Earth, one whose birthright duped him the only one capable of releasing the Titans, I had ingested his blood and at the time forced it all into my hand when placing it in the Keystone. The rest I had thought had been history.

Of course, now I knew the connection to the Tree of Souls had meant that this Venom of God had travelled to the blood of my own people. That same Venom of God in my hand had the power to strip Amelia of her birthright, which admittedly should have killed her instantly.

Which had me questioning why it started coming back to her now in such a form. But startling still was that she was not displaying the natural abilities of a vampire or the powers of an angel. Naturally, this had me questioning who she truly was since that day I reclaimed her back in the soul fields.

Or should I say, *who she was becoming?*

These questions plagued me along with dozens of others as I located the right portal that first took me straight to where the Lost Temple of Olympia was. The moment I made it through, I was up in the air and searching for any signs of this ruined castle. The portal inside the temple had once led to the Temple of Janus, but since then, Aurora the treacherous bitch, had sealed it. After this I had my brother recycle it and open it back up as another gateway to my lands. Of course, this wasn't common knowledge, for only I, my brother, and Dom knew, believing its change might one day come in useful if any old enemies were ever to return. Meaning the threat of the Titans once more.

Unfortunately, getting to the other side of the portal in my realm had not been as quick as I would have liked, therefore I knew that time had passed between what the Eye had shown me last. Added to this was the different times that passed in Tartarus than that of my own realm.

I flew over the forest of soul weed taking note of how much it had grown since the last time I was here. Just across a stretch of wasteland I could see the castle in the distance. I shot through the air with greater speed now that I had my destination in my sights, confessing to praying to any Gods that would listen that she was still there but more importantly, *that she was safe.*

I found my eyes narrowing the moment I saw the destruction before I landed in the centre of the open space, one that had been obliterated, and from the look of things, a power that had managed to take out the majority of the Harpy race! I closed my eyes and pulled back the memory, knowing this was exactly where the Eye had been and where Amelia had been stood when holding it. This could only mean one thing, that the moment she'd let it go that almighty power inside of her had been let loose on the race of Harpies. Making me now wonder if something new had been released as well.

"Fuck me," I muttered as I took it all in.

I continued to scan the area and it didn't take me long before the scent of blood started to rise up my nostrils. This wasn't surprising considering the utter carnage left in my girl's wake. However, this particular blood I could sense was one that was still flowing from that of a beating heart. I soon found its cause in the form of a butchered Harpy, only admittedly not one I was used to encountering. For this particular Harpy, at one time must have been beautiful. However, after the beating my Chosen One had given her, that beauty was long gone and hidden under blood and dirt.

She lay slumped over, leaning against the tower wall and if it hadn't been for the heartbeat I could hear, then I would have believed her dead. I walked over to her, glad that she was still alive for I needed her memories to see what had happened to Amelia. The Harpy was unconscious, that was until I kicked her leg with my foot, not yet wanting to cause too much damage. Like I said, I needed her alive and her blood loss was a considerable amount already.

I bent on one knee and gripped her by the neck, giving her a shake until her eyes fluttered open. They were like two crimson snake eyes that soon morphed back into those more mortal in appearance. As soon as she saw me, she grinned, showcasing teeth coated in blood, which made for a sinister sight and one that didn't impress me.

Deciding quickly that I didn't have the time to interrogate her, I placed my hand over her eyes and concentrated on drawing out her memories. This was when I frowned in shock at finding myself blocked and soon had me growling in frustration and questioning my abilities. I couldn't understand how she was able to withstand my power. This was when I looked closely at her headdress, sparking something inside of me. It was the way the dark, smoky, serpents slithered around as if searching for something.

This was when it hit me that I had seen this once before, and many years ago. It had been not long after I had been changed in fact. A demon I had been hunting, simply for the fact that it had strangely been hunting me first, I had found one night in a dark alleyway. But what prompted the memory was it wore a similar headpiece that seemed alive, with these same black vapour snakes escaping his turban.

I had tried to access his mind for weeks before this point, in hopes of discovering who he worked for and why this person wanted me followed. However, I hadn't been able to and the demon had told me why after he'd been caught, telling me he had sold his soul for a second chance at life.

In my naivety at a young age of being newly turned, I had believed he had been speaking of Lucifer, and being fearful at the time of my potential new father's wrath, I hadn't pushed for a name. I did however try once more to read his mind after being, for the first time, in close proximity with him.

But this was only to find that his void was filled with nothing more than black shadowed serpents like those on the top of his head. In fact, there had been millions of them and the black space around my influence had been moving around me like shimmering water running vertical up the walls. Everything in his void was being blocked by these shadowed serpents.

That was when I knew it had something to do with the strange headpiece he wore. Testing the theory and believing all I needed to do was get rid him of it, I had ripped it from his head. I had not known at the time that this instantly killed him, quickly turning him to black sand the second that claim on his soul was severed.

I removed my hand in frustration after seeing the same thing in the Harpy Queen's void, knowing I would get nothing from her mind and had to do this the old fashioned, *threatening* way.

"Where is my Chosen One? I asked in a dark unyielding

tone, one she was right to flinch at. But despite her reaction to me, she grinned again and said,

"I am happy to tell you that your Chosen One is dead or if she isn't yet, then she soon will be." I squeezed her neck tighter, yanked her close and made her moan in pain before I told her,

"I can either snap your neck and make it quick or I can make your last moments in Hell extremely painful, before damning your soul to an endless death." After this threat, her reaction wasn't surprising, as it made her eyes grow wide in fear, for she knew what this meant. An eternity of endless suffering, one that didn't need a vessel to accomplish it, for it was an end that most of my kind dreaded the most. It was like being a ghost that felt pain and agony, loss and misery. It was the worst existence and with it the worst punishment that any of Hell's beings could receive.

"You don't have that power!" she tested, in a croaky voice due to the strain on her vocal cords trying to work against the strength of my hand. I closed even more of the space between us and snarled in a way that she would not only hear these words, but feel them also,

"Try me."

Two words. Two little words and she cracked, starting by giving me her terms,

"If I tell you, you will let me die in peace?" she asked, knowing that her death was inevitable and therefore not something to bargain with.

"I will let you die, though I doubt it will be in peace. However, it will at least be *final."* She closed her eyes at this and nodded, knowing it was the best deal she was going to get. However, by the time she was through I was regretting my word because the last thing she told me was the horrors that she released upon Amelia and Nero.

I snarled in her face, knowing that I needed to act quickly and in doing so I simply said,

"Fucking Harpies!" Then I ripped off her headpiece making her cry out, as with making this bargain for her soul, her original state seeped outwards from within and once more claimed what Zeus had taken from her the first time…*that of her beauty*.

It was only after she changed back into the hideous image cursed upon her, that she burst into a cloud of black sand just like the demon had that night in the alley. What it meant I didn't know, however looking at the same black sand that covered the floor of the bailey, knowing that it also covered the tomb the Eye usually sat in, I could only assume that it had something to do with the God, Janus.

However, I didn't have time to think on such things too intently, only how quickly I could get to my girl and potentially save her. I took to the air, my large wings blowing back the ash remains of her offspring combined with the black sands the Eye had created. I started to follow the only path they could have taken and took my time to sniff the air. Thankfully, with concentrating, I finally picked up the faintest scent of my girl, the witch, and the three Hellhounds that the Harpy Queen had told me she had released.

I couldn't fly too high for I needed that scent to guide me and surprisingly, it took me to the soul weed forest I had crossed when first getting here. It was a frustrating thought that she may have been down there as I had been flying over. But then a second thought later and I knew this was unlikely, for I hadn't seen any Hellhounds on my journey here.

I swooped lower before landing at the start of the forest, now being faced with a large tunnelled section that had been hollowed out most likely by that of a mage or a witch, making it continue to grow this way.

I quickly ran down the length of it only stopping when the scent of Amelia abruptly turned as if they had run straight into the thick of the soul weed. I paused to look back down at the tunnel the way I had come, knowing now that they were obviously being chased.

"That's my girl," I commented to myself knowing that Amelia most likely had made this decision to go where the Hellhounds could not follow. I continued to run with supernatural speed to the end, following now the scent of the Hellhounds, knowing that they wouldn't give up that easily. Not even when they had been forced to go around the forest.

As soon as I was free from the soul weed above me, I took to the sky once more and only dropped down when on the other side, back to where I could see the broken temple. After this I picked up their scent once more and it became easier to follow, meaning it hadn't been too much time that had passed before they had been here. This also meant that it most likely took them a while to make their way through the harrowing forest.

I picked up speed until eventually reaching an access tunnel that led straight down to only one place,

The river of Phlegethon.

There were six main rivers in Hell, and they all led to different places, in different realms. There was the river Styx, the most prominent of all due to its central location, as all rivers connected in some way to this one. It was also known as the river of hatred and was named after the Goddess Styx.

The Acheron was known as the river of pain. It is also one most travelled upon for beings like Charon and only one of many Ferrymen, who used this as a way to transport the dead. The river known as Lethe was said to be one of forgetfulness, aptly named from the Goddess of forgetfulness and oblivion, a Goddess known as Lethe.

The others were Cocytus, the river of wailing and naturally not known as a joyful boat ride. And the last was Oceanus, the only river known to be connected to the mortal realm, crossing over at certain parts of the world. Most common was at the place the humans had called the Bermuda Triangle. Hence the disappearance of ships and planes over the years.

But as for Phlegethon, this was known as the river of fire. It was also the only river that led straight to the depths of Tartarus. If legend was correct, the tale goes that Phlegethon runs parallel to the river Styx in only one place. It is said that the Goddess Styx was in love with Phlegethon, but she was consumed by his flames and bitterness for their lost love, and was therefore sent to Hades. Eventually, when Hades allowed them to reunite, a new river formed and connected at only one point in Hell…

The Realm of Lust.

Standing on the edge of the spiral tunnel I could see for myself that getting down there mustn't have been an easy task. In my eagerness to reach the bottom quickly, I jumped and kept my wings curled close in the free fall, only opening them to aid in my landing. The moment I reached the bottom two things struck me, the first being the dead Hellhound and the second was the strangest by far.

"Keira?" I said her name the second I felt the lingering essence that she had been here before and had unknowingly left her mark. I knelt down to pick up one of the shell casings of a bullet, raising a brow in question. But then my memories came back to me and I was soon muttering another name,

"Wild Bill Hickok." I shook my head at the character that being was and continued through the broken door with haste.

However, the moment I breached the opening I heard it at the same time feeling it.

Another heartbeat, but this time it was one that was struggling to carry on. Meaning, combined with the blood I scented, it could only mean one thing…

Nero was dying.

CHAPTER TWENTY-SIX

BLOODY BETRAYAL

After a quick scan of the cave, I found a dead Hellhound with a slashed underbelly still burning from its infernal insides spilling onto the cave floor. It was one still being fueled by the flaming river it had died close to, for its essence was still yet to be fully extinguished. I focused on the diminishing heartbeat, noting the droplets of blood that led the way, along with the faint sound of life. I rounded a corner leading to a small cave-like crevice and once there I found another dead Hellhound with a sword embedded in its skull and a dying Nero lying next to it.

She had three deep lacerations across her torso slashing open first material, then skin and flesh down to the bone. Her eyes fluttered open as if sensing my presence and I got down on one knee and took her hand in my own. Her pulse was nearly non-existent, and I knew there wasn't much time.

"Amelia, she..."

"What happened to her?" I felt like a heartless bastard for asking but I needed to know. She closed her eyes and released a sigh and I took it as a good sign that it seemed to be one of peace, not worry.

"I got her on the boat, she's safe on the boat," she said, repeating this as if needing to hear it to comfort herself.

"You sacrificed yourself to lure them away from taking the river, didn't you?" I asked feeling that question weigh heavily in my gut knowing that this woman here lay dying in order to save my Chosen One. There was no greater gift to receive or any payment worthy of such a sacrifice. However, I did have at least one thing to give if she was willing to accept it.

"She is safe now, she's safe on the boat." This was her answer and it made me smile, then I put my gloved hand behind her head cradling it with my palm after first making it smooth without armor. Then, with the other hand I raised it to my mouth and bit into my wrist where the blood would flow the fastest.

Then I asked her,

"Do you want to live, for if you do, I will own your soul as you will be one of my own, and your soul will be forever...?" At this her eyes snapped open and she said with renewed energy,

"I would make a shitty martyr, so...fucking spare me the spiel and just tell me where to sign and give me your blood, yeah...I kind of wanna live here..." I had to laugh at the brass humor even in the face of death. I would enjoy owning this one and admittedly was already contemplating making her my newest council member, for she most certainly deserved the status.

"Then say the words...say that you swear your loyalty to me and grant me your soul and in return you will gain the eternal life of a vampire, for I will gift to you my blood and you will then become one of my own," I told her and she

ROOTS OF RAGE

closed her eyes. But then as she was obviously waiting she cracked one eye open and said,

"What are we waiting for here, a cocktail umbrella and a straw?" I smirked and leaning down a little whispered,

"I need your words, little brave witch." After this it finally dawned on her, making her tell me what I needed to hear.

"I swear my loyalty to you and that of ownership over my soul. Now please hurry up and feed me before I die." I grinned down at her and readily fed her my wrist. She latched onto it and started to drink down my blood with gusto. However, despite ingesting so much of it, I knew it would be a while before she would be able to fully heal, but it was enough not to die at least.

As for her turning, well, I had no idea on this either seeing as she was a witch and had been sent to Hell first as a mortal. I knew this, not because I had checked up on her, but because this was what happened to most witches. My own witch had been slightly unorthodox in her turning and therefore it was quite a different story.

So, other than coming outright and asking her why she was sent down here, then I had no idea. But as her new Master it was my right to ask it, yet it wasn't a question I would ask until the time was right. It was something I would want answered in the near future though, for if I potentially did ever decide to take her topside, as I had the power to do so, and assuming she agreed, of course, then I would want to know. For if she was to be on my council then I would have to know the reasons why she was down in Hell in the first place. For all of those on my council, as a matter of trust, I needed to know about their history. After all, knowledge was power, and to be forewarned of any issues that may arise in the future would only aid me further in dealing with them.

As for Nero, she had made the ultimate sacrifice when saving my Chosen One and it was one that, even with my blood and saving her life, I still didn't know if I would ever be able to repay such a debt.

Thoughts of the future was all I had whilst she continued to drink down my blood. That and some small comfort knowing that Amelia was at least safer now being on that boat. After all, any ferryman was charged with safe passage, which meant their cargo was their responsibility and that meant arriving at its destination in the same state of living as when picked up.

The moment I knew that she'd had enough was when I tapped the side of her cheek, one that now had some more colour to it. Then I told her as softly as possible,

"That's enough, or before long I'll be lying next to you to take a nap and I know of a particular Wyvern who is anxious to see you." At the mention of Vern, she winced, and it was not the happy expression I would have expected to see. There was no light in her eyes in anticipation and glee, but only apprehension. I was curious to know why before she beat me to the question, with her explanation,

"It no longer matters." I only needed to raise a brow before she continued,

"No offence, but he doesn't particularly like vampires." My lips twitched because hearing this piece of information wasn't exactly a shock, for I had never set out to be a King people actually liked. Therefore, I couldn't give a fuck about his thoughts towards me, but as for the witch's life I had just saved, it obviously did matter, and I took the knowledge of this seriously enough to have care in the next few words I told her,

"If that is the case and it is something he cannot move past, then you must be the one to move and if he does not chase you down and claim you, then he is the one not worthy." Her eyes widened at this as if she was surprised such a philosophy had come out of my mouth. But then again I was the famous tyrant King, and up until now she had thought me to be one without a heart.

After this I tended to her wounds whilst she told me snippets of what had happened. Parts of this I already knew from what the connection with the Eye had shown me the moment Amelia had touched it. But everything after that moment, I hadn't seen. I couldn't help but grin when I heard about how she had taken on the Harpy Queen single-handedly and how first before taking on the horde, she had pushed Nero down the well. Doing so and letting her fall to protect her before my girl could unleash Hell. Truthfully, I couldn't have been more fucking proud of her and I could barely wait until I got the chance to be able to tell her so.

Unfortunately, knowing that she was on a boat currently sailing down the flaming river, Phlegethon, meant there was little I could do about it until she reached the other side, for only the boatman could crossover freely into the other realms. Or if those realms with free treaties held in place were agreed upon with the surrounding kingdoms, then their people could also cross freely. However, I held no such treaty, therefore it was physically impossible for me to crossover unless I found the right portal. This was so that when my kind travelled to different realms using portals it meant arriving at checkpoints and in its basic form, it was the equivalent of arriving in different countries around the human realm.

Of course, there were always those who could find a way, the right witch or mage for example. Ones who could summon a portal if they were powerful enough, although how stable it would be I didn't know. But that was up to the individual taking the chance that they didn't end up somewhere they really didn't wish to be. No, the only chance I had known was to get back to my own kingdom and have my brother create a portal to each known checkpoint the boat would cross, hopefully arriving to at least one that held clues as to her whereabouts. Or even better still, finding my girl there.

But Nero had been right, she was at the very least safe on the boat and my only hope was that she rode it to the end, meaning that I wouldn't be long in coming for her.

After I summoned material from my tower, I wrapped up her wounds that had at least healed enough for the bleeding to have stopped. This meant she had a better chance of healing quicker. I picked her up in my arms and stood, before starting to walk back to the base of the tunnel that I had dropped down.

She explained to me after I had inquired how they had managed to get down this staircase when the top portion of it was blanketed in soul weed. She explained to me how Amelia had used the Eye to draw some of its power and channel it into her so she was able to use her own magic to aid them.

Naturally on hearing this I found myself shocked and utterly astounded that such a thing was possible, that anyone was capable of using the Eye in such a way. I had heard tales of its untapped power far beyond that of simply telling the future or recalling moments of the past, but what Nero described made it more than just a tale. Much more than just a myth. It made it a dangerous, powerful force and one, by Nero's account, that was currently wrapped up in the torn skirt of a Harpy and strapped to my Chosen One's back.

"Gods, but that girl will be the reason I will wake up one day and find myself grey."

"And balding...don't forget balding," Nero added, and I smirked down at the funny little witch and told her,

"There is someone on my council I think you'll get on well with."

"Yeah, is she funny like me?" I grinned at the thought and told her,

"Most tend to think so." Of course, I was referring to the naughtiest member of my council, and something I wouldn't readily admit to anyone other than Amelia, but in times like this I missed that Imp immensely.

I released my wings and flew up the centre of the tunnel making her cling on and suck a breath of fright before relaxing again after we had been in the air for some time. For the most part of this journey Nero was silent, and I knew her anxiety was down to seeing a certain shifter.

As soon as we made it back to my own realm, I carried her inside the throne room and could already sense that the Wyvern was waiting for us. It was his brother that spotted us first and the moment he made our presence known to Vern, the shifter was storming down the length of my throne room with purpose.

"What happened, what did yer…?"

"I suggest, for your own good, you do not finish that sentence, especially not when I just saved your woman's life." At this he paused a step and looked astonished, then as if it dawned on him how I would have done this, he shouted,

"What?!"

"Erm…I think I should point out here that I'm not his woman," Nero said looking uncomfortable, making Vern scowl down at her,

"You dinnae speak!" he snapped, pointing down at her in annoyance.

"Erm, excuse me!" she barked back in return.

"You heard me, lassie, fur ah doubt yer hearing git damaged!" I closed my eyes for a second and held back my own annoyance, for I didn't have time for these two and the shit that they needed to obviously work out. I wasn't here to aid in couples' therapy even if it was clear that these two needed it.

"Yes, and if you don't watch it, then it will be your vocal cords getting it for I am this close to turning you into a posh twat again!" Nero snapped holding her thumb and finger an inch apart and in front of his face. However, he just got closer to her face and said,

"Then that wull juist mak' me sound lik' a gentleman whin a'm spanking yer ass. Noo hand her over ah wull ta'e care o' her from ere," the Wyvern demanded, making her cry out in outrage, which was one he ignored. Meanwhile, I had hit my limit and had quite enough of being in the middle of these two. So, I gladly held out my arms ready for him to take over, despite Nero's protests.

But then something stopped me when she suddenly gripped onto me so tightly, I felt her entire body freeze solid in my hold.

"Hey, ah said...wait whit's wrong, lass?" Vern asked, obviously seeing her reaction for himself and knowing that something wasn't right...it also wasn't because of him. We both knew that when she couldn't seem to take her eyes away from staring in the direction of my throne. The look on her face was as if she had seen the ghost of her ancestors speaking to her only of the death they wanted for her, like a darkness upon her soul.

I turned to look in the direction, seeing now my brother after he had just created a portal and was stepping through it. Nero then started to tremble in my arms and the scent of fear was clinging to her like a sickening veil.

"Nero, tell me what's wrong?" I asked in a stern way to get her to speak.

"It's him, oh Gods..." I frowned, looking back at my brother wondering what it was she thought she saw in him.

"That is my second in command, he rules my realm when I am absent. he is..." I started to explain more but she finished off my sentence for me with a word I prayed was wrong,

"A traitor!" she hissed as if close to spitting it on the floor.

"Why do you say this?!" I demanded, and she looked up at me with fearful eyes, ones that I knew were not lying to me when she explained,

"We both saw him there; he created a portal just like that. But then it can't be right, Fae had said...she told me she saw..."

"What, what did she tell you?!" I asked with more desperation now and Nero took a sneak glance back at the man who she believed had been there calling the shots. but she must have been wrong. There was no way he could have been that shadowy figure that I had barely seen in the Eye's visions. No, it couldn't be true!

Of course, no matter how many times I told myself this, the knowledge was obliterated the moment she turned back to me and said,

"Fae told me that the Eye had shown her who was responsible for all of this, the same man that had been there with the Harpy Queen...she recognised him, and she wasn't sure that you knew."

"Knew what, tell me Nero!?"

"Speak, lass," Vern said seeing how close now I was to the edge. She gripped onto me harder as if fearing that once she said it out loud I would toss her aside. But the only person in the whole room that I would take action against for such knowledge would be the person under scrutiny now.

Because of what she said next, there was no way possible she could have known other than that of the Eye showing Amelia the truth.

This was when she told me...

"...That he is your brother."

CHAPTER TWENTY-SEVEN

HOPE IN HAND

The second I heard this was when I knew I had to hand over the girl before I crushed her already battered body in my hold. Vern took her quickly, as if knowing I was too close to the edge to be handling his woman, because despite Nero's denials, I could see it in his face that was exactly who she was to him, his woman. Even if he hadn't claimed her to be so yet, to him she was already claimed in his heart.

As for my own heart, looking at my brother now and it felt like it was being ripped in two. I saw him frowning at me as if knowing that something wasn't right, but I couldn't let on. Not yet, anyway. So, I granted him a nod, silently telling him everything was fine just so he wouldn't escape by creating another portal. Then with clenched teeth I muttered to the shifter,

"Place Nero on the ground and pretend to assess her wounds, do it quickly." Vern didn't argue, he simply did as I asked knowing the importance of what I had just been told and my reaction to it. Vern now had his back to my brother and as he was leaning over Nero it meant that I was out of sight, thanks to Vern not being of slight frame.

"So, tis true then, he is yer brother," Vern said quietly and I nodded, for there was no reason to keep that information from him now. I looked down at Nero and told her,

"I need to access your memories, I have to be sure...do you understand?" Nero didn't argue this point, she simply accepted it and nodded her head telling me,

"Anything I can do to help you, I will do it." Vern looked surprised at this bold declaration, but thankfully it was another moment that he must have thought best to keep to himself, for he would no doubt be questioning Nero about this once this was all over. I looked over to him and said,

"Once I've accessed her memories and I have seen the proof of evidence against him, I will need your help and that of your brothers to take him down. You'll need to get word to Gryph the second I stand and walk over to my brother, for he will fight and try to create a portal, but we cannot let that happen."

"Aye, It wull be done," he said with a certainty that actually surprised me, then he went on to ask,

"Out o' curiosity how many kin he tak' thro' a portal?"

"Only himself and one other," I replied seeing where he was going with this, confirming as such soon after,

"Then it wull tak' all three o' us tae seize him at once," Vern said surprising me, and my look must have said it all because his reaction to this was to tell me,

"I'm a fucking bounty hunter 'n' ah dae this shite fur a living, trust me if thir's one thing ah dae well tis be catching folk...well, two things ah dae well..." At this he winked down at Nero making it obvious what the second thing was and she groaned before rolling her eyes, telling me

"When you're in my head, do me a favour and rid me of

the image Vern just painted so I may be able to sleep at night without having nightmares." Her comment would have been funny under any other circumstances.

"Och, ye wound me, lass," Vern said, with one hand over his heart. Like I said, I would have smiled at this but seeing how this conversation originated, then it was the furthest reaction from my mind. No, embedding a fist into my brother's face should he be the one who betrayed me, definitely took priority in my mind.

"You ready?" I asked, and then movement in the corner of my eye showed my brother's patience to know what was happening had run out and he started to walk towards us. Vern glanced over his shoulder at this and then started whispering something which at first seemed as if to himself. It was also something neither me nor Nero could understand. There was, however, one other person in the room that did...*his brother.*

Gryph, looked directly at him, nodded once in understanding, and quickly intercepted my brother. Then he started reeling off an extensive amount of information, questioning him on a number of things that he believed my brother may have been able to help him with. Thankfully, the distraction worked long enough for Nero to say,

"Let's be quick then." I nodded and put a hand to her forehead and we both closed our eyes at the same time. I went back to the moment that I needed, soon seeing it all start to play out. However, this time the figure standing on the broken castle walls was no longer blurred and void in a memory.

Although, admittedly, it also wasn't a face that I could see and this concerned me as it was far from evidence damning enough to condemn my brother.

However, after going back a little further I saw the evidence that I couldn't explain as being anyone but my brother, for he was the only one that I knew was capable of creating such portals so quickly. It was when he first appeared, as her visions were being played in reverse. he created a tear through the realm of Tartarus and slipped through as if it was as easy as breathing.

This then made me think back to the point that Amelia must have touched the Eye and gained the power she needed to obliterate the army surrounding her. It was at that moment I filled in the gaps and the voids in Nero's memory for she was currently at this point hanging down inside the well for her own safety.

The puzzle pieces I created showcased my brother creating a portal the moment Amelia's power was unleashed. I looked back at it now and I remembered that it was also the exact moment my brother had returned to my castle. This, of course, being only moments after the connection with Amelia touching the Eye had took hold of me.

This was damning indeed.

Added to this were the days of him disappearing just when those of us needed to speak with him. I also thought back on previous conversations. Like when he had declared he would be the one to find out more information about the witch instead of my general, who I had first issued with this task. Was it because he feared what Carn'reau may have found out?

I also thought back to when he had asked about the Eye and convinced me that it didn't need to be moved. Was this because he knew she would be drawn to it when she woke and that was all that was needed for him to have the Harpy Queen steal it away?

In fact, the only piece of the puzzle I didn't have was how she had been able to take both my Chosen One and Nero along with the Eye. However, the moment I released Nero, giving her back her mind she answered this lingering question that I must have subconsciously left planted there,

"It was the hex," she told me.

"What do you mean?" My frown said it all, or more like the all I didn't yet know.

"It wasn't the type of summoning hex we all thought it was, I'm just sorry that I realised it too late."

"Ur nae tae be blamed, lass," Vern said to comfort her, at the same time running the back of his fingers down her cheek.

"Tell me of the hex," I said, needing to know.

"The hex wasn't trying to summon Amelia to the witch, the hex was so that others could be summoned to her, wherever Amelia was." The moment she told me this, it was as if a light had been switched on in a dark room, spreading light on the parts I hadn't been able to make sense of.

Now I could see everything so clearly. Mainly how the Harpy had been able to get inside. She most likely had others, perhaps her sisters waiting nearby so they could transport both the girls and the Eye to Tartarus. This also meant that my brother was working with the witch, and in between had seemingly been collecting those he could use and manipulate.

It was all starting to make sense in an unforgiving way, I could barely believe that my own brother had done this to me. It would have been like finding Adam stood at my back after the knife had pierced through my heart from behind.

But then there was no other explanation, and right now I only had one option left, to imprison my brother, and interrogate him, extracting any information from him any way I could.

I gave the nod to Vern after releasing a pained sigh, knowing this wasn't going to be easy for both my brother or I.

Vern picked up Nero and carried her over to his brother for it would look too suspect had he had just left her on the floor.

He nodded toward Dariush in acknowledgement before carrying Nero over to the steps that led up to the level of my throne. He whispered something down to her that I couldn't hear but whatever it was, it made her blush. Then after this, he walked back to Gryph just as I was walking up to my brother,

"Where have you been?" I asked knowing this was the question he would be expecting first.

"I should be asking you that same question seeing as you flew out of here pretty quickly."

"I had a vision of where Amelia would be, granted to me by the Eye," I told him taking careful note of his reactions to this.

"And were you successful, for I see you retrieved the witch at least, although she does look to have seen better days?" he commented, and knowing what I knew now it was a struggle not to punch him.

"She will survive, but I need to speak with you, for there is much for us to discuss." Dariush actually had the audacity to sigh as though this was all very taxing, before running hands through his hair.

"Yes, well you charged me with finding information about this witch, that was never going to happen by having my ass sat on a throne or behind a desk," he said in his defence, and I had to say his act before today would have been quite convincing, but then I had to question just how many years he had been this convincing? For this wasn't something that had simply occurred in the last few weeks, months, or even years. No, a plan of this magnitude took decades at least, meaning that the brother I once knew who stood before me now had been nothing but a lie.

I was killing mad, beyond furious and I wanted to make him pay. But the conflicting feelings inside me were ones I wasn't used to, for it wasn't often that I had to fight against someone that I cared about or considered family. Thousands of years we had been brothers, fought wars together, battled realms of Hell to possess what we did now. But, fuck me, he was practically a King of this place for I was hardly fucking here! And I had been happy to let him rule in my place, what more did he fucking want?!

None of it made much sense, but then again, without knowing the reason from his own lips, then it never would.

I motioned the McBain brothers closer, letting my brother see openly so he wouldn't suspect anything more except believing what I had to say next concerned them also. However, the moment they approached close enough I asked my brother about the witch.

"And tell me, brother, what was it that you found out?" The moment I said this, and he heard me confessing his connection to me in front of others, he knew something was wrong. He knew he'd been discovered for his look of shock turned into a scowl. Then, before he could act, the brothers sprang into action, restraining him either side, at the same moment I took hold of his neck and squeezed. I held on tight in an unyielding grip as I choked him of air, having to force myself not to go too far and snap his neck.

"What is the meaning of this?" he wheezed out, and I got closer to his face, and snarled,

"The meaning of this is *treason.*"

A little time later I was in the dungeon wiping the blood off my knuckles and doing so with a crack that happened upon straightening my fingers. I had worked over my brother pretty good and with every single blow I inflicted, my soul darkened further. I had felt every hit delivered as if it had been to my own gut, as to know that my brother was a traitor it was like swallowing acid, one that churned inside of me and stayed there.

It was a pain I had once felt before, only not in this life but that of my first, for I would not speak his name, vowing never to do so once he passed. As for my brother, he was currently chained to the wall at eight different points of his body, and each chain was connected to different points in the room. This may have seemed overkill, but it was so he had no means of escape through a quickly created portal. He had fought all three of us to get him down here and in truth, this had been where he'd sustained most of his injuries. However, every time I inflicted more, each one had healed, meaning it became a vicious circle. For I only ended up splitting the skin once more. Fuck, but he was practically healed already, and I had only just finished punching him bloody, breaking his nose, jaw and cheek bone. But no matter how long I had been at it for, he still would not confess.

All I had wanted to do was leave to go and find my girl, but unfortunately, I also knew that without me here he would have had the power to manipulate others to let him free. Meaning I had no other choice than to play his jailor and leave the retrieval of my Chosen One in the hands of others. I had sent the McBain brothers to look for her, after first retrieving Trice to aid in their search.

It pained me to do this but having my brother escape, knowing that he was the one who had been pulling all the strings was far more dangerous.

"I want a confession out of you," I told him yet again.

"Then you'll be waiting a long time for it is not one I will ever give you."

"You won't give me the satisfaction of one then, is that it?"

"I won't give you the fucking lies of one…that is it!" he roared back in anger making me shake my head in frustration.

"Your future is already damned as the evidence against you is immeasurable," I informed him, and once more it felt as though I was just going over old ground and repeating myself.

"And all I can say is that you have been fooled, and most likely by the work of a witch for you're about to kill your own brother for nothing." I inwardly winced at the thought but hid it well, as I had been doing since I dragged his ass down here with the help of the brothers.

"I want that confession," I told him again, hating that every word out of his mouth was a lie or a way to try and twist the truth and get me to doubt my own actions.

"And like I said, you will never get it for I'm not speaking lies to alleviate your guilt when it comes to delivering my death." I closed my eyes and released a sigh as I faced the bars away from him for the sight of him pained me.

"Then your death is all I have left to offer you," I told him.

"That is not true for there is something else that you could offer me." I frowned in question and turned a little to ask over my shoulder,

"And what is that exactly?"

"Other than your benefit of the doubt." I snarled back at him as was my answer to that.

"I wish you to grant me until the morning." Now that was a strange request.

"Why? Tell me why I shouldn't just kill you now and

alleviate my own suffering at knowing that my brother who betrayed me is dead!" I snapped the question.

"Then if that is how you feel, you may class it as my last and only dying wish, for I wish to see out one more night, for if new evidence hasn't come to light by then, then I doubt it ever will and you can kill me knowing you had little choice." His words troubled me, for I didn't know if they were a trick or he actually thought with time his innocence could be proven. I fucking hated being put in this position. I hated knowing that I was to be judge, jury, and executioner against my brother. For I would have no one else take his life but that of my own hand.

I released another sigh, one this time I didn't try to hide letting him know how heavily this lay on my mind, and just before he was about to speak I held up a hand to stop him. I turned my back on him, walked to the cell door, and told him,

"You will have your night, and if there is any evidence of which you speak, I will spend the night having all at my disposal searching for it, because you are my brother and it is worth every minute spent to me trying to prove your innocence." He closed his eyes at this and was about to thank me when I stopped him,

"However, if I do not find anything, then you will not see another day past this one, on this brother...you have my word."

"In that case, I have nothing left to offer but my hope that you find something." I looked back at him over my shoulder and said as my parting words,

"You are not the only one with that same hope...

"Brother of my Blood."

CHAPTER TWENTY-EIGHT

AMELIA

MIGHTY LITTLE GREEN THINGS

The moment I realised that the man stood in front of me was none other than Trice, my reaction had been instantaneous. I had literally thrown myself at his back and hugged him as hard as I could. I then hummed,

"Thank the Gods!" Doing so as I don't think I had ever felt so relieved in all my life. His head turned and he looked down at me over his big shoulder before saying,

"Do ye mind, lass, only a'm trying tae look lik' a bad ass here 'n' that's kinda hard wi' ye clinging tae mah back lik' a dirty wee monkey." I winced at this and then as I let go I patted him on the bicep and said,

"Oh, right…yes, okay…I uh…see your point, I will just let you do your thing…go get 'em Tiger…" As soon as this new brand of stupid came out of my mouth he raised a brow, lifting his scar and the mirth in his silent question could easily be seen.

"Erm...scrap that, I don't actually know why I said that." On hearing this obviously embarrassing back tracking of mine, his bad boy smirk lightened up his hard features and he winked at me.

Then he put a hand to my belly and pushed me back into the corner. After this he took care of business, which in other words meant drawing out his long sword and engulfing it in blue sparks that displayed the threat of a dangerous power. This acted like a warning light for anyone who wanted to come near me, and it took only seconds for everyone to go back about their business. Schlong demon and his jealous lover included.

The gatekeeper threatened him to keep me out of trouble although I couldn't help but notice he did this while backing out of the door. I guess he wasn't stupid after all. Then, once the threat was all over, Trice turned back to me and just as I opened my mouth to say thank you, I suddenly found my torso being flipped upside down over his shoulder. Naturally, I screamed out in shock making a few of the customers chuckle.

"Yep, he's claiming his bounty alright, claiming it to grind his cock!" One of them said, making Trice pause his steps and with the sword still in his hand, without looking he extended it out to the side, meaning that the demon who had made the comment was now facing the tip of his blade a centimetre off the end of his nose. He swallowed the hard lump that had formed at the sight of this and held up his hands in surrender.

Trice hadn't needed to say anything in response to this, he merely lowered his blade, putting it back in its sheath and continued on towards the back of the pub. his arm remaining hooked over my waist keeping me to his shoulder, doing so as if he was carrying a tree trunk through the forest and back to his woodcutter's cottage.

"You could probably get away with putting me down right about now," I told him, and I felt his chuckle at my belly before he told me,

"Now why would ah dae that, as it seems tae me that whenever ye'r on yer feet ye git yourself into trouble 'n' lost in Hell," he said full of humour. Well, I'm glad one of us was finding all this funny! It was of little wonder why my reaction to this was me making a simple, but I like to think effective, 'humph' sound.

I watched as he made his way to a wooden staircase that was on the far wall past the bar, and was one that I gathered led to the rooms that for a coin you could stay in for the night. I watched him take the steps three at a time thanks to his long legs and his impressive strength, for it seemed as if he wasn't even carrying anything at all.

"Shit me bit ye stink, whit ye bin doaein' playing in th' mud 'n' then huv a go 'n' wash yersel' aff in th' shitter?" he said as soon as he put me down, after first kicking open a door to what I presumed had been his room. I also had to say as far as compliments went this wasn't my finest moment. However, I pushed back my mud-soaked hair and looked up at him with my hands on my hips,

"Now listen here you! I only caught half of that Scottishness but the parts I did get I didn't like!"

"Aye, a second ago ah was her hero 'n' noo ah be th' villain," he muttered to himself, still looking amused I hasten to add. I chose to ignore this and said,

"Do you have any idea what I've been through in the last twenty-four hours?"

"Well, seeing as ye covered in shite 'n' reek lik' a demon's ass, ah would say whatvur 'twas, it was ney pretty." After hearing this and after deciphering it, I closed my eyes, held the bridge of my nose and counted to ten just so I wouldn't knee my saviour in the balls.

After this I said the first thing that needed to be said...

"Please tell me there's a bath in here."

A short time later I found myself in a small slice of Heaven in the form of water encasing my skin. Of course, with this little slice of Heaven first came a bit of the Hell that I was most definitely getting used to. Meaning that before this point of the night first came the weird. Something that started when Trice picked me up by my waist and strangely, walked me over to a bucket, and stood me in it.

Then, when I started to complain and asked him what he was doing, he told me not to move. Of course, I didn't feel as though I had much right to complain, not considering I was safe and out of the rain. But I had to confess the moment I finally got my muddy butt inside a warm space then standing inside an empty bucket was not what I had in mind.

I was also concerned about the actual use for this empty bucket seeing as it was behind a wicker screen that looked to have seen better days. Which quickly told me that whatever was done behind here and in this bucket, it was most likely something the people would like to keep private.

But then I had looked down at my dirty feet and my ruined flat shoes and after that took note that every inch of me was covered in mud. I quickly made the decision not to give a shit if I was in fact standing in a bucket that people usually took a crap in, even if it was from a demon and trust me, those were some big buggers downstairs!

Yes...I was that dirty.

All I cared about was the fact that it was empty, and Trice clearly had a plan. A plan I soon discovered the moment I heard someone enter the room and of course, I couldn't help but sneak a look. A small being covered in a cloak walked over to an empty copper bath and after Trice spoke to him in a different language, one I couldn't understand, and this time not just due to his accent, the hooded being started dancing his fingertips over the bucket. I watched in amazement as it filled to the brim doing so solely by magic.

Then, after the bucket was full, he moved on to doing the same to the bath and I could feel myself getting giddy at the thought. But as my attention was still on the bath, I screamed in shock the second water was poured over my head. half of which filled up the bucket I was standing in, the rest however simply went everywhere, flooding the floor. I looked up to see Trice holding the empty bucket over the screen with a grin, I then stomped out of the bucket, rounded the screen, and whilst shaking a finger at him asked him what he was playing at.

He nodded down at me with a smirk and a mischievous glint in his eye, when he told me

"I didnae think ye wid be wanting a shite bath." Then when his gaze lingered elsewhere, I, too, was forced to look down at myself to see that he was right, most of the mud had come off meaning that I wouldn't be sat in my own filth when taking a bath. However, this wasn't the only thing I noticed, and so did Trice. As thanks to the colder air hitting me, and wearing a once white material with no bra, I now looked as though I was entering a really crappy wet T-shirt contest. One you would have found in some Hick town when nobody gave a shit what they were wearing, as long as it was white for the sole purpose of becoming see through. I looked like I had a couple of pencil erasers stuffed down my top, for Gods' sake!

Naturally, my reaction was to cross my arms over my chest and storm back behind the screen with a huff. His deep manly and throaty chuckle was as annoying as it was sexy…damn him!

A short time later and I was in that Heaven I spoke of, finding myself in the bath, relaxing back after scrubbing my skin and my hair clean. In fact, I had nearly wept with joy when Trice had handed me a simple bar of soap. After this he had left, surprisingly like a gentleman after first moving the screen so it covered me in the bath. I didn't need to question why he did this considering if anyone had just walked in the room, then seeing me starkers and ringing wet would have been the first sight to greet them.

However, the moment I heard the door open, I had called out asking who it was.

"Tis bit I, lass." As soon as Trice answered me, I relaxed back against the edge of the tub knowing that he couldn't see me. But then the second I smelled it, my hands gripped the sides of the bath and I bolted upright, making water spill over the sides and splash onto the floor.

"Oh, my Gods. If you tell me that is food I can smell, I will think you're an Angel on the wrong side of the tracks, I told him making him laugh before shouting,

"Heads up." This was before I saw a bread roll being thrown over the top of the screen, making me catch it quickly before it could drop into the tub and become nothing but a mound of soggy bread in my hands. I couldn't help but moan around the first bite, feeling as though it was the best thing I'd ever tasted, I was that hungry.

"You sound like a wild hungry bear," Trice commented, clearly amused and I answered him unashamedly, and with my mouth full I told him,

"I feel like one." It was after this that I ended up having

the strangest conversation, not only because of all the things I had to tell him when explaining to him exactly what had happened, but also because I was sat in the bath and there was nothing but a screen in between us.

Thankfully, this conversation took so much effort and explanation, that it didn't give us time to address the elephant in the room, that, of course, being me, and why I had kept the knowledge of who Lucius really was to me from him. Because this was the first time I had spoken to Trice since that day. The one shortly after I had been imprisoned in the dungeon. Since then it had been one thing after another that had kept me from being able to speak to him and explain. Which I had to question why neither of us was taking the opportunity to do so now. Especially when we were alone and quite possibly would not get another moment like this to present itself.

But then I had to confess to be following Trice's lead, as he too didn't seem to want to talk about it and knowing him, he would have simply asked if he had. In fact, the only time that we touched on this subject was when he explained to me what he was doing here. That after what happened in the field of souls, as he had called it, the King had charged him and his brothers with the task of finding anyone that had the ability to remove a hex. A person that apparently he was supposed to find here, as it was said this was his usual place to meet a particular female demon with whom he was having an affair with.

My last question I asked him before getting out of the bath was how this person was supposed to help in removing this hex, to which Trice's cryptic reply was a simple,

"Ye wull see."

A short time after this I found myself clean, fed, and well rested after Trice had suggested I get some sleep before the demon arrived. I thought this was a great idea on account of me being exhausted, but before my nap I had asked him where his brothers were if they had all been tasked with the same job of finding this hex removal guy.

It turned out that only a few hours before I turned up, word had reached the brothers that Lucius needed them back to help him find me. Of course, hearing this and I inwardly winced at this painful image of what Lucius had been through in the time that I had been taken. I had to wonder if he would have found us by now, and more importantly if he had found Nero?

Telling Trice about Nero had been one of the first things I had said, even before I found myself being unceremoniously showered in a bucket. Naturally, I then tried to get him to go and save her. Trice was clearly frustrated and worried for Nero's life, as I was, and I could see it pained him to have to tell me that he couldn't do this. Before I could argue he held up a hand and explained to me why.

He told me that where I had come from, he did not have access to. I asked about the boat, thinking that he could simply take it back to where it had brought me from. But the moment he started to shake his head I knew that this was obviously not possible. He explained that this type of boat could only be called from the other side unless you had the right coin to bargain with, which he did not.

I couldn't help but wipe the frustrated tears from under my eyes, turning away from him so he wouldn't feel guilty for being the one to tell me this. This meant that my last hope lay solely with Lucius not only finding her but getting to her in time.

After all this on my mind I had been surprised that I had been able to sleep at all. But then again, exhaustion won over worry. I woke up to the feeling of having my hair pushed back from my face and I opened my eyes to find Trice looking down at me.

"Time tae be getin' up now, lass," he told me softly, before his gaze dropped ever so slightly to my naked shoulders. I had got out of the bath and slipped under the covers on the bed, having no choice but to do so naked, as I didn't have any other clothes to put on. Seeing this and making me feel self-conscious, my natural instinct kicked in and I folded my arms over the covers making him smirk. Then I told him,

"That's going to be a little hard considering I'm naked."

"Och, ah will ney be sure about th' wee part, but as fur clothes 'ere I got ye some." After this Trice got up after leaving a bundle on the bed so I could get dressed, but then my mind went over what he had just said, only making sense of it by the time he reached the door,

"Oi!" I shouted knowing he'd referred to his manhood as not being little but hard. Hence why his chuckle could be heard even after he closed the door. I got up and unravelled the medieval style dress that reached down to the floor and cut across my collar bone. It also had long sleeves that hung down well past the wrists and was a plain rust coloured red. But it was clean and warm and soft to my skin, meaning that I couldn't have been more thankful.

This was something I was soon on my way to tell him as I slipped out of the room, knowing I would meet him in the pub below. I had also plaited my hair and used a small strip of my already ruined outfit to tie off the end. Little flat shoes were of the type you strapped to your ankle and around your foot, meaning you could make them fit your size. I also looked as if I'd just stepped out of some movie about medieval England.

Once downstairs, I cautiously made my way to the bar

area soon finding myself in the arms of Trice who suddenly had my back against the wall. He was also caging in my entire frame in what looked like an intimate embrace. He had a hand positioned next to my head and was leaning down into me making me believe he was about to kiss me. I placed my hand on his chest ready to stop him when he whispered,

"Thee Hexion demon is over mah shoulder currently feeling up th' drooling redhead wi' tusks." As soon as he said this, I couldn't help but sneak a glance to the side so I could see for myself. And he was right, there was a woman with an orange tone to her skin, had long red hair flowing past a very large backside. She was on the larger side and it was clearly working for her, as the demon with his hands all over her clearly couldn't get enough. I also had to say that for a demon his vessel was incredibly handsome! What with all those bulging muscles that look chiselled from stone combined with his devilishly handsome face, Gods, but he was a thing of beauty. He almost reminded me of Gaston from Beauty and the Beast. In fact, he almost didn't look real.

"Wow, I have to say that is not who I was expecting. I mean just look at the guy with all those..." It was at this point that Trice cut me off, and he did this by taking hold of my cheeks and steering my head in the right direction. I then saw hidden under the stairs was a small creature with green skin. In fact, I could barely believe what I was seeing as he looked remarkably like you would imagine a goblin to look like. He was also making the same exact movements that the handsome and musclebound demon was making when feeling up the woman.

That's when it dawned on me,

"Oh, you have got to be kidding me," I said once Trice had let go of my cheeks. He grinned down at me and said,

"Nae everyone kin be as handsome as me, lass." I rolled

my eyes making him chuckle and went back to looking at the goblin who, despite this despicable act of deceit, seemed to have the incredible ability to create any illusion of himself that he was able to project like a real being.

"We have tae be careful we dinnae spook him, as they're nae normally easy tae catch," Trice informed me, as I watched when a waitress went past him catching his attention and making him for the moment lose concentration. This made his projection drop its hold and become like a vacant ghost, making the woman slap his arm in outrage because he had stopped showering her with his attention.

This gave me an idea, seeing as the little green guy obviously had a weakness. So, I winked up at Trice and told him,

"Maybe I can help with that but first, you have to buy me a drink, handsome." He gave me a questioning look in return that made me chuckle.

After this I told him my plan and let him buy two pints of something called soul water mead. Then I muttered six words I never thought I would ever hear coming from my mouth as I played a waitress, walking up to him…

"Time to bag me a goblin."

CHAPTER TWENTY-NINE

MURDEROUS MISTAKES

"Well hey, aren't you a cute thang," I said wondering why the hell I had decided to put on a southern belle accent!? For starters, I didn't need to disguise my voice and why I picked the voice I did, I had no idea. Either way my plan worked as the goblin saw me and started to look very excited that I had shown interest in him.

He wagged his over pronounced eyebrows at me, ones that were so hairy they looked like he had to comb them. His nose was big, his chin was over pronounced like his eyebrows, and his ears were the size of side plates. They were also full of hair that looked as though he had twisted it around in his fingers from habit.

His beady yellow eyes scanned the length of my body and it made him look like a little menace or sex pest. He was also wearing a little dark green suit with a blue shirt, green bowtie, and to complete the look, he wore a wrinkled top hat that looked as though it had accidentally been sat on by bigger demons quite a few times.

The sound of a slap coming from behind me and the cry of a woman's outrage made me turn to see the redhead was trying to knock some sense into her now vacant partner, who suddenly looked about as interested in her as someone does when staring at a painted wall waiting for it to dry. Needless to say, she didn't take too kindly to this, which was when the ghost of her partner simply turned around and walked out of the door.

I turned quickly to see what the goblin was doing, to catch his fingers making a walking motion through the air, telling me this was how this puppeteer had made him disappear. The female demon stomped her foot in outrage and the weight of such made a few tankard's spill to the floor on the table next to her. However, by the time she made her way across the pub to the bar she already had three of the demons show their interest, so I didn't feel too badly for her.

"So, you think I'm cute, do you?" the goblin said, turning my attention back to him and I was surprised to find he had a sort of cockney accent.

"That depends, handsome," I said in a strange way because halfway through I forgot the accent I had started this off with. He raised bushy eyebrow which in turn raised the rim of his hat that had been resting on them.

"On what exactly, how much coin I have?" he said, insinuating that I was a prostitute and to be honest I couldn't be surprised considering I'd stopped and chosen to speak to him over all the others. I mean yes, granted I was in a pub filled with demons but there was definitely better choice than this little green pervert.

Suddenly Trice, who had been slowly sneaking up behind him, placed a meaty hand on his shoulder and squeezed, answering his question for me,

"No, oan how much ye enjoy pain." This ended with a

squeal from the little goblin man when Trice picked him up by the hold on his shoulder, plucking him off the floor. The next thing he knew he was being tossed into the room Trice had paid for. He quickly picked himself up off the floor, straightened his suit jacket, pulled down on his cuffs and then straightened his little hat.

"Hey, if you wanted a threesome all you needed to do was say," he said waggling those eyebrows at me, making me look to Trice and say,

"This one is all yours."

"Aye," was his stern reply, folding his large arms across his chest and looking menacing. I also knew that he was putting on a show for the goblin.

"Okay, no threesome, but just so you know I'm not into dudes," he said, looking Trice up and down and then finishing,

"But I can...should we say...pretend." Then he winked at him.

"Euwww," I said scrunching up my face, knowing that he meant he was going to bring back his projection hunk man if this was what Trice wanted. That would have been like getting it on with a sex doll and having some creepy little guy in the room controlling it.

"Don't knock it till you try it, chickie," he replied with a toothy grin.

"You kin remove a hex," Trice said getting straight to the point and at this, the goblin looked to have paled. Of course it was hard to look sick when you were already green but he managed to pull it off.

"I don't know what you're talking about, nope you most definitely got the wrong He uhhh, demon with no name there."

"Wow, that was original," I commented dryly making him give me a dirty look.

"Yer a Hexion demon, ah ken fur ah hae bin tracking ye fur days," Trice said, making the little guy shake his head before looking at me and asking,

"What did he sa…?" I opened my mouth to answer only to close it again before looking up to Trice and asking,

"What did you say?" At this Trice growled which I didn't take as a good sign for our little green friend here. I knew this when he stomped towards him making the goblin back up quickly, bumping into the few bits of furniture that were dotted around the plain room.

"Okay, okay, so yes I'm that guy." It was only on hearing this that Trice stop stalking towards him.

"Good, then you're exactly the guy that we need," I said, making him ask,

"It will cost you, I don't do this shit for free you know!" He once again tugged down on his little jacket.

"But we don't have any…" Trice cut me off and said,

"We hae enough coin." Making me whisper,

"We do?" His answer to this was to untie a small leather bag that hung from inside his jacket and throw it on the floor by the little demon's feet. This made gold coins spill from it and scatter along the wooden slats. The goblin (who I really needed to start calling by his real name) frantically picked them up before any could get lost down the cracks. Once he was assured he'd got it all he threw his little bag up and caught it before lifting up his hat and placing it on the top of his head. This awarded us the sight of his bald head, except for the hair that brushed the top of his ears.

"Alright, so let's do this and no names are given, that's my rule, take it or…okay, okay…so come on then who's the unlucky bugger that's got himself a hex?" the demon said, after changing his tune when Trice was once again threatening. I released a sigh, knowing it was best to get this over with, making me say,

"That would be me."

A short time later, I found myself on the bed once more with the back of my dress unlaced. I didn't think it was a good sign when the little demon sucked air through his teeth when seeing it. Or the fact that Trice had taken hold of my wrists and held me down.

"No touching anythin' bit whit ye hae tae...got it?!" Trice threatened, making the little demon hold up his hands and say,

"Hey, I'm working here," as if this was a great insult. I turned my head to the side and watched as the little goblin started to remove his clothes, making me shoot Trice a worried look.

"Tell me we didn't pay him for anything extra?" I said making Trice smirk down at me before asking me to trust him.

"I do trust you, it's the hex removal guy over there I don't trust."

"Hex removal guy, I like it...you know I might get cards made."

"Really?" I asked falling for it.

"No sugar tits, what's this look like to you..."

"Wow, you're cranky...hey, did you just call me sugar tits?" Trice's growl made him glance his beady yellow eyes at Trice and say to me,

"I wanna say yes but the big guy here looks as though I will lose an appendage if I say that."

"Then don't say it and just get back to work," I advised him just as he was removing his shirt, and the sight I saw was one that now had me sucking air between my teeth. He was completely covered in hexes.

"Holy shit."

"You like?" he asked motioning down his half naked body as he was wearing nothing but little briefs, showing me that even his skinny legs were covered.

"It's cheaper than tattoos, and these ones I get paid for," he said proudly and then looked at mine and admitted,

"But this one here will be a doozy. In fact, I might make room for this one on my chest and make it my biggest one yet," he said as if getting excited about the idea. Well, he could have it on his bloody ass for all I cared as long it was off me!

"I hope you've got good hold of her as I have a feeling she's going to be a fighter."

"Erm…what now?" At this Trice's response was a strained,

"Aye," before he nodded for the goblin to do his work, giving me a piece of advice and a warning all in one,

"Be brave, lass."

After this the goblin started to touch me and that was when I knew all experiences in Hell before this one had been a piece of cake.

For this was...

true torture.

"Tis a'richt noo, lassie, ah hae you…i hae ye." The sound of Trice's voice was what woke me from my unconscious state, for I had soon passed out due to the overwhelming amount of pain that I could no longer take. I came to with my back frozen, feeling as if it had been covered under a veil of ice and I was wrapped up in Trice's arms. He was cradling my head to his chest, and I could feel his shirt was wet from all the tears I had cried.

Thankfully, I no longer felt the pain and I think this was down to what Trice had done, for as soon as the hex had been removed he had started breathing on my back. The goblin was still in the room and currently stood swinging his little bony green hips in front of a cracked mirror, admiring his new addition.

Like he said, it was in the middle of his chest and the biggest one of all, and what had looked painful for me looked barely even a cat scratch for him.

However, it was in this moment that the other two McBain brothers suddenly burst through the door, and they were awarded with the sight of me in the arms of their brother with my dress still untied and a half naked goblin dancing in front of the mirror. Their looks said it all, for surely even in Hell this would have been a strange sight to find.

"Brothers?!" Trice said in surprise to see them, but like I said it was nowhere near as surprised as they looked.

"Whit in a' th' Gods names hae ye bin daein'!?" Gryph asked, making me look up at Trice and say,

"I gather you know what that meant?"

"Aye."

"Whit th' fck does it look lik' we hae bin doin', havin ourselves a fckin pairtie?" Trice said, making Vern glance back at the dancing goblin who didn't seem to notice this was going on and say,

"Aye, it kinda does."

"He juist lifted th' damn Hex, yer ninny!" Trice told them and as if to add strength to this claim, this was when the goblin decided to jump to face them and shake his little body at them, whilst dancing his hands up and down his torso in some sort of proud display. The brothers' faces were a picture, making Gryph rub the back of his neck in an awkward way and Vern raise a brow before telling him,

"Aye, very bonnie that." The goblin looked to Gryph and he agreed in a gruff tone,

"Aye, bonnie."

I had to say the whole scene made me giggle and I was just as surprised at hearing it coming from myself after the horrific ordeal I had just been through. Shortly after this our little goblin friend excused himself after first getting dressed and tipping his squashed hat our way before whistling his way out of the door.

I also finished lacing my dress up and I had to say now the Hex was removed I was feeling so much better. I ran over to Gryph and Vern giving them each a hug telling them how glad I was to see them. But then I found my hands framing Vern's handsome face and having no choice but to tell him about what had happened to Nero.

"I'm so sorry to tell you, but Nero...she...well she..." Suddenly Vern was grinning at me and I soon found out why when he told me,

"Nero is fine lass, she wis found 'n' tis back at th' King's castle." The second I heard this I collapsed in his arms and started sobbing into his chest as the emotions hit me all at once. I couldn't believe it, as much as I had hoped for that very thing! Nero, my friend was safe. She was alive!

"But wait, that means if she was found that Lucius came for us…and if you're here now…wait, why are you guys here? Of course, not that I'm not happy to see you but why didn't Lucius come, why didn't…?" Gryph looked to Vern and then back at me before telling me,

"He had tae deal wi' his brother." I sucked in a startled breath and practically screeched,

"He knows he's got a brother and he found him?!"

"Well, he wasn't exactly hard tae fin', lass," Gryph said making me frown, as suddenly with that comment, something didn't seem right here.

"Why wasn't he hard to find?" I asked, but it was Vern who answered me this time,

"Nae whin tis Nero who told him whit ye said 'n' his brother turned oot tae be his second in command," Vern said with a grin as if we had caught the bad guy, whereas I stumbled back a few steps in utter shock. My hands flew to my mouth and I felt the colour drain from my face.

"Lass?"

"Whit be wrong?" Vern and Gryph both asked as well as prompting Trice to come up behind me and take hold of the tops of my arms before turning me around to face him.

"Amelia?"

"What does Lucius plan to do to him?" I asked instead of answering them.

"Whit th' treacherous bastard deserves, he wull be dead by mornin,'" Vern told me making me suck in a horrified breath.

"Amelia, speak tae me," Trice tried again, when I told him,

"Nero, she has made a mistake…"

"Bit she…" I quickly interrupted Vern.

"She said only what I told her…that Lucius had a brother who was his enemy, one he didn't know about…Oh Gods, we have to go, we have to stop it before it's too late!" I shouted in desperation running to the door and only stopping when Trice held me back.

"Amelia, stop…"

"No! I have seen his brother's face, Trice, and his brother isn't…"

"He isn't…?"

This was when I told them the grave mistake that had been made.

"It wasn't his second in command and that means he is about to kill his own brother…one who isn't…"

"A traitor."

CHAPTER THIRTY

MATTHIAS

ROOTS OF RAGE

The moment I materialised through the portal I took in the smell of another puppet, three of them actually if you could call them that. Oh, my brother Lucius had worked them over good, but then again, he always had a way when extracting information. Thankfully, I had an even better way at keeping it from him.

After all, I had been doing it since his rebirth.

The Keepers of Three limped their way out from the cave in which they hid, no doubt nursing their wounds that were still yet to heal. Of course, they would do that until my presence returned, and this was the first time since our foolish lovers had stepped into Hell.

"Master, we did as you asked."

"We completed our task."

"Mmknd…"

"Ah, ah, you know how I loath to hear from that one," I

said, preventing the murmured ramblings from a head that should have been severed years ago. However, it was told that one couldn't live without the other and I had needed to keep them around for this very purpose, for all my plans were finally coming to fruition.

However, I had been surprised for there had been one aspect of my plan that I have not been expecting. This being the power of the Eye that had decided to choose Lucius' little bitch over me.

In the end this would be nothing more than a mere inconvenience, for I would find a way to simply make another puppet out of the girl. I would get to her somehow. Oh, I doubted that I could rely on getting another use out the Hex before it was removed. I also doubted to have another opportunity for Dalene to cast another upon her flesh. For no doubt one of Lucius' shifter dogs had found some way of removing it, meaning that the girl would be protected from another Hex.

This, however, was of little bother, for I would just have my own witch come up with a new way. She was vicious and cunning and more powerful than any other witch alive. And for the most part completely loyal and easy to control. Well, that was if the other side of her behaved as she was supposed to. But admittedly it was every now and again I had to put her back in her place just as I had with these three cretins, stains upon the Earth and yet another failure of my father's.

They were pitiful to look at and a mere drain upon our bloodline. But then there was no greater insult than there was in being forced to endure sharing my blood with the likes of that vampire. My father's greatest accomplishment, it was fucking laughable! Precisely something I would do when they were all burning at my feet, for the entire vampire race I would see crumble, exploding in ash where they all fucking belonged!

Despite this hatred, I still told them what they wanted to hear, for their use might still serve me yet.

"You did well, my brothers, for you accomplished your task…now get out of my sight!" I said, making them sink back into their hole. Then I walked across the space of the Temple cracking the stone floor and making the infection in the roots respond to their true Master.

Hatred and rage.

Yet, despite the power of the Tree of Souls not yet fully belonging to me, this Temple, I had made my home and the veil that I had placed at the end of the tunnel evaporated the moment I walked through it. I'd had Dalene cast it for me, so that when finally getting Lucius and his Chosen One down here, I had a way to prevent him from stopping her going into Hell. It was also why I had the Keepers of Three show her exactly what she needed to see to make her believe in this heroic attempt at trying to save the Tree of Souls. Everything had been orchestrated to get these two back into Hell and into my realm, where the wheels of my plan could finally start turning faster.

I felt the presence of my witch the moment she appeared. She had most definitely been playing her part very well, even going so far as to take control of her own little vampire army, making them into nothing more than zombies. She assured me that she could do what needed to be done to get Lucius and the mortal girl down into Hell. This meant going as far as planting the box for her father to find, and also the map inside, all of which were connected with the same blood that ran through my veins. The same that ran through that of our father's.

It was how she had managed it, using my blood as the anchor.

Every single action the witch had made had been to lead her to this point, for she was the true key and puppet I needed in manipulating my brother, and the best part was that she didn't even know it. But yet I still needed that Eye of Crimson for my plan to end the way I intended it to, for that was where the true power lay.

I had to admit that manipulating our other brother into becoming my personal portal master had been fun and now knowing that he was the one that was to be blamed for my actions was another death that I could cross off my list. Oh, how I couldn't wait to see the look on my brother's face when he discovered that he had killed someone so loyal to him for all these years. it was a bonus that I hadn't even thought of until this day.

Now if I just had that Eye I'd be congratulating myself a lot more. However, the second her power had erupted, then I had to confess it wasn't often I was shocked and admittedly a little impressed. Perhaps there was another use for her other than just sacrificing her life for my gain.

Perhaps I would make her my Queen. Now this was a notion indeed, for it was temping, stealing her away from my brother and forcing him to watch as I took everything from him, including his powerful little bitch. A woman, admittedly, I was starting to like more than I should, for she wasn't anything I expected her to be. I'd had her watched for years, knowing who she was to Lucius almost at the same point that he did, for I was the one who orchestrated her kidnapping the first day he saved her.

The mortal life she lived repulsed me and I believed her nothing more than a fly trapped in my web, but then when I saw her today something snapped inside of me. Something was awakened. It was true my nature was drawn to powerful beings, collecting them for my gain. But this was something else entirely. Fuck! But I think I was still hard just thinking about her! Of course, this was an unfortunate moment, Dalene walked closer after using the portal I had Dariush unknowingly make.

I wondered if he was currently begging for his life in some shithole cell somewhere beneath my brother's castle....a castle that should have been mine. Fuck, how I hated my brother!

I hated him with a passion like no other, the roots of my rage were connected to Tartarus, just as that fucking hand of his was. But the Venom of God was yet another immense power granted to the wrong fucking person.

I would make him pay.

I would make them all fucking pay, and Amelia made for a nice sight in my mind of her on her knees before me.

"My Lord Master." Dalene's voice echoed in the space I had made my home lifting its veil and revealing the underground palace fit for the real King of Hell.

"My dear, I trust everything went well?" I asked, recalling the next stage in our planning.

"But of course, however, I fear the Hex will soon be severed as the shifter found the Hexion demon we too had been looking for." I waved my hand, telling her,

"It is of little matter, for I know a better way to reach the girl and after all, we have manipulated her every step up until now, we will merely continue to do so."

"Yes, my Lord Master." I took a look at my witch, one who had been with me for very long time and like most of my minions, it was through their own roots of rage and the promise of revenge that led them to me. However, I believed Dalene's was the strongest need for vengeance, and almost as great as my own considering the connexion she had to Lucius or should I say...

Judas.

I held out my hand for her to place hers in mine and I walked her to the seat, one lower than my own throne, once there I asked her,

"Two thousand years is a long time to seek revenge and it's been so close on the horizon, tell me, my dear..." She leaned in as I whispered like a lover's deadly kiss,

"Are you ready to kill Lucius...*are you ready to kill*...

"Your Husband?"

To Be Continued...

ABOUT THE AUTHOR

Stephanie Hudson has dreamed of being a writer ever since her obsession with reading books at an early age. What first became a quest to overcome the boundaries set against her in the form of dyslexia has turned into a life's dream. She first started writing in the form of poetry and soon found a taste for horror and romance. Afterlife is her first book in the series of twelve, with the story of Keira and Draven becoming ever more complicated in a world that sets them miles apart.

When not writing, Stephanie enjoys spending time with her loving family and friends, chatting for hours with her biggest fan, her sister Cathy who is utterly obsessed with one gorgeous Dominic Draven. And of course, spending as much time with her supportive partner and personal muse, Blake who is there for her no matter what.

Author's words.

My love and devotion is to all my wonderful fans that keep me going into the wee hours of the night but foremost to my wonderful daughter Ava...who yes, is named after a cool, kick-ass, Demonic bird and my sons, Jack, who is a little hero and Baby Halen, who yes, keeps me up at night but it's okay because he is named after a Guitar legend!

Keep updated with all new release news & more on my website
www.afterlifesaga.com
Never miss out, sign up to the
mailing list at the website.

Also, please feel free to join myself and other Dravenites on my Facebook group
Afterlife Saga Official Fan
Interact with me and other fans. Can't wait to see you there!

- facebook.com/AfterlifeSaga
- twitter.com/afterlifesaga
- instagram.com/theafterlifesaga

Acknowledgements

Well first and foremost my love goes out to all the people who deserve the most thanks and are the wonderful people that keep me going day to day. But most importantly they are the ones that allow me to continue living out my dreams and keep writing my stories for the world to hopefully enjoy… These people are of course YOU! Words will never be able to express the full amount of love I have for you guys. Your support is never ending. Your trust in me and the story is never failing. But more than that, your love for me and all who you consider your 'Afterlife family' is to be commended, treasured and admired. Thank you just doesn't seem enough, so one day I hope to meet you all and buy you all a drink! ;)

To my family… To my amazing mother, who has believed in me from the very beginning and doesn't believe that something great should be hidden from the world. I would like to thank you for all the hard work you put into my books and the endless hours spent caring about my words and making sure it is the best it can be for everyone to enjoy. You make Afterlife shine. To my wonderful crazy father who is and always has been my hero in life. Your strength astonishes me, even to this day and the love and care you hold for your family is a gift you give to the Hudson name. And last but not least, to the man that I consider my soul mate. The man who taught me about real love and makes me not only want to be a better person but makes me feel I am too. The amount of support you have given me since we met has been incredible and the greatest feeling was finding out you wanted to spend the rest of your life with me when you asked me to marry you.

All my love to my dear husband and my own personal Draven... Mr Blake Hudson.

Another personal thank you goes to my dear friend Caroline Fairbairn and her wonderful family that have embraced my brand of crazy into their lives and given it a hug when most needed.

For their friendship I will forever be eternally grateful.

I would also like to mention Claire Boyle my wonderful PA, who without a doubt, keeps me sane and constantly smiling through all the chaos which is my life ;) And a loving mention goes to Lisa Jane for always giving me a giggle and scaring me to death with all her count down pictures lol ;)

Thank you for all your hard work and devotion to the saga and myself. And always going that extra mile, pushing Afterlife into the spotlight you think it deserves. Basically helping me achieve my secret goal of world domination one day...evil laugh time... Mwahaha! Joking of course ;)

As before, a big shout has to go to all my wonderful fans who make it their mission to spread the Afterlife word and always go the extra mile. I love you all x

ALSO BY STEPHANIE HUDSON

Afterlife Saga

A Brooding King, A Girl running from her past. What happens when the two collide?

Book 1 - Afterlife

Book 2 - The Two Kings

Book 3 - The Triple Goddess

Book 4 - The Quarter Moon

Book 5 - The Pentagram Child /Part 1

Book 6 - The Pentagram Child /Part 2

Book 7 - The Cult of the Hexad

Book 8 - Sacrifice of the Septimus /Part 1

Book 9 - Sacrifice of the Septimus /Part 2

Book 10 -Blood of the Infinity War

Book 11 -Happy Ever Afterlife /Part 1

Book 12 -Happy Ever Afterlife / Part 2

Transfusion Saga

What happens when an ordinary human girl comes face to face with the cruel Vampire King who dismissed her seven years ago?

Transfusion - Book 1

Venom of God - Book 2

Blood of Kings - Book 3

Rise of Ashes - Book 4

Map of Sorrows - Book 5

Tree of Souls - Book 6

Kingdoms of Hell – Book 7

Eyes of Crimson - Book 8

Afterlife Chronicles: (Young Adult Series)

The Glass Dagger – Book 1

The Hells Ring – Book 2

Stephanie Hudson and Blake Hudson

The Devil in Me

OTHER WORKS BY HUDSON INDIE INK

Paranormal Romance/Urban Fantasy

Sloane Murphy

Xen Randell

C. L. Monaghan

Sci-fi/Fantasy

Brandon Ellis

Devin Hanson

Crime/Action

Blake Hudson

Mike Gomes

Contemporary Romance

Gemma Weir

Elodie Colt

Ann B. Harrison